Amnesty

Aravind Adiga

PICADOR

First published 2020 by Picador
an imprint of Pan Macmillan
The Smithson, 6 Briset Street, London ECIM 5NR
Associated companies throughout the world .
www.panmacmillan.com

ISBN 978-1-5098-7903-8

The exchange between Danny and the Australian immigration officer
on pages 39–41 is adapted from a real exchange which appeared on
an online immigration forum about seven years ago.

1 3 5 7 9 8 6 4 2

A CIP catalogue record for this book is available from the British Library.

Printed and bound by CPI Group (UK) Ltd, Croydon, CRO 4YY

Visit **www.picador.com** to read more about all our books
and to buy them. You will also find features, author interviews and
news of any author events, and you can sign up for e-newsletters
so that you're always first to hear about our new releases.

For Mark Greif
To thank him for twenty two years of friendship

Within the four seas all men are brothers

—Inscribed on an arch
in Chinatown, Sydney

Amnesty

Home

All of the coastline of Sri Lanka is indented, mysterious, and beautiful—but no place is more mysterious than Batticaloa. The city is famous for its lagoon, where extraordinary things can happen. The fish here can sing: true. Absolutely true. Place a reed to your ear, lean down from your paddleboat, and you will hear the music of the fish of the lagoon. At midnight, the water's skin breaks, and the *kadal kanni*, mermaids, emerge out of the lagoon dripping with moonlight.

From the time he was about four or five years old, Danny had wanted to talk to a mermaid.

From the rooftop of his school, he could look over the palm trees and brightly painted houses of his city to the spot where the many-pointed, many-lobed lagoon narrowed before flowing into a greater body of water. Just before joining the Indian Ocean, the lagoon's face burned like fire, like the unriddling of an ancient puzzle: the motto beneath his school's coat of arms. Lucet et Ardet. Translated by the gray-robed priests as Shines and Burns. (But *what* shines? And *what* burns?)

Now Danny, standing up here, understood.

This lagoon shines. This lagoon burns.

He knew, as he watched the burning spot in the distance, that there was a second place where the lagoon joined the ocean; and that this spot was a secret one—hidden for most of the year, in a spot called Mugathwaram, the Face of the Portal, near the old Dutch lighthouse. Danny was sure it was there, at this hidden portal, that the *kadal kanni* came out into the open.

He had to wait till he was fifteen, a few years after his mother's death, to find the Face of the Portal. One Saturday, telling his father that he was going to a school picnic, he sat pillion on a friend's bicycle and went, for the first time in his life, to the old Dutch lighthouse and then beyond it, to the hidden beach, from where, he was told, you could see the second opening. When he got down from the bicycle, he was disappointed, because all he could observe in the distance was a continuous sandbar blocking this part of the lagoon: "There is no way it could flow out into the ocean here." After covering the bicycle with palm leaves so that it would not be stolen, his friend, a Tamil Christian, said: "We have to go out there, and it will appear." So he and Danny stole a boat from the lighthouse and then took turns rowing it all the way out to Mugathwaram. They drew nearer and nearer, beneath them the music from the fish grew louder and louder, and then it happened: the sandbar parted, its unity revealed to be an optical illusion, and now a gap of meters showed between the two arms of sand.

The Portal had opened.

In the middle of the gap gleamed the magic island of Mugathwaram, coral- and jellyfish-encrusted, on which the two boys alighted to watch—as cormorants, red-breasted sea eagles, broadwinged pelicans circled over their heads—the meeting and churning of waters. Currents of the lagoon flowing out and those of the Indian Ocean flowing in neutralized each other, producing an illusion of perfect stillness in the water: a solitary white egret stood with one black foot in the spot, to mark the gateway to the world.

Danny knew he had guessed right. This was where the *kadal kanni* were most likely to come up. Sitting side by side, he and the Christian friend waited for a mermaid. The tide began to rise, and the boat they had brought began to rock. The light dimmed; the ocean had become the color of old family silver. By now his father, who expected him home at five-thirty every evening to begin his homework, would be sitting outside with a rattan cane. Danny waited. He had a friend by his side; he was not frightened. They were not going back without talking to a mermaid.

Australia

Housecleaner, Danny was about to reply, sixty dollars an hour, but instead smiled at the woman.

Strapped to his back was what resembled an astronaut's jet-booster—a silver canister with a blue rubber nozzle peeping out and scarlet loops of wire wrapped around it—but it was just a portable vacuum cleaner, Turbo Model E, Super Suction, acquired a year ago at Kmart for seventy-nine dollars. In his right hand, a plastic bag with the tools of his trade.

"I asked," repeated the Australian woman, "what *are* you?"

Maybe, Danny thought, she's annoyed by the golden highlights in my hair. He sniffled. From the outside Danny's nose looked straight, but from the inside it was broken; a doctor had informed him when he was a boy that he was the proud owner of a deviated septum. Maybe the woman was referring to it.

"Australian," he hazarded.

"No, you're not," she replied. "You're a perfectionist."

Only now did she indicate, by pointing with a finger, that she was talking about his way of having breakfast.

In his left hand was a half-eaten cheese roll, which he'd made himself while walking by opening a packet of Black & Gold $2.25-for-ten cheese slices that he'd brought with him along with his cleaning equipment, and placing two slices in the middle of a sixty-cent wholemeal bun—and then the woman, who had apparently been observing him combine things into a sandwich and take a bite out of it, had made these remarks to him.

Shifting his vacuum on his back, Danny chewed and examined what was left of his self-made cheese roll and looked at the Australian woman.

So this is why I have, he thought, become visible. Because my way of eating bothers her. After four years, he was still learning things, still making notes to himself: Never walk and eat in daylight. They see you.

Now talk your way out of this, Dhananjaya. Maybe you should say: I used to do the triple jump in school. Hop, skip, and leap? Same way: plan, eat, and walk. I do these things all at once.

Or maybe a story was needed, a quick but moving story: My father always said no, I couldn't eat while walking, so now it's a form of rebellion.

Sometimes, though, with white people, all you have to do is start thinking, and that's enough. Like in a jungle, when you find a tiger in your path, how you're supposed to hold your breath and stare back. They go away.

Although she certainly appeared to be going away, the woman suddenly changed her mind and turned back to shout: "That's *irony*, mate. What I just said about you being a perfectionist."

Did she mean, thought Danny as he finished the sandwich on his way to the end of Glebe Point Road, from where he would take a left and walk up to Central Station, that I don't do anything well?

His forehead was furrowed now with the woman's word: *irony*.

Danny knew what the dictionary said it meant. In practice, he had noted, its uses were more diverse, slippery, and usually connected to a desire to give offense with words. Irony.

So by calling me a perfectionist, she must have meant . . .

Fuck her. I like eating like this.

Danny made himself another sandwich on his way to Central, and then a third one on the platform, as he waited for the 8:35 train to St. Peters Station.

His five-foot-seven body looked like it had been expertly packed into itself, and even when he was doing hard physical labor his gaze was dreamy, as if he owned a farm somewhere far away. With an elegant oval jaw, and that long, thin forehead's suggestion of bookishness, he was not, except when he smiled and exhibited cracked teeth, an overseas threat. On his left forearm a bump, something he had not been born with, showed prominently, and he had let his third fingernail on the right hand grow long and opalescent. His hair had fresh highlights of gold in it.

8:46 a.m.

The train was nearly full. Danny had a seat by a window. Stroking his fingers through his golden hair, for which he had paid $47.50 at a barbershop in Glebe, he became aware that he was being watched and turned toward the Asian man with the black-and-white shopping bag.

The man was looking not at Danny but at his backpack.

Even worse.

An astronaut faced growing competition these days, it was a fact. Two-man, three-man Chinese teams were spreading over Sydney offering the same service, at the same price, in half the time. And let's not even talk about the Nepalis. Four men at the price of one.

That's why Danny came with his own stuff. He had invested his capital. In addition to the portable vacuum on his back, he carried, in a plastic bag, a paper roll, disposable pads, a foam spray that he used on glass, and a fire-alarm-red rubber pump that would suck the problems from any toilet bowl. Sure, every home keeps a vacuum and brushes and sprays in a closet somewhere, but a cleaner impresses with his autonomy.

Aussies are a logical people, a methodical people.

Also in his plastic bag: a small but thorny potted plant with care instructions stuck into the dirt (I AM A CACTUS ☺), which he had bought for $3.80 from a woman who sat next to the park in Glebe, and which he planned to give someone later in the day.

A surprise gift.

At Erskineville Station, the Asian man stood up with his shopping bag just before the glass door opened, and Danny knew he was not a rival. That black-and-white bag did not have a portable vacuum inside. This was just a busybody on the train.

Stretching back, running his fingers through his hair, Danny sniffed them to check if the scent of the dye they used at the barbershop was still detectable—nasty stuff—and then raised his fingers to his scalp to stroke himself again.

Legendary.

He remembered the way Sonja's eyes lit up when she saw his hair. "Weird." That was what she'd said. That was a compliment. Because people in Australia were famished for what was weird, self-assuredly weird, even belligerently weird: like a Tamil man with golden highlights in his hair. A minority. And once you found out what that word *minority* means over here, tasted the intoxicant of being wanted *because* you were not like everyone else, how could anyone possibly tell you to go back to Sri Lanka and once again live as a minority over there?

To celebrate his golden head of hair, Sonja had made dinner in Parramatta the previous night, and Danny had kept looking at her as he ate, refreshing his vision of himself through her vision of him.

I'm here in Australia, he thought. I'm almost here.

True, after the flush of triumph following the first night in bed with Sonja, which was also his first time with someone not Tamil, he was confused by the idea of seeing the vegan Vietnamese girl again. He'd always thought that like marries like. How do you end up with a woman who doesn't speak Tamil, or know a thing about your heritage? Danny reconciled himself to love. There were precedents at hand. In Malaysia, for instance, so many Chinese-Tamil marriages had taken place. Not that Sonja was Chinese, of course, but he was just saying. These half-Tamil/half-Chinese children did very well in life. One of them had come to Batticaloa for a summer. He lived like a millionaire.

A root of a banyan tree, in a village near Batticaloa, burst through the corrugated tin shed protecting the grave of a *pir*, a Muslim saint, and touched his green cement grave like a giant's finger: here on this new continent, Danny remembered that transgressing banyan root, remembered it like one who knew that life had not yet expanded sufficiently through him or through his body.

So he met her again, and then again, and their relationship was now into its second year.

Sonja believed in things. Veganism. Socialism. LGBT rights. Political views. The developers control the Labor Party, yes, but the developers *are* the Liberal Party. Do you see the difference, Danny? Some of these things Danny didn't even understand, but he knew Sonja stood on them. Her Beliefs. He liked that about her. He also liked that her place in Parramatta had a spare room. After dinner, Danny went over there and sat by the duvet on the bed, playing with the table lamp, while shouting answers to the questions she asked from the kitchen.

"Yes! Vocational enrichment! I will investigate evening classes at the TAFE! You are so right, Sonja! Cleaning is not enough!"

Maybe she got the hint. Maybe she'd invite him to live in the spare room.

This morning she had called him just before starting work at the hospital—reminding him, ostensibly, to buy the cactus, but he knew it was just to hear his voice—and when she had asked, "What is your plan for this week?," for she believed that everyone needed a plan, both for life and for each of its individual weeks, Danny had replied: "The average weekly take-home pay, according to the Australian Bureau of Statistics, is one thousand one hundred—"

"That's not what I meant," she had said, laughing. "I meant what is your plan for this week regarding seeing me?"

He got up. Shifting the weight of the canister on his back, he stood by the glass door. He checked the time on his phone: its back had fallen off, and Danny had used Band-Aids to strap the battery into place. The display glass was cracked, an accident, and the time was four minutes fast, by design. The goal was to alternate anxiety—late late late—with relief—four extra minutes, remember, four extra—a pattern that intensified Danny's sense of duty.

Hissing hydraulically, the glass doors opened at St. Peters Station. Danny hefted his plastic bag and stepped out onto the platform.

Another workday began.

Four dark steel-rimmed chimney stacks, like Egyptian obelisks, rose right outside the station, as if declaring, This Is Where It Ends—though in truth it did not end here, there, or anywhere—always expanding, this city of Sydney, except for those people for whom it was always contracting. Danny walked. He saw, behind suburban fences, tropical plantains, begonia leaves whose undersides were as red as the tongue of a man chewing betel juice, and frangipani trees whose white petals, fallen over the pavement, partially covered handwritten signs in chalk—ABSOLUTELY NO FREE PARKING HERE—PLEASE

PLEASE ELIMINATE CHILDHOOD CANCER. Peeping through the charcoal-colored slats, a pitbull terrier, guardian of the secrets of white people, growled.

Danny sneezed. A blue mist sat in the trees like on a throne and the smell of smoke was everywhere: he guessed at once there was a fire in the mountains. Tonight on TV news, they would say: *Bushfires that began last night near Blackheath are being put out right now, though we might smell the smoke for days in parts of the city.*

He walked by a parked car inside which he observed a pink rubber shark, a newspaper dedicated to racing and betting, and a lovely relic, a mounted globe, the kind that the supervillain flips on a finger. Danny had stooped before the globe, searching for Sri Lanka, when from behind, someone—

Move.

—said something.

He turned but found nothing human there.

A plane flew low and loud over the suburb, passing from one building to another, the red Qantas logo appearing and disappearing.

A pair of broken classical columns had been deposited by the next gray fence; and next to the columns lay a decapitated cement statue, which represented, Danny felt, one of those gods that white people worshipped before Jesus. With the hint of smoke in the air, it was as if this Sydney suburb had summarized centuries of ruination in a night. Danny looked at the statue, wondering if it would make a good gift for Sonja, a better one than the $3.80 cactus he had in his plastic bag, when he heard it again.

It *was* a brown man's voice.

Walking around the fence, Danny saw the owner of the voice in the garden. He was wearing a gray mover's uniform, phone wedged against his right shoulder, and talking, as he ripped card-board sheets apart with casual power. Each thrust of his brutal forelimbs said: *I am here, Australians. Whether you see me or not, standing right here.*

Stopping his work, the muscular man dropped the cardboard and looked at Danny as if he meant to speak to him.

This brown man was Javanese or Malaysian, surely—not one of ours.

Before Danny could say anything, the muscular man turned to the right, shifted about as if finding a direction, then got down on his knees and closed his eyes. His lips moved. After turning his face from side to side, the brown man began to touch his head to the pavement while saying something. Ah. He's praying, realized Danny. He was looking at me to see if I was a Muslim too and wanted to join him.

Some human bodies generate time from within them. Like this man's, right now. All the ticking hands in Sydney were being reset to his heart.

They did it five times a day, didn't they?

So is this the second or the third? Danny wanted to ask as the praying man turned his face from side to side before touching his forehead to the earth again.

An angel with a red-and-green tail materialized over their heads: when Danny looked up, he saw that it was, appropriately enough, an Emirates flight. Sydney airport was not far away.

He sneezed again, and wondered if he had disturbed the praying man.

With a final look at the Indonesian, who, done with his prayer, was again handling furniture, Danny moved.

Thirty-six Flora Street rose above its neighbors, a three-story brick building, bare and basic, built for young professionals. Danny divided Sydney into two kinds of suburbs—*thick bum*, where the working classes lived, ate badly, and cleaned for themselves; and *thin bum*, where the fit and young people ate salads and jogged a lot but almost never cleaned their own homes. Erskineville was in the second category. In a suburb like this, a building like 36 Flora Street, with fifteen or twenty units, was a honeypot for a weekly cleaner. Danny sometimes couldn't believe he had just one regular job here.

First, the key.

A man could break into half the homes in Erskineville just by looking under the doormat or behind the second flowerpot. Here, the key was left someplace even more obvious. Danny raised the broken lid of the mauve mailbox and removed a shiny silver object from it.

Then he entered 36 Flora Street and ran up the stairs.

8:57 a.m.

Empty. Daryl the Lawyer was rarely at home on Monday or Tuesday. Even if you came in the evening to do the place. Sometimes you saw these clients once, on the first day, when you set the schedule, and then never again for months. Years.

Lowering his backpack, Danny dropped it on the floor; removing his T-shirt, he hung it on the bathroom door.

Rule number one: To stay ahead of the competition, always wear a white singlet. As he explained to his girlfriend, "People think the Chinese are cleaner because they don't have body hair."

Rules, it's all about rules.

Many of us flee chaos to come here. Aussies are an optimistic and methodical people and they are governed by law. Understanding the concept of the rule that cannot be broken is vital to adjusting here.

("Through my contradictions you grow: an immigrant addresses the native," page 24.)

The most useful paragraph of the book. From that one graph and its truths, Danny had forged himself so many rules, and as a result of these rules he was now charged with the weekly cleaning of twelve flats around inner Sydney and an entire house in Rose Bay with a view of blue water and yachts that he cleaned for $110 twice a month, though he did pay nine dollars each time for a car share to the house and back.

Danny tapped on his singlet. He coughed.

One more rule: Never wear a face mask, like many Chinese freelancers do—it scares the customers. Dust? Grime? Inhale, inhale.

Strapping the Turbo Model E to his back, he went to work, making sure not to trip over the dull bloodred cord plugged into the wall.

Bada-bada-bada-bum: making noise whenever he hit a tough spot, Danny moved his vacuum over the carpet. His cell phone, via headphones, played him Golden Oldies. Backstreet Boys. Madonna. Celine Dion. Nothing Tamil; everything English. As he moved, he could see three twenty-dollar bills weighed down by the wicker basket in which the lawyer hoarded twenty- and fifty-cent coins.

Danny saw, and saw, but did not touch.

Not till he was done with the vacuuming. Money left on the honor system, money taken on the honor system. Sixty dollars for cleaning the flat, two bathrooms included, fifteen dollars per extra toilet or bathroom.

Legendary Cleaner.

Danny felt sure that Daryl the Lawyer, House Number Four, had been the first to give him that name; now *everyone* said it. He had never felt comfortable with that epithet; and, as he reached around the sofa with his vacuum, he wondered if this was another manifestation of that odd, offensive word: irony. He would have to ask Sonja.

Is Daryl the Lawyer mocking me by calling me Legendary Cleaner?

Why do *you* call him Daryl the Lawyer? Maybe *you're* mocking him. That was the kind of thing she would say: point for point.

That woman.

Badabadabadum . . . He drove the vacuum nozzle under a rocking chair. "Daryl the—! Daryl the—!" Danny raised his voice over that of the vacuum's roar. Here I come, Daryl the Lawyer!

No cleaner becomes a legendary one without a certain level of aggression against his client.

Prrrompppp. Danny trilled his lips. Ever since his boyhood, he had been making these sounds whenever doing something unpleasant. *Badabadabadabump* . . .

His vacuum snout went through room after room. The canister on his bag, inflated with hot air and dust, relaxed when Danny turned the machine off.

Vacuum put away, dishes done, tables and chairs down, now for the core of the job. *You will be judged by your toilets. And your toilets will be judged by the bowls.* Removing his gloves as he came out of the toilet, he sat on the lawyer's chair and surveyed the living room.

He picked up a wine-colored leather volume from the lawyer's bookshelf: *The Reliance of the Traveller: A Guide to Islamic Law.*

Don't they ever read books about Hindu law? White people. Obsessed with Muslims. Because they're frightened of them. He flipped through the book.

One afternoon in Lakemba—a tip about a for-cash house-painting job from Abe, his Japanese-Brazilian abseiling friend—Danny had seen three Arab men on a porch, each stripped to the waist, each with a sheeshah, exhaling sultanish smoke over a garden of rust and rubbish. Some of Sydney's western suburbs—very, very thick bum—were filthy, front yards full of rotting wood, overturned shopping carts, little canals slicked over with white petals; but this Muslim mansion was easily the dirtiest thing he had seen in Australia. Danny loved it. Of course you admired the *fuck you white guy* attitude, but still you had to wonder, how the hell did people like *this* become legal, unless there was someone at the Department of Immigration who actually decided: "You don't look like a terrorist. Sorry, you'll never get into Australia. Next! Yes, you with the big beard, you can come in for sure!" See: the other day Yahoo! News had this story of an overweight extremely blind Malaysian guy, who plays the guitar, actually can't play it at all, and the Aussies had an online signature campaign for him, because he's Muslim, and gave him permanent residency. I tell you, there are Tamil men *burning* themselves alive.

Last week this man in Melbourne, this Jaffna man, covered himself in petrol and lit himself with a match when they wouldn't give him refugee status. Who gets it? This Malay Muslim.

Between Muslim and Tamil there had been frequent violence when Danny was growing up. Satrukondan, Xavierpuram, Siththandy: old names, old bloodshed.

Done with Islamic law. But as Danny bent to put the book back in the lower shelf of the bookcase, he had a clear view of the sofa and beneath it, and he saw a ball under the sofa.

It had rolled all the way up to the wall.

In Australia the unwritten rule is that the cleaner never bends down to touch anything *below* the level of a coffee table. Owner has to pick everything up from the floor before you begin work. There are rules on both sides of this business. ("We have to clean up the place so the cleaners can clean up afterward," one of his clients, possibly Daryl the Lawyer, had grumbled.) Back home, though, the rule is that while the maid will bend and scrub all you want, she will never touch anything *above* the level of the coffee table for fear of being accused of theft. Danny smiled. *Prrrpmmm. Badabadadum.*

Let's do it. Let's impress him.

Spread-eagling himself on the carpet, Danny reached with his flexed fingers under the sofa only to find it out of reach. The blue ball.

Prrrrrp. Ba-da-da-da-dum—

He extended his fingers—

"The average weekly take-home pay is eleven hundred fifteen dollars and forty cents, according to the Bureau of . . ."

". . . the Bureau of Staaaa-tis-tics . . ."

—till rubber tickled the tips.

("My strange boy," his mother used to say. When she found out, for instance, that Danny was the one cutting all the thorns out of the roses in her garden: "The thorns are here to protect the roses. If you remove them, you don't make the roses safer. My strange, strange son.")

We *are* a legendary cleaner.

Danny's fingers reached for the ball—gripped it—and extracted it from far beneath the sofa and presented the object from the darkness to Danny's nose. A ball: a blue ball. He smelled. Using his long fingernail, he scraped at the blue skin and smelled it again.

An acridity like nonliving body odor, which reminded Danny.

Don't forget the cactus: she's working at St. Vincent's today.

It was a different hospital or aged-care center each week for her. "It's all privatized now," she said. "We have to work where the agency sends us and for as long as they tell us or that's the last time I ever work."

I should go back and get that Greek statue as a gift.

Up on his knees, Danny walked over to the lawyer's table and deposited the blue ball there, pressing it with his palm to hold it in place, as he looked around the flat.

When he was a boy, he had asked a neighbor, recently returned from abroad, "What is the city of Toronto like?" The neighbor had asked, "Do you know what the Galadari Five Star Hotel in Colombo is like?" Danny had nodded. "*Every* square inch of the city of Toronto is like that."

The things they tell you about the West before you come here. No part of Australia is like the Galadari International. Sydney is filled with roaches, crickets, and flying bugs, except for any room that Danny had just gone over with his vacuum, sponge, and mop.

Legendary Cleaner.

His phone, which was certainly *not* legendary, beeped at once.

9:16 a.m.

Message from your phone company:
As we continue to build a mobile network for the future, we will have to say goodbye to older forms of technology. That means that the phone you appear to be using, a 2G phone, will no longer work from next week. Buy a new 3G phone as soon as possible from our website, our many convenient retail stores, or any of our retail partners.

The messages had begun two weeks ago. Danny had kept deleting them.

"Welcome, sir," the man at the convenience store or retail partner says, "a new phone for you, sir? Certainly, sir. What is your tax file number, sir? Do you have your passport with you, sir?"

From the lawyer's kitchen, the smell of broccoli broke into his nose; his bowels tightened. After all these years, his stomach was unreconciled to that nastiness. How could they eat it, these people, in such quantities, and *raw*? Broccoli!

Still recoiling from the smell of that vegetable, Danny picked his T-shirt off the hook and then dressed himself before paying himself, removing one by one the three twenty-dollar bills from under the wicker basket heavy with twenty and ten cents and other coins useless to white Australians.

Sixty dollars in his pocket, Danny raised both hands to his hair. He felt through his fingertips the power of his gold-highlighted strands, how they would stir envy in every man, of every race, who saw him.

No one would ever again mistake him for someone born outside Australia.

After all: in a city like Sydney, how can you tell who is a foreigner? Observe, understand, and make a chart. Danny's way.

Us and Them

1. 1st & foremost difference: posture.
2. Beards (us—too wild) and then haircuts (too docile).
3. Paunch. Young Australians don't have paunches.
4. Also don't spit in public.
5. Class (but have no *class* compared to people back home).

Mimicking a man with an Australian spine, wearing shorts in public, enjoying the low-class thrill of looking like a child again, he had kept himself, for two years, immaculately groomed. Danny's heart spoke to him in stages; and in the third year, he just grew his hair. Even as a boy, he'd wanted to grow his hair. (That and a dog: an Alsatian.) When his hair had grown so long it curled up at the back, he remembered a man in Enmore. An African who stood below a room he used to clean (House

Number Two) and talked about his tattoos. "Finally, I went to Bondi, and the man says they charge two hundred an hour, and it take three hours minimum. You only live once, right? Only live"—as he turned around to show off the tattoo of the parrot wrapping around his black leg, the African's accent changed and became British, or perhaps it had always been British—"once, right?"

That day Danny had seen his own male form, striped and sheathed in tattoos, and he, the master for the first time ever of his own body, something he could swirl round and round for his own pleasure . . .

Hierarchies exist in invisibility; there are always better ways to stay unseen.

Instead of tattoos (something *low*-class, even *uncivilized*, about them), he let his hair grow. That's not enough, though. No: you are in Sydney. Abe the abseiler colored his hair blond, and *he* was illegal—so Danny decided to go to the barber in Glebe and just ask. Reddish-brown streaks in the hair? It would cost $47.50, but Sonja approved; she more than approved.

A message from your phone company.

His machine beeped again. *As we continue to build a mobile network for the future, we will have to say goodbye to older forms of technology.*

There must be, Danny thought, some way to keep this phone for at least another month or two. Not to have to go into the Telstra office and answer questions about myself for another month or two.

The lawyer's desktop computer was covered in koalas: chintz tablecloth.

He could do it right here: get on the Internet and search for answers. What was, after all, the password on this computer? The return button. Daryl, you so-called Lawyer.

In the past, Danny *had* done great things on this very satin-covered desktop computer: he had, in fact, met the love of his life right on this computer.

But since he was going to Newtown today for work, he thought he might check his email for free in the public library there.

Though it denied him medical care, a driver's license, and police protection, the Australian state offered Danny unlimited and unmonitored access to its public reading rooms and information centers. Not far from the Sunburst grocery store was the Glebe library, a place that every illegal in the area knew well; Parramatta, Blacktown, Surry Hills, and Haymarket libraries were also good; but best of all, because of the high churchlike ceiling and the wide-open first floor where you could lie flat on the floor for hours and hours and forget who you were, was the Newtown library. Danny had even become friends with a smiling bald Indian named Ramesh who worked at the library. That guy *was* legal, though. Friendship could only go so far.

Danny packed up his cleaning equipment and heaved the vacuum canister onto his back: an astronaut again.

The next home—Danny checked his cell phone for the time—was Rodney Accountant's flat in Newtown, about halfway down King Street, where he would find, in addition to a white cat that he was strictly not to let out, three twenty-dollar bills on top of the fridge covered with slogans against uranium mining.

Right. Let's go.

But it was waiting for his final lookaround to materialize above the lintel: black and threatening, a little Shiva, with many tentative arms.

At once he got his cell phone out, scrolled down the numbers, got to

Sonja

And pressed the green call button.

"Danny," Sonja said, answering, "I'm at work, what is it."

"I'm at Daryl the Lawyer's. Cleaning? And there's a spider. Right above the door. I have to walk under it."

"What kind? Huntsman?"

"I don't know. It's big and hairy."

"Yah. That's a huntsman. They're harmless. Don't worry. Walk under it. It won't fall on you, and if it does, it won't hurt."

"But I'm a legendary cleaner. If the lawyer comes back and sees this spider, he'll think—"

"Danny. Don't hurt it. It's harmless. I have to work now. I am a nurse, Danny: I have people to take care of. It's a busy day."

He put the phone back in his pocket. All right. He stared at the motionless thing above the door.

"Huntsman," Danny gave the beast its name.

Shooo. Shooo. They can sense when you don't mean it. More sound effects (*bada-bada-bum-bum*). Nothing.

A slamming door might scare it.

He turned the knob on the front door and pushed it open to find three policemen in blue uniforms running up the stairs straight at him.

Danny stood still.

Passing him without a word, they kept moving up the stairs to the level above the lawyer's flat. There one of them began knocking on a door. Another stood still. A third looked down at Danny from the top of the stairs.

9:21 a.m.

"Mate, you live—?" he shouted down.

After nodding, Danny stepped back into the lawyer's flat and closed the door.

He came back into the security of the huntsman's stare.

Count to ten, to twenty, thirty: then he opened the door a bit. One of the three policemen, the one who had said something, was running down the stairs.

The policeman stopped and observed Danny through the open door with narrow eyes: he was blue, immensely, whalishly blue, and his belly butted against his shirt and surged over his black belt like a sac of hard blue flesh. Putting his hands on his hips, he pushed it out farther and exhaled.

"Mate. I asked you: you live here?"

". . . just the . . ."

Touching Danny, moving him to the side, the policeman poked his head in and peeked around the cleaned apartment. He sniffled as if he too were about to sneeze.

". . . cleaner . . ."

The policeman said, "All right. *Aaaaallll* right. That's what I thought. Something's going on across the street. Just checking things out."

"Yes, sir. Okay, sir."

At least they have not come for me. At least I am safe for now. Danny locked the door. The thing across the street—the police must be talking of the fire in the Blue Mountains, the one filling the streets with smoke. Nothing more than that. The big spider up there was still looking at him; but Danny knew how to distinguish, within his gut, the treble line of nervous tension (Australian police) from the bass line (Sri Lankan police). Whatever the police are here for, he reminded himself, they are not here for you. They can't even see you.

So he raised the chintz koala dress off the desktop computer, hit the return button, and waited. As soon as the screen came to life, he went to Google News and typed in: *Kiran Rao.*

Danny thought he was the only cleaner in Sydney who carried a book with him. A man must keep reading if he must keep thinking. Initially, it had been a pink paperback: *Splendid in Satin,* by Madeline Bright. Then, in the Newtown library's discarded books bin, he had found Kiran Rao's *Through My Contradictions You Grow*, seen Kiran's handsome South Asian face on the cover, after which this book, smuggled in with the toilet brushes and sprays and Black & Gold cheese slices, had accompanied Danny on his cleaning trips for over a year, until he knew most of it by heart and no longer had to bring it along.

Book of the Century, as far as Danny was concerned.

News (past 24 hours)

Rao speaks at the Sydney Festival

. . . in his customary dark suit and red tie, Kiran took questions from the audience, on the bitter and the sweet side of the immigrant's life in Sydney.

Raising his hand before the computer in Daryl the Lawyer's home, inviting himself into the audience, Danny turned a difficult situation into a question for his favorite author:

What should I do if they ask me for my tax file number when I go to hand in my phone, Kiran?

He could hear that respectable, besuited figure turn from his admiring audience at the festival to say:

You have plenty of time with the old phone, Danny. Don't think about it so much. And if I were you, Danny, I'd worry about only one thing. Keeping my relationship working. (The audience laughed.) *That's the toughest thing for an Aussie, trust me.*

Really? Danny hadn't found it so hard: his relationship with Sonja was *great*. And it had all begun right here, at this lawyer's unguarded computer. A friend, an Australian who knew all his secrets, a person full of wise sayings, had told him about the dating site, and he had logged on to it right here.

VeggieDate

Love Without Cruelty

"Vegetarians. The best-looking ones in Sydney are vegans."

"But I eat—"

"Listen, you idiot: they think all Indians are vegetarians because they worship cows. Don't you have a feel for a good scam?"

Of course he knew it was wrong: wrong to use the lawyer's personal computer and wrong to contact the women. Vegetarian? Danny loved mutton. He loved pork.

This is wrong, all wrong. They call me Honest Danny. But he did it anyway. He did have a feel for a good scam.

Sonja was the third vegan woman he contacted. They met that weekend in Parramatta.

He got there to the pub first, and waited for her in a wooden booth, observing himself in the wall mirror as he did so. Light settings designed to optimize the sex appeal of a fairer-skinned people garishly illuminated, he felt, the cuticles of his dark fingers and the whites of his eyes. "Look intelligent," he cajoled his image, and had interlaced his fingers with the thumb bent backward to touch his mouth—a *thinking* pose—when she found him.

"You know what I like about Indians? Indians are the world's only fat vegetarians. Happy, fat vegetarians."

She was a short, not unattractive, determined girl, wearing a T-shirt that said VEGANS FIRST and with eyes eager for otherness. And she was Chinese.

Vietnamese. Gentlemen *did* know the difference?

She ordered beer for both of them, a kind that she said was organic. As she spoke about the injustices done to animals, Danny strained the muscles above his ears and smiled. "You know what milk is? A kind of pus. Think about that, you're guzzling pus." She said this and sipped her beer thrice before putting it down. Danny thought, She is also nervous.

About to pick up her beer again, she asked: "Are you a Muslim?" His answer clearly disappointed; but she recovered and noted, "At least you're not a *suit*."

This was confusing because Danny had always thought of himself as a man who had come to Sydney to wear suits. Tip-top woolen suits with silver buttons and a silk handkerchief in the pocket. Only one tailor in Batticaloa could cut a high-class suit like that, and only four people in town could afford something like it.

"What do you feel about milk as a food source?"

"How actively do you support animals' rights?"

"Are there vegans where you come from?"

Steering the conversation away from food, he explained to the vegetarian about Sri Lanka and then Dubai. Yes, he had been there. Had worked there for a year, in a business motel in Deira, Dubai. Had worn a green suit and green tie and checked people in with a smile. No, seriously: that had been Danny's job before he came to Australia. Here? He was a cleaner. Housecleaner. Yes, he was looking for something better.

After a while the two of them went walking by the Parramatta River.

It was unlike any he had seen before: its banks were perfect and green, as if punched into the earth by a river-making machine.

"What does that thing mean?" she asked. "Do you know?"

He noticed that her eyes had wandered to an old building by the river.

"Why do they put letters like that in old churches. What does it mean?"

Danny peered.

MDCCCLVVII.

"Eighteen seventy-seven," he informed her.

Her mouth opened. "How do *you* know all this?" Romans, he explained, had a very peculiar way of writing numbers, which was hugely improved when they stole decimals from Hindus.

She looked at him and demanded: "Did you read a dictionary as soon as you came to Australia?"

Without his saying a thing, she darkened and smiled, realizing how offensive what she'd said was.

From then on, he did most of the talking.

Eventually, she asked: "You live by a real lagoon in Sri Lanka? Why did you give up all that and come to Australia?"

"I have a condition," said Danny. "It is called a deviated septum." He touched his nose. "Means I get fever quickly. My sinuses get heavy."

It was true.

Sinus Safety List

1. Warm water: as soon as the sinuses become heavy, start gargling.
2. No smoking. Strict. No bad habits.
3. Menthol spray on days one and two.

Life with bad sinuses the main subject, he walked with the vegetarian girl all the way to a small dam where the water fell and joined a darker body. She turned to him and said: "Will you stop talking about the deviation in your septum and answer my question?"

"Sorry."

"My question was this: why did you give up a lagoon to come to this country?"

Now I'll have to start lying, Danny thought, when the Parramatta River saved him: a white feather came floating along its surface, and he pointed it out to her.

"That's because they've privatized everything in Sydney," the vegan said, assuming that he was referring to the floating rubbish. "Even this river."

"The fishes in my lagoon," Danny told her, "can sing."

Really, he told the incredulous woman, showing her how you just placed a reed to the surface of the lagoon back in his unprivatized home, and heard them buzzing and humming beneath. Batticaloa, city of the singing fish. Jewel of the east of Sri Lanka. Fire-walkers at the temple. Tongue-piercers. Silver beaches. Mermaids living in the lagoon. *Kadal kanni*, we call them.

"Do you understand a word of what I'm saying?" he asked her, and she shook her head before saying, "Not necessarily, but go on."

And he *did* go on, not necessarily about the lagoon.

"Do you follow football?" she demanded.

"No."

"Cricket?"

"No sports at all for me," Danny said. "See: the range of human achievement in sports is only one to one point four."

"What does that *mean*?"

Danny grinned. "Achievement means ment that is achieved, no?"

She laughed. "What the *fuck*?"

After two years of great care with his accent, Danny had never repressed this peculiarity in his speech. *Sugar-free means no sugar, no?* Singsong tautologies came naturally to him. Yes, inside his accent (not quite Australian but neutral), there was an animal from another English, and now, after two years here, he let it purr.

Now he explained to her the essential fraudulence of all sporting glory.

"Average twenty-one-year-old male, given basic training for one month, can run a hundred meters in about fourteen seconds.

Okay? Fastest man runs same distance in nine point nine seconds. Not much of a difference. One to one point four is the range. Now, what is the difference between an average man's intelligence and Einstein's? Cannot measure it."

Facts came from Danny like this, strange facts, connected only by a vibrant thread of subversion, as the two walked up and down the river in Parramatta. A small bird zigzagged around them, as if he had found a field of sugarcane all to himself.

The next morning, while Danny was filing cans in the Sunburst grocery store in Glebe, when someone phoned and it turned out to be Sonja, he felt his heart pound and remembered all the race horses together thumping past Tom Cruise in that great, great scene in *Mission: Impossible* 2.

9:43 a.m.

"It must be over now," he said out loud.

That "thing across the street" must be over. The blue uniforms must be gone, so Danny rose from the computer, stood by the door, and put his ear to it.

Can I ask you, Officer, if something is wrong.

Sorry. Just standard procedure. There's been an incident across the road. We were just taking photos of the place from here. Standard procedure.

Incident?

Yeah. A murder.

Holy shit. Who was it?

Did you know your neighbors?

Not really. No. Which building? What did you say her name was? No, don't know any woman by that name.

He stepped back from the door.

27

He wondered how long he would be stuck in here now, and whether he had to call and warn Rodney Accountant he might be late.

And this reminded him too that he had not yet killed the big spider overhead.

9:47 a.m.

Holding a can of insect repellent kept under the sink by Daryl the Lawyer, Danny drew near the brown-legged spider. He started humming the theme music to *Mission: Impossible* to give the creature one last chance. But the spider just twitched its legs as if enjoying the music and the joke. Too late, it understood; it began to move. But Danny already had pressed the white button of the spray. It curled up and fell.

Compacted, redder, in death it resembled something much more dangerous, thought Danny as he lifted it up in a paper napkin.

The window above the sink, the only one in the place facing the back road, was always bolted down; holding the dead spider at the end of an extended right hand, Danny unbolted and lifted the window with the other. The first time in months he had done this and looked out onto the quiet road that was behind Flora Street.

Down below on the street, like something that had been conjured there just to punish him for his decision to open the window, a blue and red light turned silently on top of a van, parked right in front of a building.

A police van.

The only occupant of the street, a man in a blue uniform, stood with his back against a big gum tree, exhaling stallion-strength cigarette smoke.

The gum tree was a giant, and its mottled white-and-gray bark was peeling, like old paint. When you first come to Australia, the skin of these trees can frighten you, because they remind you of leprosy and other things that are still feared back home.

Danny's eyes turned back to the police van and then to the new brick building right behind it, which they climbed up floor by floor.

There. The fourth floor. Danny stopped to check.

On the fourth floor of that building behind the police van was a window in which red tulips grew in a black tray.

Now, the policeman he had seen outside the door had clearly said, *There's been a murder* across *the road*. Not *behind* the street. So this, Danny told himself, can't be the building—can't. Just can't.

Because this building in front of which the leprous gum tree grew, the one with the tulips on the fourth floor, you know this one—it is *her* building. Radha's.

Danny's throat scratched.

Every Monday morning for two years, nearly two years, he had gone to that flat with the tulips with his vacuum and kit. That was House Number Five.

There's been a murder across the road.

The dead spider! He had forgotten all about it. Danny let the napkin drop and saw the weightless red form swirl down to the street. He lowered the window and fastened it.

He breathed one-two-three, one-two-three, like they taught in Dubai in the business motel staff training program. Then he scratched the back of his neck. Removing his cell phone from his pocket, he went down the address book, taking a while to find the number . . .

He scrolled down to the eighteenth entry in the phone book. Which was identified only as

H5

Meaning, House Number Five.

Yes. There she was. The owner of the flat with the red tulips on the windowsill, right *behind* the street.

Or across the street. The way Australians speak English. Across, behind.

Just call her, call and make sure she is all right. Make sure it was some other woman *across the street.*

He was about to press the dial button. But there was a police van down there with a revolving blue and red light. If he called her phone and they were inside her place . . . They can trace anything back to anything these days, the police in Sydney.

Standing by the wall next to the kitchen window, he slowly looked down onto the road below.

The cop leaning against the leprous gum tree threw away his cigarette just as another blue policeman came over to join him.

Danny stepped away from the window. Then he stepped toward it again and lowered the blinds.

He looked at the blue ball on the desk; then he picked it up, bounced it on the floor, and nudged it with his shoe until it rolled under the sofa again. There. Go back.

This dark spot under the lawyer's sofa Danny recognized now as another of the forbidden places of the city of Sydney: should never have put my hand in there.

Back at the desktop, sitting down again, he typed in: *Sydney murder news.*

Still waiting for the slow computer to turn up the search results, he brought out his cell phone, opened the address book, and scrolled down, moving his thumb higher up on the list, all the way to the first entry

Home

and pressed the green dial button on the phone. Four rings, then a click, then an old man's voice, slow, with a 1970s pop song in the background.

"Why you calling me? I have so much tension," said his landlord. "Very bad morning it is for us. Very bad."

Tommo never used the pronoun *us* for anyone but the Parramatta Eels—his football team.

"Tommo. Can you check the TV for me?"

"They say that Joey Mitchell can't play next year. And don't call me on your cell phone, Danny. You know this."

"Urgent. Can you see if there is a murder?"

A pause.

"In Erskineville. Near Flora Street. Are they saying anything on TV?"

"Murder?" Tommo Tsavdaridis's voice dropped low. "You are working in Erskineville today, no?"

"Yes. Can you check the TV for news about a murder in Erskineville?"

The phone went dead.

Fuck him. Danny went back to the kitchen. He raised the window again.

Playing with the address book again, he scrolled down to the nineteenth entry on the list, which was identified only as *H6*.

If something had happened to House Number Five, then House Number Six would know, surely.

Instead of calling *H6*, though, Danny rang

Sunburst

again.

"Tommo, please turn on the TV. I can't get TV on my phone. Old phone."

"Danny, why are you calling? I told you once never call me."

"Just tell me if the TV says a woman named Radha was murdered."

After a pause, Mr. Tsavdaridis, the owner of the Sunburst grocery store, where Danny had lived for four years, asked: "Why?"

"Just see if there is a woman named Radha Thomas who was murdered last night. In Erskineville. I'm waiting here till you tell me."

Mr. Tsavdaridis's voice stayed low. "Danny. Danny. Joey Mitchell was suspended today. We are finished."

And with that, his landlord and protector hung up.

A pair of perfectly round yellow eyes peered at Danny from the windowsill. A crow—but not the animal called by that name back home—some other creature, twice as large, with cartoonish eyes, sat on that side of the glass, the sun beating down on its glossy skin.

These beasts—Australian crows—had been one of the puzzles in the first few days. What did they feed them here to make them so big? And so loud?

All at once, home is just around the corner.

He could hear from the street murmurs of the police, and the pedestrian indicator that was emitting the *beep-beep-beep* noise.

Danny stood at the window, watched those red tulips—they looked so vivid, so alive—and thought once again about phoning Radha Thomas, House Number Five. If she picked up the phone, he could tell her to come to the window. Just so he could see her.

But when the tulips shook together, and the window opened—it was no woman but a man, a white man, who peered out of the window to show the policeman the view—Danny knew at once who that white man was. Mark. Her husband. His face was red, and he had been crying.

And she—

9:54 a.m.

The lawyer's home filled with sound; another plane was descending through the suburb of Erskineville toward Kingsford Smith International Airport.

9:56 a.m.

"Drugs."

Danny said the word again and again and felt better. He had washed his face three times and chosen not to wipe it dry. Nothing in Australia is hard to understand once you know that all the young people have glassy blue eyes because they're on drugs.

He made sure he had taken everything with him.

So, Danny. Someone on drugs broke into her home, and shot her dead, or strangled her, or . . . She may not even be dead. You don't know why the police are there, Danny. No triple jump on this.

He locked the door behind him, went down the stairs, left the key in the mailbox of 36 Flora Street, and stayed calm, very calm, when two enormous blue creatures, two beat officers, two New South Wales policewomen, walked straight toward him from the other side of the pavement, and Danny froze, thinking, They've seen me.

His leg started to vibrate. He felt his teeth bite each other. Villawood!

The two policewomen walked right past him, and he exhaled. Withdrew his hand from the mailbox and ran it through his hair.

Safe?

He could see the four gray brick towers in the distance, with St. Peters Station next to them—but the road in between here and there was thick with Zebra Crossings, 50 signs, dots, dashes, curves—a forest of white arcs, swerves, enigmatic numerals, and zigzags of thick paint on asphalt—because this was no longer a road, it was the painted and tattooed war body of the hunter. Called the City of Sydney. Small things fit into bigger ones, automatic toll booths fit into ATMs, and they fit into swipe cards and into pay-wave cards, and all of this adds up to one anytime-and-everywhere machine. Which is hunting for a man named Dhananjaya Rajaratnam.

Danny.

10:11 a.m.

SURVEILLANCE CAMERAS CONTINUALLY MONITOR THE INTERIOR AND EXTERIOR OF THIS TRAIN, said the sticker on the glass door, although the electronic message in orange letters on the monitor board of the train reiterated the message—with one emendation.

. . . *continually monitor interior and the exterior of this train.*

Sitting in the last compartment of the train, Danny studied the discrepancy between the sticker and its electronic restatement.

The blue canister on his back, the spray gun and foam brush in his bag, grew heavier.

He looked around. He was going to play an old game.

This woman reading *The Sydney Morning Herald*, for instance: her blonde hair in a bun; lines of tension visible in the tight strong jaw. If the Sri Lankan military police or immigration sat that one in a cone of light, she'd just suck her lips in. And say nothing. How she'd eat up taunts: reverse psychology, insults, slap to the face . . .

But a cigarette in your thigh, miss?

The blonde turned the pages of the newspaper. Danny cupped his hands around his eyes. Ridiculous. You are in Australia. You have been here for four years. Start thinking like them.

House Number Five. Now, she could have beaten the torture. Yes, *she* could have.

Strong woman, House Number Five, Radha: wide-hipped, muscled, he saw her now, wearing a white shirt that fell over tight-fitting black gym pants. There was strength in this woman, yet she was light; she was a dancer, and Danny saw her on that rooftop in Hong Kong, doing the Lindy Hop. She was quick.

It wouldn't have been easy, killing her.

If she's dead. Maybe the police were asking her husband about something else. He's a real estate agent, isn't he? One of them was arrested the other day for fraud. It was in the paper.

Just call Radha, Danny told himself. House Number Five. Ask if she's all right.

The creaking of the rear compartments grew and grew, as if, any minute now, the back of the train would detach itself from the rest.

But if she's *not* all right, the police have her phone.

Near Central Station, a gray-shirted employee of the railways with glossy silver hair and a silver beard, an Aussie version of the Tamil sage Thiruvalluvar, his hands behind his back, hunted for something on the tracks.

The train passed the sandstone clock tower of the station: Danny remembered a minaret with a timepiece set into it near Batticaloa that glistened in silver light all through Ramadan. Quick. Stare at it, Danny, note down the time. People used to think like this when he was a boy because they had nothing, not even a wristwatch, in those days. How near it feels again: home.

Just then the silver-haired railway man on the tracks raised his head and found Danny's eyes.

"O-kay," Danny said aloud.

That was how she said it: her one peculiarity of speech, the only alien thing that came out of her Australian mouth, a breath of *H* on the vowel, and the *kay* exploding, a nervous tic, an attempt to placate trouble.

"O-kay," he repeated.

The air inside the train circulated a reek of rancid animal fat that no other passenger seemed to notice, making Danny worry that it was the smell of his cleaning equipment or his fate.

In the seat opposite to him, someone unfurled the newspaper. Danny saw an advertisement facing him: *Chinese Dragon, $8 Menu, 7 Days!*

The animal fat smell in the air tightened. Do not do something stupid, Danny warned his stomach, do not vomit. To be invisible for four years, you need the *tongue* of an Australian, we all know that.

When I was new to Sydney, and I still spoke with an accent like some new immigrants do, I was picked on in school, but I talked sense and reason with the bullies, and they became mates. ("Through my contradictions you grow," page 12.)

Even before he got to Australia, Danny was practicing becoming Australian. All the way back in Batticaloa. In front of a mirror. Slowing down his *V*'s. Biting his lower lip when saying *volleyball*.

Later, in the Sunburst grocery store in Glebe, while filing cartons of longlife milk and chocolate shakes, he searched for the magic keys to Australianness. He remembered what he'd heard in Dubai, that villagers in China were asking doctors to cut a groove in their tongue so they could speak English without an accent. If they can do that, I can do this. I reckon I can. Because what is the thing that makes an Aussie an Aussie? *Sounding*

Aussie. Eliminate the tics that Tamils bring to their English: the undulating rhythms, *yo* and *ree* tagged on to words, the use of *no* for emphasis or a pause in a sentence.

He *enjoyed* this change.

Because compare and contrast, point for point, with how people back home argue. Smoking causes cancer, you say one morning: *O, no, no, re, no!* What about Eswaran over there who has lived to ninety-nine years, no, smoking beedis morning, evening, and night? *Exception* to the rule, buddy, the Aussie points out. Danny liked that. Logical. Other day, cleaning House Number Nine, in Ashfield, he flooded the bathroom, but once he'd explained to the owner of the place, a red-haired marketing woman, that the water faucet was broken, and he was able to prove this by demonstration, she calmed down. Not Danny's fault—and she even felt she owed him twenty-five dollars for the extra time he had put in. Logical people. Your life is yours, my life is mine.

The tongue of an Australian. Never say *receipt* with the *P*. Be generous with *I reckon*. Add a loud *Look*—at the start of the sentence, and *ridiculous* at the end. If you are happy, talk about rugby: "Go Eels." If you are unhappy, talk about rugby: "What about the Rabbitohs?"

And do not *ever* call it rugby.

You need the tongue of an Australian, sure; but to stay invisible, you also need, at the opposite end, the bowels of an Australian.

Chinese Dragon, $8 Menu, 7 Days!

Please turn to another page, Danny begged the man reading the newspaper. I don't want to shit right here.

Turning away from the newspaper, he glanced behind him and to his left, and that is how he found out he was being watched.

The woman in a white shirt and jeans was reading a newspaper, but her blond child, his head on his mother's thighs, like a cat on a lap, was looking at Danny.

In the shade of his mother's newspaper, his eyes began sparkling. The highlights don't fool me, mate. I know what you are.

Obnoxious legal thing. Danny tilted his head to the side and returned the child's stare.

Little legal policeman. I am never going back home.

The child tilted his head a little more and a little more and kept staring.

Danny did the same.

I haven't lasted four years here, little policeman, to be caught by you.

First Year as an Illegal

Not even six months in, one morning at the shopping mall in Burwood, they caught him.

Holding a powerful green umbrella over her head, she suddenly stopped to stare at Danny; and then the bag in her free hand dipped, as if it had become heavier. She was Tamil, for sure. And she knew at once, he knew at once, he was from Sri Lanka and Tamil. From the fullness of her shopping bag, from her way of walking in the sun rather than avoiding it, he knew she must be legal: and from his way of doing the opposite of these things, she knew he was illegal.

At once Danny turned around and ran.

When he confessed to Tommo that a woman from back home had spotted him, or almost certainly had, the old Greek man sat down behind his counter, pointed to the street, and shouted, "Get out right now. Get out. I'm a citizen. I have a passport. I took the oath in the public hall in Parramatta, and I have my citizenship certificate, and they can't do a thing to me. Danny. I could rent this room out to some uni student for three hundred dollars a week. Easy. But I give it to you for free. Why? You are useless. Totally useless."

Running up the metal stairs, Danny lay on the sofa in the store-
room of the Sunburst grocery store in Glebe, his ears alert for—"Is
an illegal down there? Is an illegal from Sri Lanka down there?"

He knew Tommo would betray him in a second.

I am sorry for what I did, he wished he could tell the police, and
immigration, and customs, and his father back home. He wished he
could tell them more: that from the day he had become an illegal,
he had been trying to reverse things. To find some way around his
decision.

Q:

I came to Australia on a student visa, but I realized that
my college is a "ripoff." They will not help me find a job
here, so I dropped out. But I made an honest mistake and
stayed for more than twenty-eight days after I left my college. Can anyone in this forum tell me, is it now possible to
make a petition to the department, to give me an extension?

Best Answer (3 likes):

Mate, can't you read a calendar? As a law enforcement officer, I can tell you what is going to follow very accurately
because I have arrested dozens like you: I know perfectly
well that you did not overstay by mistake. You chose to be
here. Doesn't matter. Honest or (more likely) dishonest,
twenty-eight days after you left your course and had not
left Australia, you became illegal. You have probably seen
enough of this country to believe that it has zero tolerance
for illegal activity of any kind. This is not France. This
is not America. We are an island, and you cannot get on or
get off without our clearance. My recommendation: kindly
surrender at once to an immigration office and receive the
sentence of deportation immediately. Because if you keep

doing what you are doing, if you run and dodge and hide until you get arrested (and you *will* be arrested), then you face a much worse time. Understand that every police officer, taxation man, and immigration or customs officer has the power to arrest you immediately and hold you indefinitely unless you can show, on the spot, documents authorizing your presence in Australia. There is also something called the citizen arrest option. I am betting you have an accent, which in other words means: *Hey, law enforcement officers, come check out my legal status not to be here.*

Q:
And?

Best Answer (3 likes):
And. Son. Let me tell you. And you will get caught, yes, and this comes next: Spending your days in a room with lots of strangers—maybe you'll have Iraqis, maybe Pakistanis, but basically, they will be a bunch of lovely people. Hope you enjoy Arabic for breakfast! Before we deport you, you will have to face court for your illegal activities and failure to pay tax. Expect the subsequent bill from the government to be over ten thousand dollars. You will pay all of the expenses for your deportation, including the three hundred dollars or so for each day you are held in a detention center. Hey, and guess what . . . when you logged in with your question, son, your IP was recorded. Since law enforcement actively monitors Yahoo! answers for pedophiles, crooks, druggies, and illegal aliens like you, they already know what town you are in, if not what house you are living in. Do you understand what I am saying, son—do you know enough English?

Q:
Yes. Nandri.

Best Answer (3 likes):
And what the fuck does that mean?

It meant: each time a door opened or slammed in Glebe, Danny's heart contracted; he saw a brown man who held a cigarette in the fork of his fingers; a Sri Lankan interrogation officer normally stationed somewhere around Bandaranaike International Airport. Each time a door opened or slammed, he wanted to shout, I am sorry, sir. I am so sorry. But what was the point of saying that now? He was now a man without rights in this world.

10:32 a.m.

Seven exits lead out of Central Railway Station, depositing you behind the city, in the shade of Surry Hills; or directing you into the bright central business district through a U-shaped sandstone arcade; or lifting you up an escalator to the light rail; or, in the case of the long tunnel paved with mosaic tales that Danny was walking through, leaving you in Railway Square, a bus stand.

He stopped in front of a sandwich shop with a TV screen affixed to a corner of its ceiling; a woman behind the counter was wiping a plate and looking at the man with the astronaut backpack and the plastic bag.

In a minute he would be told that facilities were only for customers, but for now, mouth open and clutching his bag full of cleaning equipment, he was watching the TV screen:

. . . police are asking anyone with information about the murder

of a woman from Erskineville to step forward. The woman, a forty-three-year-old former Medicare administrator, was found near a creek in Toongabbie. After being stabbed to death, her body was wrapped in a leather jacket, which was filled with stones and dumped into the creek in a bid to sink it. But it rose to the surface and washed ashore, where it was discovered early in the morning by a jogger. Police have described the injuries to her neck and head, committed with a knife, as horrific.

Now they were showing an old photo of the dead person, a brown woman with a broad smile and strong thick arms. Unbloodied, unhurt. He immediately closed his eyes.

Prrrrrrmp. Badabadabadabum. I am Honest Danny.

Because once, as a boy, he had walked for six kilometers to return an umbrella left behind by an old relative. "Abraham Lincoln," someone remarked, "did the same thing at the same age. This boy will become a great man." He became a business motel assistant manager in Dubai. One day Danny found dollars in a wallet dropped by a guest who was already in a taxi to the airport. The guest sent him a PDF attachment letter of appreciation for his honesty. You had no choice where Danny grew up; in Batti, even criminals had to be law-abiding. One evening, see, the government declared a curfew. Every shop has to be shuttered before eight. Two policemen, walking about the market, hear a noise behind a shutter: "Open up!" Turns out the shopkeeper and his son are having dinner behind the closed shutter. Technically, the two police say, since we could hear your eating noise from outside, you *are* breaking the curfew. Come. Father and son wash their hands and go into police custody. Father comes out that evening, drunk as a dodo. Police are misunderstood chaps, really. Lovely people. Son doesn't come out the next day. The father goes to the station daily to check. A week later, a naked body is found floating facedown in the lagoon, piece of wood around the ankle. Father spends hours trying to identify it. So if the curfew was at eight, you observed the curfew starting at 7:45. If the law said, *a*, you said, *A*.

One hundred percent Honest Danny.

Prrrrrrrrmp. And opened his eyes.

The TV was still showing an old smiling photograph of Radha Thomas, his former employer, the owner of House Number Five.

So they didn't break in to her flat with the red tulips. It wasn't for drugs or money. The police were there only to question her husband, maybe. Another set of police must be down at the creek, where they recovered the body.

Killed at a creek. Wrapped in a jacket and dumped into it.

A drowned body, he thought, looks nothing like this. Like the TV was showing. He knew. A day after the tsunami of 2004, he'd been standing in a crowd on the Kallady Bridge, which connected Batticaloa to the world, and peering down at the water, watching as those who'd gone missing were now returned one by one by the swollen lagoon—each new bloated, milk-white corpse greeted by a cry of recognition from the bridge.

That's what Radha Thomas would've been like when she washed up. Except she was dead even before she drowned.

Stabbed. What does it feel like, when the blood spurts out? What does blood look like? Shark liver oil, maybe. Danny had been fed it as a boy by his mother. She had told him it was shark's blood, to make him strong.

A hunger for meat twisted his stomach: a short eat with pork or egg inside, a triangular wedge of paratha with dark flesh wrapped snugly inside, a fried samosa, all the compact fried stuff kept behind glass in Sri Lankan teashops for difficult moments in the day. But no more meat, ever again. That was the price of being with a vegetarian woman.

He shifted the weight of his backpack about, glanced around, and saw a clock.

Wait. He turned back toward the television. What color was the jacket? Did they say that?

10:37 a.m.

"Everything okay, buddy?" asked a lady from behind the sandwich counter.

Danny smiled at her.

The TV was now saying:

The fire burning in the Blue Mountains is expected to last most of the—

Turning around, Danny walked back toward the trains and ran up the stairs to the first platform he could find. He stood there without knowing where that train went.

A crushed can of Diet Coke, trapped in a vortex of little winds, rattled complicatedly about the tracks.

Call Dr. Prakash. Just call. See if he has heard the news about House Number Five. That's all.

You could smell the forests burning all the way in the Blue Mountains even here on Platform 17, Central Station. Standing right by the yellow line illuminating the edge, Danny turned from the tracks toward the people behind him.

A weak-eyed boy wearing a Sikh's turban was staring at the electronic noticeboard as if it were something he had been told to eat. Three Catholic nuns gossiped in what Danny thought might be French, or perhaps Spanish—and he heard Hindi, and also somewhere else on the platform (far away), Tamil: this was inner-city Sydney, and a crowd like this, warm, expanding, like the convection-powered liquid molecules he remembered from his physics textbook, would envelop and conceal Danny—unlike the other sort of crowd he had seen in Australia, on the platform of a country town or bus station far from Sydney—cold and Caucasian, contracting into itself and stranding you farther and farther away. Danny felt safe right here, on this yellow line, at the edge of this platform.

But when he turned back to the Sikh boy, Danny caught his eyes: and they were hazelnut in color.

The color of Dr. Prakash's eyes. Radha Thomas's lover. The man whom, for nearly two years, Danny had called House Number Six.

What color, Danny wanted to ask the Sikh boy, was the jacket? The one the killer wrapped her in? Do *you* know?

Down on the tracks, the metal can rattled louder and louder, because the next train was approaching.

10:44 a.m.

Behind the glass door of the train, an Indian, wearing a blue suit, waited with her eyes to the floor; the moment the doors opened and the commuters stepped down onto Platform 17, she raised her eyes, threw her hair back, and gazed straight at Danny.

Radha Thomas.

Weren't you killed last night? Weren't you dumped into the creek, and didn't you wash up this morning, and weren't you discovered by a jogger, who must have, I assume, screamed at the sight?

The Indian woman in the blue suit went past, and swallowing

45

down the lump in his throat, Danny followed, until he lost her in the crowd.

10:54 a.m.

Seven exits lead out of Central Station, and up above the flight of steps, out there in the sunlight, stands the seventh.

That bright street beyond it is Chalmers Street, and when you are there, you are behind the city.

This time the man bearing the silver jet-booster on his back was trying to leave Central Station by the rear exit.

Still on the dark steps, as people took the stairs or the escalator on either side of him, he watched the trees beyond the thick black line, on the road. Prosperous with the Sydney light, the leaves swayed and wooed him. *Come on, Legendary Cleaner. Cross the black line. Ask Prakash what he knows of the murder.*

But there is a black line Danny had to cross to get to the leaves. No Aussie saw this line, which followed Danny around the world; but anyone who grew up in Sri Lanka in the 1990s knows this black line, what it loudly commands of one, what it quietly permits.

Taboo.

And the black line states:

Survive.

Don't be involved in this.

You're a man without rights in this world.

But on the other side of the thick black line, every incandescent leaf tip, each sun-darkened vein in the trees, was saying in a dead woman's voice:

There's a reason I can't ever leave Sydney and it is the light. You know I had an offer to work in the biggest hospital in Hong Kong as

*an administrator. Offers from Dubai too. Everything's tax-free there.
I could have gone anywhere—Hong Kong, Malaysia, Singapore.
But I can't leave this light.*

Looking at the sunlit trees, Danny, an expert negotiator with
taboo, proposed this: he had another hour and a half to make
it to the Accountant's place. Another hour and a half before he
returned to his day's duty.

I'll go out into Central for just five minutes. Then I'll come
back.

What are you doing? The black line thickened.

If he had free time, he should spend it in Glebe. In the
storeroom. Or in the library, talking to the other illegals. Not
out here.

With each new arriving train, he could hear steel carriages
pulverizing that stray Diet Coke lying on the tracks at Platform 17.

Brushing past Danny, a white man hurried up the steps and
toward the bright road, turning to check him out from the corner
of his eye.

Danny felt it like a punch in his stomach. I must look ridiculous. He could feel the comic weight of all those gold-tinted,
shampooed strands of hair on his scalp. It was a huntsman sitting
on his head and he was carrying it around Sydney. Go back at
once, said his shame, to the storeroom in Glebe and wait.

But then all the leaves rippled in the wind and glowed in
southern hemisphere light.

*But for you, Nelson, this must be a terrible city, right? Some
mornings, it must be. A prison of light. I will try to help you, Cleaner.
I know people in the government, and I'll ask them, without men-
tioning any names, of course. I'll ask if there's a way for you to say
sorry and be forgiven for what you did. I will ask.*

In the end, it was too strong. The dead woman's voice was
just too strong.

10:57 a.m.

Commuter trains packed full of honest suburban people were still drawing into Central Station as he walked alongside the trees with glowing green leaves.

He had done it. Breaking his taboo, he had left the station and run across the road.

Immediately, he wanted to eat something fried, something with chicken, or pork, or egg. Mutton.

If he can't have meat, a man has to have a friend.

Danny set his teeth and walked.

Down Chalmers Street, he saw a twenty-four-hour convenience store and moved toward it, because he knew at once who ran a place like that.

The door chimed as Danny pushed it open, looking about for the owner.

11:01 a.m.

In the city of Sydney, the shopper is a child in a fairy tale: sweets and colors surround her in a magic castle, and the Wicked Witch squints from government messages.

Behind his mountain of $2.50 candies and $3.50 pink greeting cards stood a brown man, his head blocking a SMOKING KILLS sign, as he guarded his most valuable cargo: scratch-off lottery tickets and cigarettes, both of which were encased in protective glass.

The man behind the counter was burly, bearded, probably Bangladeshi, and, Danny thought, extremely legal.

You can tell from the way he watches you.

The brown man in a white man's city who is watching other brown men. Danny had studied all the ways this was done, from the amiable glances of the Western Suburbs Indians, smug in their jobs and Toyota Camrys; the easily acquisitive *Sab Theek Hai, Bhai?* (or, more recently, the mysteriously Jamaican *Hey, maaan*) of the fresh new students in Haymarket, the ones who are running madly across roads; the ostentatiously indifferent *I've got nothing in common with you, mate* glances of the Australian-born children of doctors in Mosman or Castle Hill (Icebox Indians, Danny called them, because they always wore black glasses and never seemed to sweat, even in summer); and worst of all, those families visiting from Chennai or Malaysia, clicking photos of the beach, or loudly double-checking on the phone with relatives back home exactly which cholesterol medication or marsupial souvenir was needed from Australia. *Man who has run from his family, you're not natural,* brown people told Danny, and he, with his innate instinct for double or nothing, had streaked his hair in a barbershop. Standing in front of a mirror, he had imitated the gaze of an Australian-born man: *My father is a surgeon at Westmead Hospital. I don't have time for immigrants like you.* He had fixed his posture too. On the streets of Sydney, Pakistanis, Indians, Sri Lankans still looked at Danny, but now they looked with envy.

Easiest thing in the world, becoming invisible to white people, who don't see you anyway; but the hardest thing is becoming invisible to brown people, who will see you no matter what. Since they must see me, Danny thought, let me be seen this way—not as a scared illegal with furtive eyes but as a native son of Sydney, a man with those golden highlights, with that erect back, that insolent indifference in every cell of his body. Let them observe that Danny is *extremely* icebox.

Not *here*, though. Because no one is icebox around Central Station.

49

Here in these streets still resounding with the bodies of trains passing over old iron tracks, Chalmers and Devonshire, Danny had seen only the raw gaze, the Central Station stare, eyes that convey a desperate truth from one immigrant to the other: *every brown man in Sydney, one day or another, has to beg.*

Today is my day to beg, Danny pleaded with his eyes to the Bangladeshi, for I am in such trouble today, my legal brother.

Legal? Much more than legal—this young Bangladeshi was a brick wall in which each block said: Ideal Bloody Immigrant.

Returning Danny's gaze, he folded his arms across his chest, the image of respectability, diligence, and responsibility to family, everything the whites wanted in someone they let into their country: he did not have to talk about the weather, or about cricket or football, to curry favor with his clients; secretly, they envied his faith, his purpose, his strong alien core.

To win him over, step by step, Danny touched the top of a stack of *Daily Telegraph* newspapers, curved his spine, hunched, and smiled.

Meaning: Can I look at the paper without buying? Cricket? Only for cricket?

All this without words. South Asian to South Asian, ignoring the highlights.

Without a smile, the Bangladeshi relented, adding: "Don't make dirty."

Danny wandered past more greeting cards, small useful metal things hung in plastic, and a freezer just for Magnum ice cream, before he reached for *The Daily Telegraph*.

Danny turned the pages. Don't make *it* dirty. Legal idiot.

Nothing in the paper. So it must have been late at night. Still gazing at the paper, he played the knife murderer and made thrusts into the air. You'd have to be bloody strong to do it. Even if it was a big knife. She was a tough woman. She would have fought.

From where he stood, he now overheard the Bangladeshi store manager whispering into the phone: ". . . real malik is Louiebhai, he is the real . . ." and Danny was charmed momentarily by that name, Louiebhai, before he thought, Unless she knew the murderer and wasn't expecting to be stabbed, so she didn't, until he was summoned to the present by the snapping of fingers:

Danny looked up. The Bangladeshi was pointing straight at him. *Time's up.*

Folding the newspaper, Danny replaced it with a big smile. *Thank you, brother.*

"I have a cactus," he said. From his bag, he had removed the thing wrapped in thick plastic.

The Bangladeshi looked at it almost curiously. Danny knew why his eyes were sparkling like that.

Instead of the bonsai version with branches, Danny had bought the other, less endearing, domelike kind of cactus.

"For my girlfriend. Sonja. Nurse. She is a nurse. At St. Vincent's today. Very good nurse. She'll like the cactus, I reckon. Yes, I reckon."

The domed cactus was sixty cents cheaper than the branched kind, and didn't the Bangladeshi know it? Look at him grinning.

"Do you have *Knitting* magazine?" Danny raised his voice. "She likes stitching. Aussie girls don't stitch, but she does. Very good stitcher."

"Over there." The store manager knew Danny by now. "Don't read it for free."

By the time Danny had moved over to the rack with the women's and craft magazines, the TV newsreader had begun talking about sports.

As Danny browsed through the only knitting magazine on the shelf, another customer came in and actually bought something.

"Do you want the receipt?" the Bangladeshi man asked this customer, and Danny smiled: He still pronounces it with the p.

But the Bangladeshi man had nothing to hide: he was a legal, and whether or not he pronounced his p, Danny's time inside this store was now over.

Louiebhai, Danny thought as he left the store, Louiebhai, the new Malik, the new Boss of multicultural Sydney. *He* is the one I have to talk to, Danny thought, right outside the Bangladeshi's store, as the trains moved over their noisy tracks. Louiebhai, louiebhai.

Stress always made his sinuses painful. Danny felt the holes inside his skull become heavy; the deviation inside his nose hurt; and he shivered. Louiebhai, louiebhai . . . He looked around for a cigarette butt on the pavement. Please. Even the smell of tobacco made a man more rational.

Walking around Central Station, searching for something to eat or something to smoke, or just to sniff, Danny saw, instead, shards of glass.

A hole had been knocked in the middle of a window, and the pieces lay on the pavement. You don't ask why in Sydney, because young white men just do these things. Punch, smash, and wreck.

Danny could not stop staring at what lay on the ground. It seemed too horribly intimate a sight. Too eloquent.

It reminded him of death.

. . . a sudden image: Radha Thomas, healthy, thick-armed, in the luminous glow of a Sydney city swimming pool kids' section, with a giant water snake of red and blue tiles, a *Nagadeva*, right above her head, and children in their goggles and swimwear squealing for joy while this woman with her powerful neck, her powerful shoulders, splashed water on them . . .

Yes, that evening the doctor and Radha had bought Danny a two-dollar spectator's ticket so he could stand, watch, and offer funny comments while they swam and played in the kids' section of a public pool.

That woman who had been so alive in the turquoise water, that woman, House Number Five, Radha Thomas, was dead.

Murdered!

He felt a tightening all along the cord that connects pleasure to terror. The last time he had felt this, Danny thought as his shoe tried to move a piece of vandalized glass, was the twenty-eighth day after he had broken the terms of his student visa in Australia. And become illegal. Forever.

The broken pieces of glass had been painted with black letters . . . and the moment Danny saw the kangaroo-and-emu coat of arms of Australia, he guessed the original name and began to . . .

M

. . . restore the broken word with his shoe.

All things in life, all good things, take time to emerge, like a glossy plantain shining deep inside a dark coconut grove. Be slow, Danny. Think this one through.

He moved the first letter into place and stepped back.

E

What do you know, Danny?

They fought a lot.

So? Everyone does. Don't you and Sonja?

Danny remembered his uncle Sankar, who took a Vicks menthol inhaler with him everywhere he went, and sucked on it through a nostril . . . If only I had a menthol inhaler to suck on right here, he thought as he approached the next piece of broken glass.

I

Dr. Prakash was her lover, yes. Radha's lover. And he is a strange man, yes. He drank a lot. Sometimes he drank twenty beers at a time. But he wasn't bad. He wasn't one of the gutter men of Kings Cross. He was a private school boy. He had a cupboard full of ties.

Blocking one nostril, Danny inhaled with the other, an old trick to ease sinus pain.

A train moved noisily into Central Station. As the rattling of the train grew, the bright glass buildings cast incandescent reflections all around, while the great four-sided clock tower of Central, like Lord Brahma with His four faces, rose over the conflagration displaying the time of day to all the meridians of the city. Danny stared in wonder at these familiar things.

Down on the ground, a piece of glass caught his eye. He moved it with his shoe.

C

Black-and-white-striped ties. And next to them was a leather jacket. Which he wore all the time.

But it was a red leather jacket that he wore.

And they didn't say anything about the dead woman being found in a colored jacket, did they?

Danny saw himself now: at the top of Kings Cross, right by the Coca-Cola sign, looking down at the row of Californian palms that divided the traffic. Radha was by his side, waiting. It was one of those mornings in August, when the weather is boiling over in Sri Lanka and the rest of the normal world. But here, it was freezing, and air condensed when Danny breathed. Radha had come so close the shampoo from her hair blew into his nostrils. *There,* she said. *There.* True enough: walking up William Street, wearing a brand-new leather jacket—not black, but red—was Dr. Prakash, waving back at them—yes, Prakash, in that red jacket of his, exuberant and grinning, looking like a risen leaf, come to inform everyone that their long Australian winter was over.

You're crazy even to think it's him, Danny said to himself, walking over to the next piece:

A

And then **R** and **E**.

Now Danny realized he had missed a D somewhere. Didn't matter. Working his shoe with expert, subtle movements, he pushed the pieces of glass tighter together until each shard now glinted like a tooth of the sun.

ME ICARE

Here's the thing, though.

Her body was found at a creek in Toongabbie, they said. And she was killed yesterday. Which was a Sunday.

If her body was lying by a creek, and it was on a Sunday, then I think I know which creek that is.

Danny felt himself standing before an audience like the one Kiran Rao had addressed the previous day at the Sydney Festival. Yes, sir: that's it. I knew something about the dead woman no one else did. My very position as an illegal gave me, strangely enough, this unique power, and I used it to do some good. Through my contradictions, you grow.

But when he looked up and saw the hole in the window from where the Medicare sign had fallen, the back of his throat scratched.

I was just the cleaner, he now found himself pleading with the audience. Once a week, vacuum and toilets, that's all. He hoped the audience of rational Australians would understand. I like to show off a bit, that's all. I am very sorry.

Yes, Danny had assembled a name out of the broken glass pieces, but perhaps it was the wrong name.

ME ICARE

A white man was now watching him watching the broken glass. Danny turned and walked away, but then another train began to rattle through Central Station, and in the middle of the road, he froze.

The convex glass of the building across the road twisted the zebra crossing he was stepping on into a curvy chalk spine, and Danny caught himself, caught himself incoherent. Gold streaks in the hair, vacuum canister on his back, falsity in his heart, and an Australian accent on his tongue. Thin bum. Thick bum. I reckon. *Prrrrrrp.*

Crossing the road, he stood plumb in front of the curved glass. Astronaut.

As he watched it, the image of the weird astronaut before him changed: it became that of Cousin Kannan. Oh, you remember Cousin Kannan, don't you? The same time Danny flew to Australia, Cousin Kannan had paid a gang of people smugglers who would get people from Batticaloa to Rameswaram and, from there, around Africa and across the Atlantic. Kannan sat inside a boat for seventeen days, eating brown bread and boiled potatoes, watching for sharks, collecting rainwater, until the Coast Guard of Canada arrested everyone in his boat. Eight months in a prison. Then—like a miracle—legal status. A man needed a certain level of self-confidence even to become a refugee.

Danny had come to Australia by plane and then applied for refugee status and been told to fuck off. Could he really blame the Aussie government for doubting his story? It was the same with that interrogating officer back home, the man holding the lit cigarette in his forked fingers: people easily saw through Danny, but they saw through to the wrong thing. The fraudulence, the grin, weren't concealing any bigger secret.

There are some thick old walls on which poster has been stuck on poster. Peel away the posters—and the whole structure falls.

Honest Danny. Intelligent Danny. Reliable Danny. Reliably Intelligent Danny.

A train sounded a whistle from afar.

All at once, someone began humming the *Mission: Impossible* theme song. Danny slid his hand into his pocket and found the cell phone. Good. It felt good and solid in his hand as he looked at it. Scrolling down to the nineteenth entry in the phone book, he found

H6

House Number Six

And he pressed the green call button. He waited to hear it ringing.

"Ridiculous," he said, "ridiculous," and ended the call right there.

His leg was trembling as if it had seen a policeman; but his lips were parted, and there was joy in his heart.

As Central Station rocked with another incoming train, all around the sandstone wall that formed its perimeter, trees glowed, and their leaves took on the translucence of green grapes. Danny saw in each trembling and incandescent tree the peacock's tail of fire on which Lord Murugan rode. Vibrating with the locomotive's passing, the peacock's tail rippled and promised: *You will be whole again.*

Murugan: and he closed his eyes.

Buddha was *their* god, protector of the Sinhalas. Murugan, deity of Tamils in need, sat on a peacock holding a *vel*, a spear: he had temples devoted to his worship in India, in Jaffna, in Batticaloa, and a golden statue outside the Batu Caves in Malaysia.

When Danny opened his eyes, his phone was ringing, because the nineteenth number on his list, *H6*, was returning his call.

Murugan, god of minorities, protect me today, as you have for four years.

Danny answered the call. "Doctor Prakash," he said. "Is that you?"

Second Year as an Illegal

The cactus job in Campbelltown was one of Mr. Tsavdaridis's tips. In addition to ownership of the Sunburst grocery store in Glebe, and a pawnshop in Petersham, Tommo also ran a little Someone Else network extending across the city into the suburbs.

Five saguaro cactuses in a backyard in Campbelltown. Word came down to Tommo in Glebe. Good money. A local gardener, shown the five "gentlemen from Texas," had quoted a figure for removing them. Too high, felt the owners. "Get someone else to do it," said the local. That was when word got around, on the Someone Else network, to Tommo, who himself went to Campbelltown. Now, the old man, even in his arthritic state, was always ready for extra cash . . . but when he stood in that backyard in Campbelltown and saw the five cactuses, even he fell silent.

Danny was Someone Else's Someone Else.

Tommo gave him the morning off, and the address, and even paid for half of his train fare, on the understanding that it was to be a 50/50 split. Danny agreed. Before he went to Campbelltown, he bought himself three cigarettes from a store near the train station, smoked one, wrapped two in a white handkerchief, and then picked up a copy of a free local newspaper.

Another Death in Villawood

Once again an illegal immigrant awaiting deportation inside Sydney's Villawood detention centre has killed himself even while he was on "suicide watch." The Department of Home Affairs acknowledged media reports that a man, identified as a 33-year-old Afghan national, swallowed a razor blade and perished of internal bleeding overnight. Unofficial reports suggest

that this is the 698th attempt at self-harm this year
among the facility's estimated 3,500 inmates.

It was a long train ride. Three young men sat in front of him with
a pair of two-liter Coke bottles between their bare white legs. "So
my grandfather was half Scottish, right?" said the one in the middle
to the others. "Means they have to give me Right of Admittance in
the UK, and then I get an EU passport . . . not that I want to go to
Scotland, mind you—"

As Danny got out of the Campbelltown station, passing a row of fish-
and-chips shops, he saw four fat Aussie mynahs strutting about. These
were not the demure mynahs of home, but plump and noisy, fonder of
walking than of flying, gangsterish around french fries. Because Sydney
is a city without raptors. The meek can become bold here.

He found the house: outside, cut turf was stacked in dark rolls of
earth bristling with grass, like homemade chocolate stuffed with nutmeg.

Danny licked his lips.

An Aussie woman in her thirties answered the doorbell and
walked him to the backyard to show him what she called "the gentlemen from Texas." Saguaro cactuses. Five Texan giants, the tallest
a foot and a half taller than the other four, pale, U-branched, thorn-
proud, deep into the pebbled backyard; Danny walked around them.

"The guys who lived here before us, they fed these things fertil-
izer, and now look how dangerous they are, and we plan to have a
baby next year."

The man who had cut the grass had not agreed to cut the cactuses,
Danny guessed. He touched a thorn.

"—when we have a baby, we don't want our baby's eye in one of those
things." In a shed in her backyard, she showed him tools that included
a battery-powered buzz saw. ". . . taken out by the root, because you
know these things can grow again from a stump—and then I want
them rolled to the corner. Do you understand what I'm saying?"

Danny unwrapped and lit his second cigarette.

He understood.

On festival days, in the temples of eastern Sri Lanka, Hindu men walk over burning coals, because that is just how people in the East are. In the dargah of Kalmunai, the Muslim faithful pierce their tongue with a metal skewer; in the heat of April, a man opens his forearm with a stiletto. Because this is how people in eastern Sri Lanka are. All through the civil war, the worst things were done in the East by people from the East to people from the East.

When Danny extinguished his cigarette stub on a cactus, the Aussie woman let out a noise. She closed her glass door and watched from behind.

He loosened up the earth around the first cactus with the shovel. He did this for twenty minutes, attacking the base around the plants and tentatively tapping each one with the shovel. He began singing— and turned the buzz saw on. Thorn and milk and pulp flew out from the cactus. "Wait. Put these on," the woman shouted from behind the glass door, holding up a pair of goggles.

Hacking at the Texas gentleman with the buzz saw, he sang louder and louder.

The thorns are there to protect the roses. Danny grinned as he cut into the cactus. The thorns are there to—

"Are you an illegal?"

He turned the machine off, removed his goggles, and turned to see the white woman in the doorway, arms folded.

"You agreed to work for so little."

Danny put the saw down and got ready to run. But she just went back into the house and closed the door, before opening it to shout: "Once you're done cutting the gentlemen from Texas, you're also supposed to roll them away to the wall."

She left him alone for three-quarters of an hour, and when she opened the door again and came out, she saw the five dead cactus trunks rolled up the wall of the garden. The buzz saw had been put away. Danny was washing his hands in the outdoor sink. When she got there, she saw the color of the basin had changed from his blood. "Go to a hospital, it could get infected, which would be suboptimal. Seriously sub—" But she looked at him and knew he couldn't go to a hospital, of course.

She had antiseptic inside the house. And soft white towels. She swathed his hands in them for him.

"I used to be illegal," she said. "Not here, but in America."

Her name was Sam. And she was not Australian either. She was from Zimbabwe. Did Danny know why people were leaving that country? He should look it up on Google. He looked straight at his wrapped arms and waited for her to give him his money. Sam talked. She had tried for seven years to settle in America. Had Danny been there? Sam had lived in Colorado, in Texas, in Las Vegas, everywhere, always trying to get a green card. It never came. She kept extending her visa for years, but then one day it wasn't renewed. And so she stayed illegally in America, running from one immigration lawyer to another, for eighteen months.

"You know when I finally gave up?" she asked Danny. "It was the day I talked to Jose Diego, this man—this cleaner—at my lawyer's office. He told me how he became American. His mother, six months pregnant, had walked across the border in Texas—waded through a river—to get into American territory, just to give birth to him on U.S. soil. You had to have such passion to get that fucking green card thing. On the other hand," Sam added, "some get it just by luck." See, there was a cousin of hers, Anna, a British cousin, born and bred in the city of London—or so Cousin Anna thought. Because at the age of eighteen, her parents suddenly told her: "By the way, Anna, did we never mention you were born in Hawaii?" They just forgot to tell her, all these years. She was an American citizen by birth. "She lives over there now. Ohio. It takes

prodigies of effort or prodigies of luck to become American, and I was capable of neither.

"Australia isn't too bad," she said as Danny unwrapped his towels and examined the state of his hands. "It's outside human history. There's no torture here, there's no evil in the soil. Is it hard being illegal here?"

"I am," stated Danny, "not illegal."

She went into the house to get him his money.

Thanking Sam for the towels and refusing her offer of a beer but giving her his phone number and telling her to call him directly next time, and not via Tommo Tsavdaridis and his Someone Else network, Danny walked over to the Campbelltown station, where he discarded the bloodstained towels and waited for the train.

11:11 a.m.

"Dr. Prakash," said Danny again. And then, not knowing what else to do, added, "Sir."

There was a pause, and then a voice he hadn't heard in months laughed.

"Nelson. Nelson Mandela. That's you, isn't it? Nelson our cleaner."

"Yes, sir. It's me." Danny sighed. Too late now to change a thing.

On the other end of the phone, the man laughed again.

"Haven't seen this number in so long. In *so* long. Our Legendary Cleaner. And how nice to hear from you, today of all days."

The impetus to communicate often came to Danny as mimicry. He heard himself saying:

"Today of all days."

The doctor's voice was as clear and unhurried as the headlight of a car in Batticaloa after a late-evening storm has cleared. *How could I be the murderer?* it asked, quietly, serenely.

Clap your hands, son, and the day will start again.

Thinking, Aussies are a logical people, mistakes can be undone in this country, Danny said, "Just hit your number by mistake, Doctor. Was looking for House Number Seven. He's an accountant. On Brown Street in Newtown. Have to clean his place. Hit your number by mistake."

"By mistake. Today of all days," said the voice of House Number Six, Dr. Prakash, the man he had once called the King of the Nile.

Danny coughed.

"A bit strange, Doctor sir," he said preemptively.

There was a pause, and then the voice on the phone laughed.

Danny waited.

"Mr. Cleaner. Nelson the cleaner, it's great you called today. You know why? I'm flying to South Africa in a few hours. By the day's end."

"South Africa?"

"Yes, South Africa. I told you how much I love that country, right? Gandhi was there as a young man. You remember that. I told you all about it." The doctor chuckled. "And guess what I need? Someone to clean my place. Potts Point. Someone's got to give it a clean, then I can head out. And you were the best. You were a legend, Nelson. Come over."

"Busy busy busy," said Danny. "Too busy. Have to go to Newtown."

"Not too busy to call me but too busy to come over. Funny man, our Danny. That is your *other* name, isn't it?"

The voice sounded calm, cool, rational: above all, it sounded Australian.

"Sorry, Doctor." Danny took a breath. "Big mistake—just a mistake. Have to go work in Newtown." And he hung up.

Overwhelming relief. There. He had done it. Done his duty: he had checked, just to see if Prakash sounded normal, and found him perfectly so, which meant he had had nothing to do with anything. Fine. Life was fine. Back to cleaning Rodney Accountant's flat now. *Ba-da-da-da-bum-bum*.

A middle-aged man passed him with a dog on a leash. No breed of dog Danny could name, the animal was the color of blueberry ice cream from New Zealand; around its fist of a neck was a black collar with spikes, and hard white nipples stood erect under the flat belly. How good it would be, Danny thought, to see a fat and familiar Sri Lankan dog right now, like an Alsatian.

German shepherd, they call them here.

His phone began to glow again.

H6

Dr. Prakash was eager to resume the conversation.

It must be past noon now. Surely.

Clap your hands, son, and the day will start again. Inhale some menthol, son, and the day may start again.

He walked into Glebe clapping his hands.

Maybe it was the time in the hotel business in Dubai. You have to keep selling your customers your shitty hotel, your shitty room. A man who overpromises to others will overpromise to himself. He says: "Danny is going to solve this murder—Danny is going to be a hero." And *this* is what happens.

He calls the one man he shouldn't be calling today. The day of Radha's death.

The smoke was thicker here in Glebe than around Central, and he sneezed again, thinking, Where is everyone, where is the world, as the keening noise of construction rose in the background.

Just two days ago it had been a different neighborhood: the weekend fair was on, and he and Sonja had held hands and gone into a row of white tents where they saw hand-beaten steel jewelry, leather belts, soaps wrapped in colored paper, and fragrant fat candles. A rock band played behind the tents. Sonja looked for the type of black jeans that are slashed open at the knees; also for colored thread for her knitting; and she discussed woolen knitwear with the people under the white umbrellas, and different styles of darning and stitching, a sort of homeliness that Danny did not associate with Australian women, and which made him smile. In the background, the other illegals, who knew he was there, and knew Sonja was coming, stood at a safe distance, grinning.

Saturday. That had just been on Saturday. Today Glebe was like a ghost suburb, darkened by a film of woodsmoke.

Past the white pillars of the Glebe post office, the empty parks, the wrought-iron terraces reminding him of homes in Batticaloa, he ran to the library.

Hide in the Sunburst, or sit with your own kind, Danny. That's how you'll survive this day.

Most weekday mornings, the illegals gathered in front of the Glebe library: it was their own market, of damaged goods to barter or sell, and information about jobs and changes to immigration laws. Sometimes Danny read to the others from Kiran Rao's book, or described to them what Rao had said that morning on TV:

Every morning Mum put me on a train from Penrith to the city to attend Knox Grammar, where I was dux of my year. On the way to school, I read a book a day. Thanks to my mum's "never give up" attitude, today I'm a trained psychiatrist and an adviser to Channel 9 on multicultural affairs.

There was no one sitting in front of the Glebe library today.

Though Danny knew their names—Lin, the Chinese-Malaysian, and the two Pakistanis, Ibrahim and Razak—he had no way of finding them. That was the agreement. That way, if one got caught, the others were safe.

Just two months ago . . . right here, in front of the library, Lin, the Chinese man from Malaysia, had met a European back-packer who was in tears, saying he had been cheated by a farmer in Tamworth for whom he'd been picking oranges for a month, at the end of which the farmer had paid him a dollar per bin of fruit, so that he left Tamworth with just $120 for a month's backbreaking work. Lin, amazed and appalled that this white boy had apparently never before been cheated in his entire life, was delighted by the fellow's habit (he must have been a Britisher, Danny felt) of saying "See you in a bit. In a bit. See you in a bit" to everyone who passed by. Lin smuggled out two sets of free tacos from the Mexican restaurant where he worked, and he and the European ate the tacos together outside the Glebe library. To make the poor boy understand that he was not the only one in trouble, Lin even confessed that he was illegal in Australia, and then the European, would you believe it, after thanking him for the tacos, after saying, "See you in a bit, see you in a bit," had gone back to his hostel in Town Hall and *called* immigration, yes, *seriously*, and when the officers drove in a van to the Glebe library to hunt him down, who saved Lin? One of the librarians, a university girl, who hid him in her car for two hours. Two hours. After that Lin changed his phone number and wouldn't give it to Danny or the others . . .

From the library, Danny ran down the right-hand side road, following its plunge and vanishing quickly from the main road, past block after block of eyeless houses, to a garish spray-painted mural of the Lord Krishna, portrayed as a blue-skinned Rastafarian on a surfboard, which meant he was nearly home.

He could hear, already, golden oldies playing on 2CH 1170 kHz before he saw a pale old white arm dangling out the open win-dow of a grocery store, tapping a lit cigarette onto the pavement, adding smoke and warm ash, its own pollution, to the bush fire's.

The owner of the burning cigarette said:

"Why are they always picking on us? Everyone's picking on Eels. You remember last year, Rugby League Judiciary gave Joey Mitchell a dangerous-contact charge, and it was a clean tackle. Perfectly clean tackle. They pick on us always."

"Tommo."

Summer may be the cricket season for the rest of Sydney, but not in this store just off Glebe Point Road, whose name was announced by an old white sign: SUNBURST.

"Mitchell, he's the one with bruises on his head, and the Judiciary make him the bad guy."

"Tommo!"

The cigarette fell to the pavement, and the arm drew back into the window, as Danny entered the store, walked past all its shelves, turned left, and ran up an old metal staircase into a storeroom whose door he closed behind him.

He was home.

11:16 a.m.

Two panda bears welcomed Danny from above a cupboard filled with stocks of tissue paper. Cardboard cartons were stacked up on the walls, but a blue sofa and a black swivel chair dominated the room. A small cracked mirror hung on the wall.

UNDERSTAND RUGBY

In Australia three types of rugby (never call it rugby) exist
Rugby League (just call it football)
Big teams
Eels—Parramatta (Tommo's team)

Dragons—Illawara
Rabbitohs (very bad team)—South Sydney
Bulldogs—Canterbury
Also they play this game in Brisbane

Next to the mirror, a handwritten sheet of paper was pinned up on the wall, with stickman illustrations.

2. Rugby Union (just call it Union)—played by very rich people. This game has the "scrum."

One of the stickmen jumped high up and caught an oval object.

3. AFL (Aussie Rules)—played in Melbourne. Teams are Collingwood, Fitzroy, etc.

Removing his backpack, Danny dropped it over his plastic bag; then he removed the cactus from it and placed it beside the panda bears.

"Why are you here?" a voice asked, and Danny, opening the door, looked down the staircase of seven metal steps.

Tommo Tsavdaridis's pale face stared from below.

The sunlit cash counter of the store was visible in the distance. Right behind Tommo were a shelf of baby formula cans (Shelf F1) and a shelf of air sprays, tissues, toilet paper (Shelf G1). The numbering of the shelves was Danny's invention. This reminded him he had to open the cardboard carton with the ramen ready-to-eat noodles and place them on Shelf E, next to the canned soups.

"You have a job today. Two jobs. Did you cancel?"

Tommo placed a hand on the staircase to draw nearer. He had a weak smoker's voice, and an eye that stored up punishments.

"You have to pay me twenty dollars, even if you cancel. I won't forget. I won't ever forget twenty dollars. Danny. You believe me, don't you. I won't ever forget."

Without answering his boss, Danny closed the door on him.

He sat down on the black swivel chair. He drew in the air that smelled of wet cardboard, spices, and carpet. And he knew this was something he did not want to lose.

He had furnished it well and for free. Because Aussies threw out a regular living room every two days. Inside the cupboard, there was even a small electric heater that he was allowed to use, but only for forty minutes a night, even in midwinter, because, Mr. Tsavdaridis said, it consumed too much electricity. Still, the winters were not too bad, especially after he had found the swivel chair, discarded by the Glebe library.

Whooooosh. Danny began spinning round in the chair. In Dubai he had guessed for the first time the size of the world at whose very lowest level, instinct told him—a Tamil from the east of Sri Lanka, a minority within the minority—he dwelled.

Here in this storeroom in Glebe, Danny had added a swiveling chair to his prison. When he sat on it, he became someone else. Kiran Rao, usually. The blood pressure was coming down. He felt it.

Then from down below, from the store, he heard someone shout: "Danny. How much money did you make today? Danny."

"Tommo," he shouted back. "Go away."

"You have to give me the money even if you canceled the job."

"I haven't canceled. I'm just resting."

"Resting?" The old Greek sounded as if he did not recognize that word. "Resting?"

Moving his black swivel chair to the cupboard, Danny picked up a panda and threw it at the door. Get out!

He kept thinking of that face. Mark. Her husband. The one he'd seen today next to the red tulips. Yes, he wasn't screwing her—maybe that is what got him angry. Jealous. But Mark was a real estate agent, isn't he? A rich man. (I'm not saying he did it either, Danny felt obliged to tell his imaginary Australian audience. I'm sorry if I gave the impression that I was blaming Mr. Mark.) Who else could it be? One of those King Punch things? Random aggression? But whoever did it, and for whatever reason, one thing was almost certain.

The killer was a citizen.

"Something on your mind, Danny?" the old man's voice said from outside. "Don't think too much."

Mr. Tsavdaridis charged Danny a third of all that he made cleaning houses as middleman's commission; the advice on life was given free.

"The fire alarm went off in the store today, you know. Next door also. Everywhere in Glebe, fire alarms. There was so much smoke in the air. Maybe the smoke got into your head. You're thinking shit today," the grocer shouted from below before he left Danny alone.

And he was right: Danny knew. This time Mr. Tsavdaridis was right. He should be cleaning.

His heart pounded as if praying on its own to its own god. One greasy samosa. Just one. One egg samosa.

"Danny. That woman who died today." The voice was back outside his door. "You're not home because of her, are you?"

The cunning old man had begun to guess.

"Tommo," Danny shouted. "House Number Five. You don't know her."

"I know *everything* about you."

"You don't know her because I never told you. I used to clean . . . Then I stopped working for her. She died. They don't know the color of the jacket."

"You never told me? You never paid . . ."

Danny could hear Mr. Tsavdaridis struggling with this fact. Four years ago, he had had Danny in his store and in his grip, and with every passing day since then, he knew that his grip had loosened.

There was no need for Danny to say what he did next, except to let the old man know that they had become equals inside this grocery store.

"You remember when I was coming late some nights? I said I was in the library? I was with them. The murdered woman. And the doctor. House Number Five in Erko and House Number Six in Potts Point. I stopped going to both. About six, seven months ago."

"You were staying out late, you were having fun, you never told me, you never paid me—" From below, the voice turned high-pitched, hysterical.

Danny grinned. He was feeling sadistic this morning.

But the smile did not last long. Every mistake he had made this morning had just grown bigger: his phone was ringing, again and again.

H6

Dr. Prakash was calling again.

"Cleaner."

Danny had picked up.

"You just hung up on me."

"Sorry. I am sorry."

"You called me today, remember. You called me. Now you have to come over and clean the place. That's a fair deal, isn't it?"

"I . . ." said Danny. "I . . . I . . ." and then just hung up.

Fuck.

In his room, Danny said the word out loud: "Indians." You *knew* they were Indians. You *know* Indians are the worst thing for a Sri Lankan Tamil, so why didn't you stay away from these two Indians?

Why didn't you call us before this, police will ask, if you felt something was wrong with these two?

I am a victim of state torture.

He spun around on the swivel chair; its metal joints creaked.

Is that why you spent your father's money to come to Australia and then stopped talking to him?

Danny pressed his shoe on the floor to stop the chair from turning.

He reached for the fallen panda bear and placed it back on the cupboard. From in between the panda bears, he brought out the cellophane-wrapped cactus and set it down on the sofa. He sat facing the cactus.

The interrogation had begun.

Start at the beginning of the story. That is how the police always want it. Say, "I confess my shame. I'm an illegal. I've broken the law."

And Danny again spun around on the black chair.

. . .

Good. Now, how did you start cleaning the dead woman's place?

When you do a professional job in this country, people appreciate you, it is one of the things I like about Australia. You do a great job, they say, my friend needs a cleaner too. Someone must have sent me to Radha's place. I can't remember who . . .

Remember harder. Who sent you over there?

. . . Danny slowed down his spinning a bit. Sorry. Can't remember that now.

This is what he did remember:

The first week, it was just a place to clean, her flat. Yoga mats and gym clothes on the floor, spaghetti in the sink. Radha Thomas, the owner, was watching him as he cleaned, but that was normal enough. They want to see how you do it the first time you clean. There was a photo of her along with a white man on every wall in the place. Her Australian husband. She paid sixty dollars in cash. No problem.

The second time Danny came to clean her place, she stayed on the phone as he worked. He listened in on her conversation. "O-kay," he said to himself under his breath, mimicking her. "O-kay." Through the window, he could see the four dark obelisks, the four brick towers, at the end of Erskineville.

Suddenly, these strong feet came pounding up the stairs, and before Danny could turn the vacuum down, the door simply slammed open, and the man had already put his arms around Radha and simply lifted her off the floor. Danny dropped the vacuum handle. Raised above the earth by the powerful intruder, fighting off his kisses, the woman of the house shouted at the hired help: "It's o-kay. I know this man. I know him. Wait downstairs. Wait. I'll call you up. We'll pay you more. O-kay? Oh my God, Prakash, stop touching me in front of—"

The Indian man who had lifted up House Number Five in his arms turned to Danny and said: "Get out for a while, mate."

Did you wait for them?

What else could Danny do?

Closing the apartment door behind him, he went out onto the street and waited next to a white gum tree, leprous and magnificent, wanting to touch its bark, to tickle the mushrooms at its base. He watched the tree and kept mimicking that word. *Okay.* A hand grenade of a word: guttural *o*, explosive *kay*. From above, a woman's moaning filled the courtyard. Danny looked up: Radha had been growing red tulips in her window.

O-kay. O-kay. Listening in on their pleasure, Danny once again saw in himself a man who had not even been able to express his rage at the world *cleanly*, as so many less gifted men had done. A friend from school, not a good student, not good at the triple jump, had joined the LTTE one evening, fleeing by motorboat over the lagoon, then climbing onto the back of a truck and going all the way to a training camp in the north, where he had become a soldier and died fighting the Sri Lankan army. There was honor in *that*. Picking up a knife and stabbing a racist policeman in the heart again and again, honor in *that*. Getting on a boat and hitting sharks with your paddles and shouting at the Canadian Coast Guard, "I am your refugee," there was honor in *that*.

But look at *you*.

Before Danny's eyes, a mural materialized—which he had seen on a wall in his wanderings somewhere or other in Sydney, the artwork done realistically, hair and fur painted with minute attention to texture—of three dead animals. A deer with curved horns, a heron, and a rabbit. Three animals, three corpses, trussed up by wires from the ceiling of a kitchen, and below them, on the butcher's table, a ram lay, its mouth bound with ropes, its tongue sticking out. The heron in profile had one eye open wide, as if to say: *We didn't even scream when the world was stolen from us.*

Forty-six minutes he waited there.

Danny's knuckles were chafing at the papery bark of the gum tree, peeling it away in white strips, adding them to the crushed mushrooms below, when the woman's moaning rose and then stopped. When he looked up, the tulips shook after a few minutes, a window opened, and Radha's vivid, sated face summoned him back into the building.

He ran up.

"Are you a spy, buddy?" up in the unit, the Indian man, still in his boxer shorts, demanded, his hands on his torso. "I can smell a spy: they always send a brown man to spy on a brown man."

He was still talking about spies when he gave Danny his cash—sixty dollars plus twenty extra—and Danny knew he ought to say nothing, but he had spent a year and a half living in a storeroom. "Are you two rednecks?" he asked, at which the woman just burst out laughing.

"Did you learn that word after coming to Australia, mate?"

"It's American," Danny said before leaving.

Halfway to the train station, he heard footsteps behind him and a woman shouting: "You're right!" Radha came running up to him. "It is American. We looked it up on Prakash's phone. Come back and have a drink with us. Have dinner."

After a pause, Danny followed her back.

The routine was set.

Have you remembered yet who sent you to her place?

No, not yet. It'll come. Danny spun around again in the chair.

Every Tuesday he went to the place in Erskineville. But she had another place too, in Potts Point. House Number Six. She was letting him live there: Dr. Prakash. Every Wednesday to that place. But it was the same routine in both places, really.

Which means?

Means he was told to wait outside while they did the part they liked best—fucking in the apartment when her husband, that man, wasn't around. Danny put up with that. He put up with everything as long as they paid him on time, which they did, with tips thrown in.

Then there must have been an incident, perhaps her husband nearly caught them one day, because one day Prakash stopped coming to Erksineville. From then on, they met only at his place in Potts Point.

Her place in Potts Point, which she let him use.

Now, after Danny came to House Number Five and cleaned it from wall to wall, Radha drove him in her car ("Every other cleaner we have is like, 'I wants to change bedsit,' and you arrive with polysyllables! How could we let you leave us?") all the way to Kings Cross, Sydney's red-light area, right behind which, in one of those sudden shifts of tone typical of the city, was a suburb of whitewashed classical buildings ("seriously thin-bum," Danny would later tell Radha, making her laugh). This was Potts Point. She stopped her car in front of a building called Regents Court. House Number Six. She went in first; Danny was supposed to wait outside, or buy himself a coffee, or walk about Kings Cross, or stand at the Coca-Cola sign and watch the traffic below until she texted him—*All done mate*—and then he hopped, skipped, and leaped back to their place, just like in the triple jump, went in through the glass door and up to Dr. Prakash's sixth-floor flat, straightening it all up, the bed and the bedsheets.

The black chair had stopped spinning; Danny had picked up his cell phone from the sofa.

H6

It buzzed and glowed nonstop now; interrupting his imaginary one, Dr. Prakash was calling to have a real conversation.

You keep calling him a doctor. A real doctor?

Reaching forward, Danny adjusted the position of the cactus plant a bit; then he spun another round on his chair.

She called him that, Officer. It was her idea of a joke. She called him Doctor because it's the price you pay when Radha Thomas helps anyone. Prakash got into the spirit of the joke. Sometimes when he was walking about Kings Cross, he would point at people and say, "That guy's got a fucked-up bladder. I can tell from the way he walks." Or, pointing at a jogger: "*Arrhythmia.* That man's got a bad heart. Won't jog long." Yes, he played along with the doctor joke.

What was *the joke?*

He was a private school boy, an icebox Indian, and he should have been a doctor. Not a miner. That was the joke.

Inside his flat in Potts Point, or the flat that was hers and which he was occupying, you *did* believe that the man was a private school boy: there was a cupboard full of ties, striped ties, and there was a silver shield he had won in rugby at school, with a motto in Latin. Beside the ties and the school shield, there was a photograph of Prakash in a foreign country, somewhere in Africa, judging by the people around him.

Did you remember yet the name of the person who sent you to Radha Thomas?

No. Still trying, though.

Do you think Dr. Prakash killed her?

No. (Danny looked again at the glowing phone: *H6* still calling.)

You see, each of them could laugh at himself *and* at the other. That saves a relationship. I'm telling you. That's why Sonja and I get along so well.

An example: see, one day Radha stood next to her man and said, "I did what everyone of my generation did, I worked for the government. You're having an affair with a bureaucrat. Dangerous, aren't you?"

"Everyone in *my* generation became a doctor," replied Prakash with a bow. "So did I."

And they both laughed.

See what I mean? Danny raised his arms for emphasis. Those two were great with each other. They had the gambling. And the fucking.

Of course they talked about running away together. Yes, like lovers in Tamil films, they talked about running away, leaving Sydney, leaving Australia.

But Danny never thought they'd do it. They owned property. She owned property. Two places in Sydney.

Danny closed his eyes and remembered that place again. The one in Potts Point. The one she let Dr. Prakash live in rent-free. As he ran the vacuum around the sofa, Danny had a view, framed by the apartment blocks of Elizabeth Bay and the arch of the Harbor Bridge, of a pile of broken porcelain, the Sydney Opera House—which trembled, on humid days, inside a haze of air that seemed to have been blown from Batticaloa.

And she let Prakash stay there rent-free. She wanted him *that* much. Why would he hurt her?

Maybe *that man* did it. Her husband, Mark, the fellow with the red face whom he'd seen in the window, beside the tulips. But why would she have told him of that creek or taken him there? That place, that flowing water, those stars: those were only for her and for the doctor.

Or maybe it was a stranger, someone who just saw her at the creek that night . . .

Wait. There was that time when Radha and Prakash were at the creek, and two white boys were jumping in the water with their black dog. And how that dog was howling.

Danny opened his eyes. The metal staircase outside was trembling, which meant Tommo had placed a cardboard box on it, his way of indicating that Danny had to get to work at the store rather than lie and dream in his room.

Getting up from his chair, he opened the cupboard and looked about for the Yellow Pages—he kept it there to call cleaning services and check on their rates. He flipped through the big old book till he found what he was looking for:

Important numbers

Crime Stoppers 1-800-333-000
Crime Stoppers operates 24 hours a day, 7 days a week, and allows members of the community to anonymously report criminal or suspicious behavior or activity. Your information may be the vital missing piece the police need to solve a crime.

He took the cactus with him as an accomplice.

Opening the door of the storeroom, Danny saw that the seven-runged ladder that led down was blocked by the cardboard carton of ramen noodles, which the old man must have moved over to give him a message. If he wasn't cleaning for Tommo, he was expected to be filing for Tommo.

The ladder tittered in a bout of metallic nervousness. Holding the cactus in his right hand, Danny went down, taking exaggerated steps over the cardboard box.

Can you tell us more about those two white boys in the creek? And about their black dog?

Placing a finger on his lips, Danny urged the policeman to be quiet—just for a second.

While Tommo Tsavdaridis watched from the counter, Danny did the triple jump: hopped past the old man shouting, skipped out of the store, and leaped out into Glebe, while a frenzied voice screamed, "Danny! Come back and pay me my twenty dollars! I will murder you, Danny, I will never forget twenty dollars!"

Not far from the famous mural of the Lord Krishna, a local landmark, stood another treasure of the suburb, a shop called Gabrielle. It baked its own bread, served coffee at a cost 20 percent above the citywide average, and closed every weekday at three p.m., while on a timetable on the glass window, beside *Saturday* and *Sunday*, a nightgowned body emitted luxurious Z's. It was the kind of place run by people who are not migrants to Australia.

As he walked in front of Gabrielle, inhaling the smell of fresh baking, Danny pressed the potted plant to his T-shirt and felt its domed shape against his chest.

From the dark window of the 7-Eleven, which is the kind of place that is run by immigrants, someone was watching him.

Though he took a step back from the window when Danny returned his gaze, the brown man's eyes grew, like a camera expanding its aperture even as it pulled back, ashamed of wanting Danny's image and thirstier than ever for it because of that shame.

Danny mimicked his actions. He took a step back; he kept watching the receding face of the brown man in the 7-Eleven.

All at once it materializes before your eyes: the visage of an Egyptian pharaoh on an electronic gambling machine. King of the Nile. He is broad-shouldered and regal, with sleek, understanding eyes, a worthy consort to the tiara'd Cleopatra, who gazes at you from the next machine, the Queen of the Nile.

Danny's heart began pounding. *It is coming,* it told him. *It is coming.* A dog ran panting by Danny's shoes, found them uninteresting, and went back to its master, and then, as he expected, it came. His phone buzzed, and the panel glowed:

H6

House Number Six.

Aware that he was still being watched from the 7-Eleven, Danny walked on toward the Glebe post office.

He pressed the cactus into his chest but raised the flesh of his palm just enough so he could see the number he had written on it.

1-800-330-000

And he answered the call by saying: "Yes, Doctor, sir?"

11:43 a.m.

"Isn't it funny," a voice on the phone said, "you calling me today of all days, Cleaner."

Calm, unhurried. There's no guilt in this voice, Danny told himself. None.

"Today is a special day. You do know why it is a special day?" Dr. Prakash asked.

"Yes, of course I know," protested Danny. "It's Guru Purnima day."

"Oh, you know," the doctor said, as if surprised by Danny's answer. Then he stayed silent.

Has he not seen the TV news yet? Should I just tell him that his girlfriend, his secret girlfriend, is lying by a creek in Toongabbie, stabbed to death?

The voice on the other end of the phone laughed a bit now, before sucking in air as if to cool a burning tongue.

"Guru Purnima day means Purnima that is Guru. Isn't that how you always talked?" The voice laughed again, and then it dropped to a whisper: "How much you want?"

"Excuse me?" said Danny.

Again the whisper on the phone asked: "How much?"

"For what?" asked Danny, saving the situation.

There was a laugh. "That's right," said the voice on the phone. "For what? For cleaning the place, of course. And the place needs a final clean. Come over. You're just the man I need to see."

Maybe that's why he doesn't know what happened to Radha. He's leaving. He's been packing.

"You know, they made me clean it after you left, Nelson. They made me do everything. The place is a mess. Come over."

Now the doctor's voice dropped. "Danny. Don't worry."

Danny asked: "Don't worry?"

The voice on the phone said: "Yeah, don't worry. Your secret is safe."

Before he could stop himself, Danny retorted: "You mean *your* secret."

"No," the doctor's voice grew louder, "*your* secret."

Like children playing with the word.

"*What* secret?"

"I won't tell anyone, Danny. Your secret, it's a terrible secret."

"What secret?" Danny asked helplessly.

He's threatening me. He just openly threatened me on the phone. But with what?

"Yes, *what* secret. Exactly." The doctor paused. "You live in a grocery store, don't you, Danny? There's a painting on the wall next to where you're hiding. A Hindu painting. Right?" A pause. "Is it a painting of Ganesha?"

That secret.

Danny felt the cold phone on his neck—She told him. Told him everything—and tried to find his foothold on what had recently been firm earth. Breathe in, breathe out.

Before she died, Radha Thomas must have told Prakash every secret of Danny's that she knew.

"Come to my place in Potts Point and clean it. Okay?"

When Danny stayed silent, the doctor, like a reasonable man, changed his proposal. "Or we can meet at the Clinic. You remember it, don't you?"

Danny simply hung up.

He *must* know of the immigration dob-in number. If he calls them first and tells them what he knows of me, I'll be in the Villawood detention center by evening.

Right outside the Glebe post office, a shirtless white man had prostrated himself like a Hindu, his head bowed to the ground, with his hands around a plastic cup marked HELP ME, as if in a yoga of abasement.

A new text message arrived. *You hung up.*

Thinking fast, Danny texted, *Sorry. Im coming.* And then: *see you at the clinic*

And Prakash texted back: *Secret is safe.*

Danny exhaled. But why is he threatening me unless he has something to hide?

Maybe he just knows something about the murder that he doesn't want to tell the police.

Fuck her. Danny wanted to smash his cell phone. Fuck that woman—that Radha. She told him I was illegal.

Plenty of water, he remembered. Sonja said that would help with sinus trouble. Plenty of water all day long.

Looking at the bent-over white man, at his white begging cup, Danny thought: I have just cursed a dead woman. By way of atonement, Danny drew out his wallet and threw the smallest piece he had, a five-cent coin, into the plastic cup. Like a machine that had been activated by the coin, the yogi suddenly looked up and said, "Thanks."

Before his head sank back to the pavement.

A great curved building, like a stage set, announced the end of Glebe and the start of Broadway. Now no part of the city was really safe from the immigration machine, but Glebe was a glade inside Sydney's rain forest of light—leafy, lefty, defiantly full of churches—and when you came and stood here, on Broadway, and saw, a few feet away, two palace-like shopping malls, identical twins, each crowned by a green globe, then you knew you were at the end of Glebe's special protections.

These were the portals of Sydney.

12:03 p.m.

Danny breathed in.

Flags, neither Australian, rippled above a pair of dark well-articulated brick towers connected by a balcony like the one the pope gives his blessing from.

This is another of Danny's safe spots: the Lansdowne Hotel, across the road from Glebe.

Stepping out of the black door of the pub, letting out a blast of air-conditioned air, a woman spilled ice cubes from a plastic bucket into a tin box captioned REFRESHMENT FOR DOGS, making a racket as Danny approached the pub.

"You're late, buddy," the white woman said without looking up from the tin box, which now dazzled with diamonds, but there was no mystery there. She had just mistaken Danny for some other brown man who worked at the pub.

"Sorry," said Danny.

She'd never remember the golden highlights in the hair, or anything else about this particular man, if she was asked later on.

Inside the pub, he saw, by the pool table, the flashing screen of Big Buck, the video game in which you aimed black plastic rifles at caribou and reindeer that fled through simulation snow and icy water—each deer, when shot, revealed itself to be a girl who blew you a kiss—and then he went up the flight of stairs: past a pornographic oil painting, there was a lounge with a view of the portals of the two identical shopping malls across the road, with their glass globes.

The lights had not been turned on in the upper level, and as Danny searched for the pay phone, he soon found himself in an area of darkness; but with the first step he took, the lights clicked on by themselves and exposed, in front of toilet stalls with WET PAINT signs on them, a black pay phone.

With the flat of his right palm, Danny compressed his golden hair. This is what he had come for.

So pick up the phone, dial, Policeman, House Number Five was having an affair with Number Six, that's all I know, bye-bye, hang up.

And run.

"Mate, is that a cactus you've got?"

Of course, you're never alone in a pub, not even in the morning. This fellow even wore a suit and a tie, and he was drinking on a Monday morning.

Danny looked helplessly at the green thing in a pot that he was holding. He expected to hear a laugh, but instead, in the young man's red face, he saw a deep sympathy—either alcoholic or Australian in origin—with something visibly out of place in the world.

"It's a cactus you've got," the drunken man said unhappily, and left him alone.

In an alcove before the toilets, Danny saw a black phone in a flickering light. Within the misfiring lamp in the alcove, the naked bulb beat like a bird's heart.

On his palm, in black ink, in the throbbing light, Danny read the number.

1-800-333-000

He put his twenty-cent coins into the pay phone and dialed. *Insufficient credit.*

One more coin.

Now the New South Wales Crime hotline was ringing. Answering it, a woman's voice said: "Police hotline. Can I help you?"

"Excuse me," said Danny.

"Yes?"

"Excuse me."

"Yes, what are you calling for, please? This is the crime hotline. Do you have a crime to report?"

"I have knowledge." He paused.

"What kind of knowledge? Of a crime?"

"Knowledge of a crime."

"That's the kind of knowledge this number is for. What is the crime?" she asked.

"Today is . . . Guru Purnima," he said.

Because there is another hotline and another number, isn't there. And Danny knows *that* number by heart.

1-800-009-623

<u>How to make a report to the Immigration Dob-in Service (Border Watch Hotline)</u>

What types of activities should you report?
We encourage the community to provide information about any person you think:

> *has overstayed a visa (such as no longer having a valid visa)*

> *is working illegally*

> *has breached visa conditions—example: a student visa holder who is working more hours than the visa permits*

> *deliberately lied on a visa application*

> *provided false documents to the department*

> *arrived in Australia without a valid visa*

> *is on a student visa but is not studying*

> *is in a fake marriage or relationship to obtain a visa*

> *is providing immigration advice but is not a*

"Sir? What is the crime, and what do you have to report?"

In the flickering light, the alcove became the Embassy of Batticaloa.

A paraffin lamp hissed and cast shadows around the alcove: the sharply outlined shadows were of humans, humans he might know from home, and the weaker shadows were from all their bicycles, propped up against a wall.

Danny touched a bump on his forearm.

Never going back.

He put the receiver back into the pay phone and ended the call.

He noticed pink-and-white letters stating that the Pay Phone Identification Number was 02379286X2. He followed the long black cord coming out of the old pay phone to its source in a socket of the wall. Electrical wiring rose up from the socket in banded columns before jagging left, like art deco decoration. Now, where are those wires going? One big listening-in machine, the city of Sydney.

The lights in the alcove went out on their own.

Leaving the pay phone and the temptation to be a hero behind, he ran down the stairs, past the pornographic painting, and caught the eye of the woman behind the counter, who said, "Did you get the cheese? The special's burger tonight."

He kept walking, pushed the doors, and stood outside, with a view of the twin palaces, the portals of Sydney, across the road.

Below each green globe on the twin buildings was a giant clock, visible for miles around.

As Danny watched, the minute hand on one clock moved.

South Africa.

He said he was going to South Africa today.

That's where *he* always wanted the two of them to run away to.

She would say: "If you want to leave, fine, I'll come with you, Prakash. But not to South Africa. Let's go to Hong Kong. I have a job offer there. Or India. You're from India, aren't you?"

"There's *blood* over there. There's blood on the highways in India. The way they drive there, I don't have the nerves for that," and Prakash would shake his head. "I'm never going back to India. It has to be South Africa. You know the taxes are low there. People *live* over there. It's not stuck up, like

87

here. You don't have to fill out three bloody forms to go to the toilet over there. You can see lions and giraffes right outside the city. *That's* civilization. And they've got honest casinos. Really honest machines. We'll win every single night we play over there."

Danny started.

"Hey. I asked, did you get the cheese for burger night, or did you fucking forget again?" From inside the pub, the white woman was shouting at him.

"Sorry," he yelled back, just to keep her quiet.

If Prakash is innocent, why did he threaten you, why is he saying he knows you're illegal? You *should* call the police.

But even if the police believed you, and phoned the doctor, he would guess at once you were the one who dobbed him in, and in return, he would dob you in as an illegal. He would call the immigration dob-in number about the Legendary Cleaner who was illegal, give his name, and what he looked like, and where he lived, because the dead woman had told him everything.

On the other hand: if you know who the murderer is, you should call the police. It is that simple.

(But if I tell the Law about him, I also tell the Law about myself.)

On the threshold of the pub, Danny neither moved in nor moved out.

The tin bowl that had been so noisily filled with ice cubes for dogs was now brimming with water. Small hard bubbles were forming in the water. The day was already so hot, and the door of the furnace hadn't yet opened. Danny drew the cactus nearer to his chest.

Girls in white were playing cricket on the green next to Sydney University. Danny watched the young bodies run and turn and scream. *I have not even started to live in this city, and you are asking me to leave.*

12:06 p.m.

A new text message from House Number Six: *On your way?*

Yes, Danny texted back. On my way. Yes.

He kept his eyes on the twin palaces, on the twin green globes and twin clocks, opposite him.

His sinuses responded to the clocks: he felt a lump in his throat expand and the temperature in his brow rise.

Someone yelled at him. Leaning out of the window, holding under each of her arms a fat gray pug wrapped in an Australian flag, a heat-crazed white girl screamed, and then screamed again. Licking the summer wind from within their patriotic covering, the dogs grinned at Danny in unison.

Mission: Impossible 2, my arse.

Danny sighed.

I should have stopped cleaning for them right at the start, Officer, I know this. They were both crack. I knew it.

With the cactus to his chest, he was walking up Broadway.

But they laughed at my jokes, Officer. They wanted me there.

Casually, while reaching under Radha's sofa with his vacuum, Danny might state: "There is a saying in Tamil, the kingfisher shows off, and the eagle hovers all day over water, but the crow is the one who always gets the fish." She *loved* that one. "I think the cleaner's making a reference to you, Prakash." Or putting his vacuum down, Danny might say, "I used to do the triple jump in school, hop, skip, and leap. Watch."

One evening he disemburdened himself of a question that had bothered him for two and a half years. A question about the water in Australia. "Do they put blue color every night in Sydney Harbor?" Radha ordered him to explain the question. "They spray wax on the apples in supermarkets," he said, "to make them red. Right? Maybe they do the same with Sydney Harbor. The ocean in Sri Lanka does not look this blue."

"Are you being ironic, mate?" Radha double-checked, and then called Prakash over and asked Danny to repeat it.

When they were done laughing and wiping away their tears, Prakash said, "I'm telling you, this fellow would have fit right in at Middlington. He's a private school boy."

Radha made an O with her mouth. "Have you seen his private school ties, Danny?"

Of course. Danny had had to pick so many of them up off the floor. Striped black and white all the way down to its broadest spot, where it was stamped with a golden smudge, which, the foreign cleaner was made to understand, was the sign of a very private Sydney school, proof that Prakash was part of the elite, marked out for big things in life.

"Very nice tie," acknowledged Danny. Of course, he had worn a tie to school too: back in Batti.

"Prakash is so proud of his ties, isn't he?" the woman said in a manner that might have been, Danny felt, ironic. "He wore the tie to court, didn't he? To impress the judge. And now he wears them all around Kings Cross."

"Spying on me?" Prakash asked the woman. "Are you spying on me with your cleaner? You fucking bitch."

"So civilized. So classy."

"Civilized?" the doctor asked. "What is civilization?"

"Don't get angry again, Prakash. You're mean to me."

"I asked, 'What is civilization?' Lots of blonde women serving you black coffee is not civilization, is it. And that is all we have in Sydney. You tell me, Radha, you worked for the government. You're really smart, aren't you?"

"I don't know. Helping other people, like Gandhi. That's it."

"No. It is not going to other countries and giving brown or black people your money. Do-gooders. They're the worst kind of people. And we know one of those people, don't we, Radha?" he asked.

Radha Thomas changed moods like a lightning bolt. In a moment, grinning wide, she had begun attacking him: "Oh, baby. Baby's just jealous because we went to a café in Dee Why and all the hot waiters flirted with me. All of them. Now I get it. The doctor's jealous."

Prakash said nothing. He rubbed his palms together and winked at Danny.

"Doctor," the woman said, egging him on. "Do you hate the fact that I call you that? Doctor? Doctor?"

Apparently, yes, for the man suddenly aimed a silver pen at her and threw it.

"You are so fucking low-IQ," Prakash said. "You really are. Really."

Removing his reading glasses, he tossed them on the table in front of the woman and began advancing on her.

Radha turned suddenly to Danny, who thought she needed help, before he heard her shouting: "Get the fuck out of my place, you dumb cleaner. Drop everything and run out. Now!"

They live like pigs, Danny told himself as he closed the door behind him. Pigs. He could hear them starting to make out even before he had left.

Walking through Potts Point, he entered Kings Cross and went to the Coca-Cola sign, looking down on the palm trees that led into the city; he knew he had to give them about forty minutes. He turned around and looped back aimlessly, down into the area known as East Sydney, which had a view of Sydney Harbor. This part of the city was empty throughout the day. There was food in these quiet streets for something inside him that had been starved in Batticaloa and in Dubai: something needing unmonitored solitude. Danny talked to himself. "No one ever *saw* Shakespeare in Shakespeare's own lifetime, it is a fact. A total fact." Through a vista of palm trees, he saw blue ocean and, near it, the white opera house. He talked faster. Until the city, in retaliation, presented to him one of its own wonders. A bleating noise. Turning to his left, following the smell of feces, he found, inside a wooden enclosure, tied to a post, a white goat, belly distended as if it were pregnant, a trapped unicorn, gazing back at him like the emblem of everything the West was meant to be. From somewhere above, whispering. "He really shouldn't be keeping it there." "We should tell the cops. Have you smelled its shit? Phenomenal. Stinks up the whole street."

Forty minutes later, when he had returned to the apartment on Potts Point, the door was open and Radha was smiling and more or less dressed. "C'mon, Cleaner. We're going out." Packing his stuff up, wrapping the red cord around his astronaut's backpack, he brought it into the car with him and sat in the back, accepting this ride as another unicorn, smeared and smelling of shit, which was the best he could expect from Australia. Prakash drove the car, and they were off to explore Sydney.

That mad couple had taken him to bar after bar over those eight months he had cleaned for them. Sports Bar. Jackie Chan Bar. Cricket Corner. Wizard's Lair. Live excitement. A throbbing neon dragon pointed down the steps to a hidden lair, the frisson of something James Bond–y down there as Danny followed Prakash and Radha into an air-conditioned gambling den, his skin shivering in the luxury cold, he remembered what had been promised about the West. Every square inch of it was like the Hotel Galadari! But when he turned to share this discovery (the West!) with his benefactors, Danny found those two were already changing, right before his eyes, into the King and Queen of the Nile.

It was as if Danny had parted a veil and looked into the heart of this new country. And what do you see there?

Gambling!

The *pokies*, they called them.

King of the Nile was the pokie that they always started off on—and only if they lost there would they migrate on to the other glowing machines: Aztecs, Wild West, Zodiac Symbols, Taj Mahals, Bengal Tigers, Lightning Bolts, Mexican Sombreros. The doctor played by either inserting a white magnetic card or simply feeding the machine dollar after dollar, while Radha watched as the electronic screens flipped and flickered; then man and woman switched places, and she played while the doctor lowered his reading glasses and watched, and then they switched places again, gradually ceasing even to talk to each other, man and woman slipping into a sort of trance in front of the machine, relieved only when they turned to buy another round of drinks, or when men in black vests, the guardians of the VIP room, smilingly escorted them to the men's or the women's toilet and back from there into the gambling room, outside which a small sign stated, to no one's benefit but Danny's, that the odds of winning the jackpot were worse than one in a million.

"Look at the cleaner's face. Just look at his face."

"Don't mock him, Prakash. Cleaner. Don't just look. Go and play on the machines. Here's a dollar. Play."

"Look at him. I think he's scared of the machines. Give that man some courage!"

"You!" declared the woman. "Cleaner. Have a drink. On us."

"No."

"That's outrageous," said the woman.

"Yes, it is," agreed Prakash. "What kind of Tamil are you, anyway?" he asked the cleaner. "The Chinese are sullen, solitary, and then they become bitter. It's not the way the Indian gambles. Do you know what the bhangra is? It is a Punjabi dance: you dance it on the full-moon night, and I tell you, anytime an Indian gambles, there's a full moon above his head."

If they ever won, the two of them began screaming together, and holding hands, and she might even sit on Prakash; and once, when they must have won big, the two of them started dancing together by the machines: doing something that they called the Lindy Hop, while the others watched and clapped.

One day, after they had known him awhile, Radha shouted from the bar: "I *am* getting you a drink today, Danny."

She returned with a Diet Coke and said: "A man's drink! I'm being," she added, "*ironic*, genius cleaner!"

Danny sipped his drink and looked at his employers.

"Cleaner. Do you know this man—this Prakash—once won the Flexi Trifecta and made fifteen thousand dollars on his original seven-dollar bet? Tell him the story, Doctor."

"Six thousand three hundred and seventy-four dollars," said the man, concentrating on the screen of his pokie machine and ignoring the woman, who began pulling on his red jacket with her fingers. "Not fifteen."

She kept at his red jacket with her fingers. "So sensitive. Dr. Prakash. Doesn't the name suit him perfectly?" She giggled. "I missed you, Doctor. Danny kept the house clean while I was away in Hong Kong. Didn't you? It was a shit holiday, though.

Mark is sitting there in his hotel room, sick, and expects me to baby him, but we're in fucking Hong Kong, and I want to enjoy, so I go up to the terrace of the hotel, and we're doing the Lindy Hop up there with all these beautiful young Chinese men. And I'm telling you, it's like I'm a rock star. Do you know what the Lindy Hop is, Cleaner? I know what you are going to say: Lindy Hop is Hop that is Lindy, no?"

"I don't know why you go on holiday with that man."

"Well, it's not like you're in a position to take me on holiday, are you, Doctor? You spend all your money right here, gambling."

"Fuck you," Prakash said. "That man—he's a fucking real estate agent. They're vermin. The lowest kind. Sells houses to the Chinese, you said it yourself. Here's another great bit of Sydney for you, friend. And another. I'm the one who goes to the army, and he's the one who owns a place in Potts Point." Prakash repeatedly tried to brush away the woman's hand from his jacket.

"Don't ask *me*," he said later that week, standing before the mirror to straighten his striped tie, when Danny, having cleaned his Potts Point flat, had gently brought up the question of payment. Sixty dollars? Prakash never paid anyone sixty dollars. You know she pays you, the woman. Where is she? Gone out? Let's go find her, Cleaner. After a moment in the mirror, fixing his appearance, Prakash led, and Danny, his astronaut's backpack strapped on, followed him down into Kings Cross.

People stopped on the pavement to look. In his gorgeous red jacket, wearing his striped private school tie, the doctor walked past the bankers of Potts Point, a prince among princes, and from there into Kings Cross, past the morning drunks, the drug addicts who were bent over and frisking the pavements for cigarette butts to sniff, the blonde call girl who spent mornings obsessively plucking petals from every single daisy in the Cross, past the man with the pet black cockatoo on his shoulder at all

times—until, placing a foot on the splashing disco ball–like fountain, surrounded by the thrashing white wings of jabiru, Prakash
stood regally over this little kingdom that he occupied rent-free;
before moving into an air-conditioned bar, the Vegas, to play his
gambling machines, bet on his greyhounds and horses, and wait
for Radha to join him in the place she had nicknamed the Clinic.

It was there, from Prakash, that Danny found out Radha's
story; there he learned that whether or not Prakash was the right
doctor, she certainly was a patient.

"You never know with that woman, Cleaner. You just never
know what she's doing the moment she leaves this place and goes
home." He lowered his voice. "She's got a bit of criminal in her, see."

Just three years ago, Radha Thomas had been the manager of
the Blacktown Medicare office. She was a star in the bureaucracy,
yes. She sat in a big air-conditioned office in Blacktown and was
in charge of all the receipts. Now, the cash in any Medicare office
is checked only at the week's end; and since from Monday to
Friday, there can be fluctuations in the kitty, no one will know
or care, just as long as the manager squares things up by Friday.
So, one Monday evening, in her white uniform, she stuffed a
shopping bag full of crisp new government notes from the vault
and walked across the road to the Blacktown RSL club. She
gambled five thousand dollars that night and lost it all. The next
day she returned and won every single dollar back. What was the
point of being young unless you lived young? That was how Radha
Thomas thought about things. She had everything her Indian
parents had dreamed for her: she was married, to a real estate
agent who sold houses in the eastern suburbs to the Chinese for
ridiculous prices; had a great government job, the best kind to
have in Sydney, and more than twenty-three hundred friends on
Facebook; but she finally found what she needed as she walked
out of her office at Medicare, in full uniform, across the road,

and into the Blacktown RSL club, to be greeted at the door with an Oriental bow by a besuited white woman, and shown into the hall that was radiant with automatic poker machines. Pokies! Oh, they knew in the club that she was from the Medicare office, they saw that her notes were government-issue-fresh, and they smiled and said, "Welcome." Though she gambled and lost, she came back the next day and won, and somehow, by Friday, she had always squared the money perfectly: the kitty at the office always added up. And then it happened: starting one Monday, she gambled over three consecutive days, her luck ran out, and she gambled and lost more than seventy thousand dollars of the Australian government's money. On Friday morning, instead of going to work, she took her passport and drove to the airport to fly to India, but they were waiting at immigration to arrest her. See, Mark, her husband, found out at the last minute and dobbed her in. For her own welfare, he said. The judge didn't send her to jail. Mark, her good real estate husband, promised the court he would support her. The judge sent Radha Thomas to therapy and group discussion for six months and ticked her off his list as a successful rehabilitation.

That is where she saw him for the first time. Salt-and-pepper hair really goes well with a dark face, doesn't it? And those thick-rimmed glasses! They were the only two brown people in their gambling addiction group discussion, and they just looked at each other the whole time, and when the discussion ended and the self-congratulatory clapping was over, the two of them, hooking up right outside, went straight to the nearest pub and began gambling again. Even in the Australian summer, Prakash had a face that did not perspire and eyes that lowered the temperature around them. She had never had an Indian boyfriend before, she confessed. Same here: had never had an Indian girl before.

Prakash told her he needed a place to stay. What a coincidence. Her Potts Point apartment, with a view of the fucking Opera House, was empty right now. Her husband's apartment, technically. Prakash could stay there, and that would be the perfect revenge on Mark for dobbing her in. She wasn't going to divorce Mark, of course, because that would lead to all kinds of issues (money, food, housing), so she went home and made Smiling Lasagna for both of them; but in the evening she texted the *doctor* and set up an appointment either at her place, when it was empty, or over at "his" place in Potts Point. So she began to run two households: a good wife in one and the Queen of the Nile in the other.

The King of the Nile had charmed her with his etiquette, his powerful male body, and his black-and-white private school ties (Danny imagined the doctor wearing them all through the fucking), and in return she fed and housed him. And went gambling, night after night, with him.

Prakash and Radha. Oscar and Lucinda.

Up there in the searing light, they were nothing, but down in the bars and amid the pokie machines, they had the full moon shining above them. Because the second he entered a pub in Sydney, Dr. Prakash was by definition the most brilliant thing in it: two shades darker than the whites and two shades lighter than the blacks, a brown man with powerful shoulders and reading glasses. Everything in the room was evolving toward him.

12:28 p.m.

I did tell her, thought Danny, looking at himself in the mirror above a restroom sink, I did warn her that he might do this.

He splashed water on his face before he looked at the mirror again.

In the crazy civilization of Sydney, where bottled water can cost more than coffee, can even cost more than *beer*, the only place to drink water for free is the place you go, in the rest of the world, to get rid of it. On Pitt Street, Danny had slipped into the Edinburgh Castle pub, where if anyone at the bar noticed him, they thought he was there to clean, and he'd run down the stairs into the men's room, where, letting the water run from the tap, he drank.

When he stepped back from the running flow to breathe, he noticed that the floor of the restroom was a mosaic of small square tiles, which reminded him of toilet floors in another city, another country. How near it feels again: home. Reflected in the mirror, on whose slab he had placed the potted cactus, he saw manual chains that operated the overhead water tanks in the toilets behind him. That too reminded him of Batticaloa. As the water flowed in the sink, he was revived; but when he closed the tap and wiped his face on his sleeve, he shivered, because he saw sentences, alternately in English and Tamil:

I did tell her

நிச்சயமாக அவளிடம் சொ·ான்னனேன்

I did warn her

அவளிடம் சொ·ான்னனேன்

Wetting his finger in the running water, he continued the sequence in English
The thorns are there to protict the roses
and had started to correct the error
to ~~protict~~ the roses
when his phone rang.

99

It was Dr. Prakash.

"You are on your way, aren't you, Cleaner."

"Yes, sir."

How calm he sounds. How readily he commands obedience in you.

. . . now the darkness was penetrated by a pair of eyes: Dr. Prakash's eyes. The hazelnut color that you see in the eyes of an Indian man, toward evening, in a beach suburb like Bondi, when the setting light, low, enters his irises.

A mistake, Danny. Those translucent beach eyes said: *You made a big mistake this morning.*

"And I'm expecting you to clean my place, Danny. Before I leave for South Africa."

"Yes, sir."

"What are you doing right now? Why are you taking so long to come?"

"Working, sir."

A pause.

"Really? You are *working* right now?"

"Yes, sir." Danny pursed his lips. "Vroom—vroom—can you hear it, I'm vacuuming, vroom vroom."

Prakash's powerful voice expanded with laughter; Danny hung up at once.

The whole time he was on the phone, his finger had been on the mirror, dripping and smudging; now Danny pressed on the mirror and made a wet line. The lagoon. And then he broke the line in two places. The openings.

Someone else killed Radha. If you go to either of the openings in the lagoon, that is all you will find out.

It was crazy even to suspect Dr. Prakash. Because you know the man. You've been to bars with him.

He rubbed his fingers through his hair. But.

It's weird, isn't it. That he's leaving on the morning after Radha died. Maybe he knows. Maybe he knows something and has to leave.

I should tell the police. They'd want to know. Wouldn't they?

Won't they *applaud* Danny for dobbing the killer in—doing the right thing? In the moist mirror, within the wet lines signifying the lagoon and its two openings, he now saw the city of Sydney, when it appeared most beautiful to him, at dawn on a winter's morning in the heart of the city, with the road-cleaning machines rumbling about Danny as he looked up at the four-faced sandstone clock tower of Central Station held aloft on shattered and roseate clouds: renewing the promise to the immigrant that something as thrilling as the air-conditioned interior of the Hotel Galadari lay ahead of him. It is still yours for the taking, Danny, this city, this country, this paradise . . .

Now an old patriarch, a former Australian prime minister, a man named Malcolm Fraser, appeared in the mirror, a gigantic southern star above his right shoulder, the flag of Australia behind him. Let's bend the law for my good friend Danny. Come over here, Danny. Give this man his felicitation, Aussies.

Danny laughed. Fraser vanished. He laughed again. At himself.

There is a culture of praise where Danny came from. If you were someone, you had to be someone up on a stage, surrounded by loudspeakers, microphones, and flatterers. A man at the mike has to be introducing you: "Dignitaries on the dais and off the dais, dignitaries visiting and resident, we are all gathered here to glorify and amplify the achievements of our son . . ." The grand felicitation. It is the lifeblood of a place like Batticaloa, as it is of every small city in South Asia. You want to be recognized, honored, felicitated. Surrounded by printed posters of you, hand-painted murals showing you with a dove hovering overhead. Then the lighting of bronze oil lamps, the delivery of consecutive thirty-minute homilies, one or two preferably by a minor politician, followed by the marigold-and-jasmine garlanding and presentation of the plaque of honor, usually with your name misspelled. Thunderous clapping. You are now the town's favorite son.

Five minutes later, everything might change.

For the Felicitation comes with a twin—the whispered subversive truth of the Gutter. Anyone praised up there on the stage must be, later that very day, mocked and tarred. "Yeah, he sits up there garlanded like a big man, but I know for a fact that last Saturday, he was seen at the . . . doing . . . along with . . ." The Felicitation and the Gutter balance each other, and the result is that any celebrated figure in Batticaloa, in the manner of a pig emerging from a sewer at noon, is divided into permanent white and black halves.

Look at the face in the mirror. What do you see? Nelson Mandela, you have been called by some.

But you have heard other names for that face. Other stories.

Half Mandela, half pig.

The place for you today, he told himself, is inside a toilet stall. Go in, lock yourself in. Right. He did just that.

The little cactus, covered in plastic, was sitting on a roll of toilet paper. The owner of the cactus was sitting inside a solid structure of four metal walls, clapping his hands again and again. Clap, clap, hard enough to make that blue ball, that unwanted spider, go away. And then the blue policemen go away.

There was Clorox in the air—too much; that must mean, he thought, that Nepalis had cleaned this toilet. They always used too much of the stuff.

Pubs would be a tough place to do, and pub toilets would be the worst. "Do you fucking know what I am saying, do you fucking understand English?" bellows the white Australian in charge. The women always seemed to be the most determined to offend. "This is a bloody loo. We let you into our country to clean it." Maybe Clorox is how you retaliate.

H6

The text message from Dr. Prakash penetrated through the wall of the toilet.

Danny laughed a bit, and then he thought he'd try another trick from his childhood. One he had used to pass hours and hours by himself.

Take your face in your palms, son. Now place your elbows on your thighs, just above your knees. Think of nothing. Soon you have become a parallelogram of pressure points in the dark: the slab of a butt on the cold toilet seat, two elbow bones thrusting into knees, and a scratch of one long fingernail against your right cheek. The rest of you is . . .

Smoke.

Danny opened his eyes and lifted his elbows off his knees. He's *packing up* today. Dr. Prakash said he was packing *today*.

Of all days.

There was a printed sign, Danny noticed, over the toilet bowl:

THIS STALL IS OUT OF ORDER DUE TO
SOME VANDALISM! WE KNOW WHO! YOU ARE
MANAGEMENT HAS EYES HERE

That exclamation mark was in the wrong place, and he scraped at it with his fingernail . . . *some* vandalism. Fucking Australians . . . can't even speak their own . . .

Enough of this. Striking the door with his shoe, he left the booth, went back to the sink to splash water on his reflection and examine how the highlights gleamed brighter once his hair was damp.

It's fishy that he's packing up today, isn't it?

Fishy means like a fish, no?

Another message. The doctor wanted his reply.

H6

vroom vroom. Come soon.

Yes sir I am coming to see you soon. Danny took a step back from the mirror with his wet reflection. I am coming, don't worry.

I always knew, he declared to the vast audience of Sydney-siders he could see inside that mirror, that something was *weird* about House Number Six.

Now she, Radha, House Number Five, the dead woman—he explained quickly to them—was 100 percent Aussie. Just like you. No question.

But *he*—Prakash, House Number Six, her lover, King of the Nile, he was like me.

By that I mean, explained Danny, he certainly had not been born in Australia. He must have come over when he was a boy. You can tell these things, can't you, from the accent. Must have been born in India, come over as a boy. But he *was* in your army, so he *is* a citizen. Like you. So he's both like you and like me at the same time.

And Dr. Prakash got tough in the army, yes.

Because every brown man in Sydney has to beg sooner or later—but not Prakash. He never said sorry. Never. "You've been to the reef, haven't you, Cleaner?" Prakash used to say. "Great Barrier Reef? You've gone in the glass-bottomed boat to see all the corals, right? And what do you see? There's that filthy stingray, hiding squat on the ocean floor, and kicks up mud and it goes fleeing under the glass-bottomed boat with its forked tail, just the most frightened vermin you ever saw. I'm never going to live like that. I'm never going to be a fucking apologist."

You know *he* would stand up to torture. Have to admire that, don't you? A really tough Indian man in Sydney.

As if in response, the vast potential audience of white Australians had disappeared. There was just a dark wet face in the mirror, and it grinned back at him.

He killed her. You knew he would.

Danny splashed water on his own reflection and saw it grin some more.

Point one, Danny responded to the reflection, how *do* we know that the dead woman was found by the *same* creek in Toongabbie that the two of them liked to visit at night? Could be any creek. Point two, more important, there's Prakash's character.

You know—he looked at the mirror—what we're talking about.

Was it two years ago now? It was a Tuesday evening for sure. Yes: Danny and Prakash were waiting for Radha to turn up at the pub. Danny remembered the decor of the pub: dead animals. A zebra's trophy head rose over a fireplace; when Danny looked up, he saw the head of an animal he thought was called *kudu* directly overhead.

A disco ball on the ceiling dispersed glitter without light around the many foreign trophies of the pub.

Prakash was having beer, Danny sipped Diet Coke, and there were three men drinking at the bar.

The three men were white.

They weren't the kind of men you saw sometimes on a Saturday in Sydney—ribands of Aryan protein, sodden, tattoo-sedimented, puffed with talk of Anzac and Gallipoli and the wealth of their race and the poverty of all other races, bony and bonily eager to bump into bodies that were not white.

These three white men were wearing orange vests, which meant that they were tradies, and gainfully employed; but they were drinking as if it were the weekend already. There was sand on their arms, as if they had come, messily, from the beach.

Prakash ordered a beer, and a Coke for Danny, and kept talking:

"Cleaner, I've had enough of this country, I tell you that. It's not what it used to be. Now, you don't know what it used to be, do you?"

Prakash told a story.

A month after coming here from India, Prakash, all of nine years old, had removed his worn shoes and shown them to a cobbler, tapping on the soles, only to find the Aussie looking him up and down before asking: "Can't you just buy a new pair, mate?"

"Australia! Here, when old shoes wore out, you just bought a new pair. Amazing, isn't it? In those days, there were no Indians here, would you believe, Cleaner. Yeah. You know what my dad and me, we did, when we got lonely?"

Prakash was selling Australia to one who had nothing else to buy. Danny listened.

"We opened the telephone directory, went down with a finger, saw a name, Kumar. You called him. From India? Me too. Want to meet? That is how it was. Now, of course, whole fucking country's overrun by brown people, right. Australia's not the country it used to be, mate. Overrun. That's a fine word. Do you know it, Cleaner? Of course you do. You come from a good educational system. Unlike ours. I regret that. Didn't do well at school. Didn't get a chance. Then it was too late. IQ is fixed by the time you're ten. Did you know that?"

Danny did not.

"Wasn't given a chance. I was in a private school for a couple of years, yes, as she keeps reminding the world. But we moved too much. The IQ, it didn't set. I didn't like the army either. After that, I worked as a miner in West Australia, in the Kimberleys. Down in the mines, down where you go, there is no ambient light. Know what that means? The man in front of you opens his mouth, but you won't see the teeth. Danger. Rockslides were a danger in those days. But the pay was good. In those days, before the foreigners took over the mining. Now the top-top people are all Chinese, and the pay's shit."

Danny had been listening so closely to Dr. Prakash that he had let down his spider sense. Then he heard a loud fart.

One of the three white men had spread sensually over three dark chairs at the bar and farted—and the laughs spread across the three, and suddenly, Danny realized all the men were glancing his way.

Something was said, and though Danny couldn't hear it clearly, the long, lazy Australian vowels, given indulgence to be even lazier by alcohol, told him: *There is trouble here.*

Because the television in this pub, which the men were watching when they weren't looking at him, was not showing racing. It was showing migrants. You picked up the story right away because there were captions. Illegal migrants. There was a boat in the waters somewhere near Western Europe. The boat was packed tight with dirty men. Another boat with men in clean blue uniforms drew close to it. They were about to catch the illegals.

Prakash was still talking. "Back then every bloody Australian, you could go on vacation each year. You haven't seen what this country was, Cleaner. My wife and I, we went to South Africa. That's where we saw the statue of Gandhi, and she's bored, but I'm standing there thinking, This is a statue of an Indian. I'm Indian, he's Indian. And he's very civilized, isn't he? But my wife, she was bored. Ex-wife, shortly afterward. Ha. Dead wife, actually."

"There's a statue of Gandhi in Batticaloa too," said Danny. "It's a gold statue."

"But this is a young Gandhi with all his clothes on. Have you ever seen that?"

No, Danny had not.

"From there we flew to Gujarat, where he was from, you know. Gandhi was from Gujarat. Have you been there? Been to India?"

Catch the bastards!—came the shout from the bar, and Prakash stopped talking. He and Danny turned to see the white men.

Catch them, said one Aussie man who was watching the TV. Catch the fuckers.

Fuckers? Danny recognized that screaming man: lean, bedraggled, his neck still coated with sand, a man who had wanted all day long to murder his boss at work. You saw men like this in Sri Lanka too, the fellow who had loud things to say about Tamils.

Catch the bastards! the white men shouted. Catch the bastards!

Get ready, Danny thought, to run.

But there was no need for Danny to get ready for anything, because at that moment Prakash stood up, walked over, and just turned the TV off. With a wink at the white men, he sat down and talked. Stunned, the three white men, even that one with the sand on his neck who had been screaming, just gaped.

"I told you, didn't I," Prakash continued, "that I'm sick of this country. I told you."

In a green field outside Batticaloa, Danny had once seen a bull elephant rolling up grass into a ball and devouring it between its tusks; Danny had not been able to take his eyes off it—that solitary, defiant animal—and, under his breath, had given it a magic nickname: Prabhakaran. Or the nonapologist.

"What a bunch of fucking racists. This is fucking Australia. See why I never became a doctor?"

Later, sitting at the Flying UFO pokie machine, feeding it one-dollar coins, Prakash played and almost scored a jackpot, while

Danny, by his side, kept bringing him fresh schooners of Tooheys
lager.

"See: this is my theory. Every man today, he's got two voices
inside. He wants to say, to anyone and everyone: I am sorry. I
am sorry that I am sorry. That's one voice. But he has another
voice in him too."

Sipping his beer, leaning back to take a break from the gambling machine, Prakash ran his fingers through his black-and-
white hair and exhaled.

"Didn't your grandfather own a piece of land in the village
right by the edge of the jungle? *That* voice says to him: Whatever comes into the jungle—deer, tiger, boar, girls, and even the
mothers who followed looking for the girls—yours."

With a smile, as if daring Danny to guess how serious he was,
Prakash vibrated his forked fingers.

No wonder, thought Danny, watching Prakash play his next
game, no wonder she lets this man stay in that place for free.

Angry with Australia, angry with India, angry with the white,
angry with everyone else—a perfect crack.

After two hours on the Flying UFO machine, Prakash groaned,
"I got cleaned out, Cleaner, cleaned out. I think this machine is
fixed, totally fucking fixed," and then dug his face into his own
shoulder to let out a dirty, self-violating chuckle.

A door slammed. Danny stepped away from the mirror. Someone was running down the stairs toward the male toilet of the
Edinburgh Castle pub.

His head down so he wouldn't be remembered, he pushed
the door open just as someone came running in, and leaped up
the stairs into the pub, and vomited himself out of the door and
into raw sunlight.

12:43 p.m.

As they flew from one side of George Street to the other, the pigeons came so low they barely cleared a man's skull: Danny had to duck.

He smelled smoke in the air again, from the bushfire in the Blue Mountains. In his free hand he held two wonderful brochures, one offering *Asian Street Food to End All Asian Street Food* and the other $10 *Haircuts Not Just for Students*, placed there by opportunistic teenagers. He held the cactus, wrapped in plastic, against his chest.

Menthol. The lump in Danny's throat bulged each time his neck moved. *I want menthol.* He was back on the open Sydney street now, and the brutal illumination on George Street compressed his eyes.

Across the road, Town Hall was hidden by its own self: covered, during a period of renovation, by a realistic painting, in soft watercolors, of Town Hall.

The cellophane cover of the cactus was sweating on the inside. Like the sweat, Danny thought, that you drip inside a dream.

Beige towers soared around him. The Central Business District of Sydney. He guessed he had been moving for half an hour without a pause. Chafing his cactus against his T-shirt (and the singlet beneath), Danny glanced up at a white skyscraper studded with black windows.

But who inside those high windows would listen to him even if he shouted up at them? Those windows were full of Chinese, full of Indians. Aussies only liked houses with gardens. High towers, they left to Asians.

Sometimes Danny would see the Indian students in a group on George Street and follow them. They were the ones living up there, seven or eight packed into a thirtieth-floor flat cool with ocean views but humid with curry and discussions of immigration law. He pretended he had the same worries they did. Sometimes even interrupted them at McDonald's, or on the suburban train, to offer free and accurate advice: "Sorry, I just had to say something. That isn't right. If your work experience is from India or any other foreign country, the law is that three years is five points. But you will get five points for one year of work done in Australia. The goal is sixty points to become a permanent resident. Look, they're not unreasonable people, Aussies. Go talk to them if you think you've broken your visa and are illegal. One more thing. Don't stare at people here, it's very rude."

From there, from immigration matters, the discussion among the brown men would move on to the next big question: Why is everything in Australia so expensive?

"Because," answered Danny, the veteran immigrant, "people here are rich. Aussies are so rich."

But that only led to a bigger mystery: Why are they rich?

"Because," Danny suggested mischievously, "they're intelligent."

Universal response of the immigrant: You must be *joking*.

"Okay, okay, you're right. Australians aren't very bright. They don't work hard. They drink too much. So *you* tell me. Why are they so rich?"

"They sailed in big wooden ships one hundred years ago and stole all our money from us."

"That was the *Britishers*. Not these fellows. Do they look like they *could* take anything by force from anyone?"

"They've got gold in the desert. Sheep."

"Other countries have sheep. Other countries have gold. But they're still poor. No. It's not gold, not sheep. It's because white people have got the *law*, and we don't."

This object of wonder, this incorruptible thing, the blondest animal in Australia: their Rule of Law.

He would explain to them. "Indians are good at mathematics, right? So tell me: can a circle have more or less than three hundred and sixty degrees?"

See, Danny finally got it one evening at a happy hour in a pub, when a young male, Indian or Pakistani, leaning over the bar counter, pointing to the machine, pleaded with the Aussie bartender: "Have a heart. Start the happy-hour discount right now, it's 3:56 p.m." Only to have the Aussie woman explain: "Happy hour is—see? *tap-tap-tap*—programmed in a chip in the cash machine. Can't start a second before four p.m. Can you change the heart of a machine?" Later, as Danny lay on his sofa in the storeroom, looking at the panda bears, another image, a better one, came to mind. A circle can have only 360 degrees. The law was a magic circle, and inside its protection, Australians surfed and swam and slept like children. Danny had seen countries in which a circle did not add up to 360 degrees. In Dubai the law let employers cheat you of your wages. In Sri Lanka the law was a burning cigarette on your forearm. *This* law, as tall and hard as the cliffs that rise up at Pyrmont, was fairer, much fairer. In the Glebe library's legal aid section, textbooks and pamphlets spread all around him, Danny had studied, understood, and finally come to admire it. Fair? Yes, it seemed fair: everything in the legal code of the Commonwealth of Australia was clear, logical, point-by-point. Special consideration, he discovered, was made for people who were new to the country and couldn't speak English in court. Vietnamese, Arabic, Bengali, and Tamil interpreters would help them answer the questions posed by the judge. Free lawyers defended indigenous Australians, and those who couldn't afford their own defense. Fair? Perhaps it was more than just fair. Unless, thought Danny, turning the pages of a book on immigration law, unless all this is just a fairy tale, it was perhaps even the best law that existed anywhere in the world, but the moment he closed this fine-smelling textbook and returned it to the shelf and walked out of the Glebe library, it would immediately start hunting him down again—because that was its nature. Blind and fair.

I made a mistake, and it is after me. It will always be after me.

This much Danny knew: If I tell the Law what I know about Dr. Prakash, I tell the Law what I know about myself.

12:47 p.m.

On George Street, people looked up at the sky. A plane was writing the oldest message in the world in white foam: a marriage proposal. The first letters were already smudged; people were trying to guess the name of the lucky woman.

WILL YOU MARRY ME . . . ET—

"Etta?" shouted one observer.

"Etty?"—another. "Write it quickly, man!"

Danny felt it too: their desperation that the name should be spelled out before the first half of the message was lost. Now it seemed to him that this was the most important thing in the world—the unraveling of the woman's name, up there in letters in the sky.

He had forgotten all about the murder. The body in Toongabbie.

When he lowered his eyes, something was staring back at him from the top of a black lamppost: its face stiff and expectant, soft gray feathers rippling in the breeze.

Descending from the blue sky of Sydney, it had appeared as if in response to a man's plea for help.

A seagull.

How do you know it's the same creek, son? it seemed to ask. *The same creek in Toongabbie? There are lots of little gullies there.*

Danny shrugged. I don't know for sure that it is the same creek, Officer, sir.

The seagull now had its beak opened wide, as if in mirth. *Go home, then. Don't call the police hotline and talk shit. Don't accuse someone.*

But it's an emergency.

Ha. The seagull had flown too often over Sydney. Every man had his crisis every day. *Feed me a chip, feed me a fry,* it cried, *mine is the only real emergency in Sydney today.*

It rose, on strong and taboo-free wings, while Danny looked at it glide down the city toward Pyrmont and the casino, as if it planned to gamble the rest of the day.

But this much I do know, thought Danny, resuming his walk down George Street—that exactly a year ago, on the last Guru Purnima day, the three of us went to a creek. In Toongabbie.

That had been a bad day. The kind that no number of rules can prepare you for. "Oh my God, oh my God," Radha began saying when she came near the Potts Point apartment, with shopping bags full of food, and found the cleaner waiting outside the door.

As if she had already guessed something bad had happened.

"All I did was ask him for the sixty dollars. After cleaning."

"O-kay, o-kay, I get it. Don't complain to me."

She opened the door to the building and led, and he, safely, followed her.

When the door opened, they saw Prakash sitting there, surrounded by beer cans, with pizza cartons opened.

His black reading glasses lay on a copy of the newspapers, turned to the racing page.

"Have you been spilling beer on the floor again? Why don't you do some cleaning? It's my fucking place, stop spilling beer everywhere. Why don't you get a bloody job instead of drinking all day? Danny, will you kindly fix that spot on the floor? We'll give you something extra."

Prakash said nothing, just ran his fingers through his salt-and-pepper hair.

Danny began cleaning. All at once, he realized that Prakash was aiming something at him.

He ducked just in time; the beer can missed and hit the wall, and Radha shrieked; perhaps she thought it was a joke, but when the next can came right at her head, she turned and ran outside with Danny. They slammed the door behind them, and the cans kept hitting it from inside.

"It's Guru Purnima today. Bloody Indians have a big celebration in Parramatta, but this time they didn't invite him. They don't want a thing to do with a man who is down. They just want the big cars and flashy culture. I bet Sri Lankans are the same, right? I know Pakistanis are."

She opened the door, and another can came flying at the wall.

From outside, she yelled: "Calm down, baby. After dinner we'll go to the creek, baby. That place calms you down, doesn't it?"

Still standing by the door, Danny understood that he had to go along with them to earn his wages. Why not? Dinner would be paid for. In the end, if he knew this pair, the woman, out of guilt, would give him a lot more than sixty dollars. From inside the door, the doctor's voice moaned: "I lost two hundred seventy dollars today. It's fixed. Every machine's fixed."

"Oh, you poor thing," the woman said from outside, placing her face sideways against the wooden door, "you poor, poor thing."

*　　*　　*

"We're lucky the neighbors didn't call the police."

They drove in silence for a while.

Danny watched the back of Prakash's head. Why didn't his family help when he was in trouble? Why did they let him become a miner? A man from a private school had to take off his tie and dig mud for iron? But that's Australia. No high or low here, no class. For instance: in Australia the signs say, MALE TOILET. FEMALE TOILET. Danny was still appalled by this. Toilets are neither male nor female. A toilet doesn't have a cock, does it? Men's or women's. Australians don't know their own language. This is what happens when you wear tattoos all over your body; when there are no black lines that say, *Do not cross this.* Land without taboo, land without class.

That was the first time he thought: I should leave these two. Something bad is going to happen if I stay on.

The woman spun in her seat viciously to face Danny.

"Say something. Make us laugh. That's why we bring you along and give you free food and drink, you know."

When they got to the creek, hand in hand, she walked down to the noise of flowing water, Danny trailing.

"Danny," she said, looking back with a smile, "you know Prakash and I come to this creek every Sunday."

Lovebirds again, the two of them.

The King of the Nile put a finger to his lips. "There's a kangaroo somewhere around us," he whispered. "I can hear it."

"You're insane. Prakash, there's no roo here."

"I can hear it. I know kangaroos. I've run with kangaroos."

"And when have you ever fucking run with a roo? Is this another of your stories?"

"Hey. Quiet. You haven't seen what I've seen of this country: this was in the Kimberleys, in the mining days. You're out there at night, in a caravan or in a tent, and you hear them gnawing. They chew on bones all fucking night long, kangaroos."

"Why?"

"For the salt. The minerals. They chew and chew, and after a while you fucking want to shoot them dead."

"You see why I like this man, Danny?" Radha raised her voice. "He's been everywhere. He could've been someone."

"I don't know where that roo is hiding," said Prakash. He turned and looked at Danny. "Cleaner. I hate apologists. You know this, right?"

"Right," Danny replied. He understood that this was an apology of sorts.

"There's beer in the car. You want?"

"No more drinking, Prakash. And don't corrupt the boy."

Trying to listen only to the burbling water behind him, Danny looked at the night sky and saw another immense white cloud of the Australian night, as big and bright as a lagoon.

"Has anyone been to Randwick?" he asked suddenly.

Both the Aussies began laughing.

"Randwick? How the fuck did we get to Randwick?"

"It's in *Mission: Impossible 2*."

"Mission what? Oh, Prakash dearest"—Radha began laughing all over again—"we really should adopt this cleaner as our baby, shouldn't we."

"He's not my baby."

"Let's take him and elope to Hong Kong. Or to India. What do you say?"

"He's not my baby." The Indian man shifted his big body about in the grass.

"Yes, he is. Our high-IQ cleaner. He's our little third-world baby. And this is our little brown Noah's Ark drifting through Sydney. Hey, Prakash, Danny's been through torture, do you know that? He's like Nelson Mandela. You're not listening, are you? Hey. Danny. Why are you silent? Entertain us. Say something."

"Even the peacock must scratch its ear now and then," Danny replied, making them laugh.

"And what the fuck does that mean?"

"It means: even a wise man must go quiet now and then."

"That's actually pretty profound. Even the peacock . . . what was it? By the way: I've been meaning to ask you, Danny. Do you have a girlfriend? Oh, that's a shocker. A real shocker. Prakash! You listening to this? Our poor Nelson Mandela. We've *got* to get him laid. Danny. I'll tell you what, I know what you should do, you should go on this site called VeggieDate. All the best-looking women in Sydney are vegan."

"I'm *not*," Danny protested.

"Who gives a fuck? Aussies think all Indians are vegetarian. The other day, Mark and I went to a beach party in Manly, and these guys turn up, all gorgeous, all vegetarians, and I danced the Lindy Hop there, you know. And the young vegetarian men looked at me and said, 'You bloody rock star.' We're getting our cleaner laid with vegetarians, Prakash."

"I've got better things to do with my life."

"Like what?" The woman waited. "Surgery?"

Danny, making a mistake, laughed, and Prakash turned around before grumbling.

But Radha was aroused; Radha could not stop now.

"I keep telling you, Cleaner, this man could've been someone. We Medicare people, we know things. Take Westmead Hospital. I tell you, there are some doctors out there who shouldn't be allowed to do surgery. Murderers. Complications every case. This girl, I know this for a fact, was operated on for stomach cancer, and guess what? She gets pneumonia during surgery. Dies from that. That surgeon, a white guy, he's still there, at the hospital. Imagine if an Indian man got that wrong? It'd be in the papers. That's why you never got to be a doctor, Prakash. It's all fixed at the top-top level."

She paused and smiled.

"That and the fact that you didn't actually go to university. Unlike every other Indian boy who wore a tie and went to Middlington."

He's going to do something, Danny thought, tensing; instead, Prakash laughed. "At least I'm not a criminal. I didn't get caught stealing money. Ha," he shrieked into the night.

Her voice changed. "So mean. You're so mean to me." Danny thought she was sobbing. "Everyone's mean to me. Men are always mean. I've got these big shoulders, don't I? Guys don't like women with powerful shoulders. I hate my shoulders."

"That's a trapezius, dear patient, not shoulders," said Prakash, holding her for an instant.

Radha kept sobbing.

"Where's the moon tonight?" asked the man after a while. "It's Guru Purnima tomorrow. Should be a big moon up there. And tomorrow's going to be a great day for the punters, I tell you, I'm going to win on every horse tomorrow."

Pieces of living black opal, roaches, ran over Danny's forearms. He lay passive, looking at the stars, and he thought, I am almost here, stars. That is what I am doing here. Almost being here.

"I should tell Mark I won't be home, shouldn't I? I'll say I'm at the pub with the girls."

The woman got up.

As Danny lay looking at stars, something pulled the woman down to the grass again. Something hit her. Not hard: just a light slap, the least force necessary to establish that it was a slap. "Don't say his name. I've told you."

"I'll say his name if I want to, stop being a fascist."

"Don't say his name."

"He's my fucking husband. And I'll say his name if I—"

Radha went silent. This was not, the slap had established, a discussion of equals.

Danny tensed. A finger had touched him on the back. Is he going to hit me next?

But a voice whispered to him: "Buddy, she's no rock star. You know what I say? You're forty years old. You're no rock star. Now look at this, Cleaner."

He showed Danny something that he'd had concealed in his sleeve the whole time. Dark with meat grease and gravy, but its serrated edge still shone in the moonlight. *"That's* a rock star. Isn't it?"

"Put that away," whispered Danny, but before Prakash could do so, the woman shrieked, "Did you bring that fucking knife here? I told you not to take it places with you. It's gross. Danny. Take that knife away from him. What do we pay you for?"

But before he could answer, they learned they were not alone by the creek. Something was splashing in the water. The three of them rose to see.

It was a black dog, and it was shivering, uncertain of the edge between land and water; and in the creek, two white boys, stripped to the waist, buoying up and down, laughed and mimicked the animal each time it howled, raising their heads to the sky and letting loose long doggy noises—which confused or enraged the black thing that staggered about the rocks, adding its weak protests to theirs.

So that was exactly a year ago. Guru Purnima day before this one. Fine. You went to a creek in Toongabbie. He had a knife with him that day. But how do you know it's the same creek where they found Radha Thomas's body yesterday in a jacket, weighed down with stones?

How do you know a thing for sure, though you keep walking toward the clinic to meet Prakash?

12:57 p.m.

On the sunlit face of an old brick warehouse was a white stenciled sign that looked as old as civilized life in Sydney: REX SIMPSON FINE CLOTHES FOR MEN. Beside the letters emerged a ghost-like silhouette of a hatted gentleman. Danny wished he had a hat like that. It would hide his stupid golden hair. How proud he had been of it just an hour ago.

He looked down at his phone.

I am hungry now cleaner

Like a chain tugging him along to Dr. Prakash's clinic, the text messages kept coming: *and someone has to clean this place before I fly to South Africa!*

See him now, lowering his reading glasses from his waving semi-silver hair and focusing his hazelnut eyes on the racing sections of the newspaper, Dr. Prakash, former miner, former soldier, King of the Nile. Would the possessor of a pair of eyes like that have anything to do with a murder? A civilized man, a private school man.

On the other hand, he did sometimes carry a knife around, didn't he?

He looked to the city of Sydney for help and saw, on the side of a building, fading letters that said: SWITCH TO TEA.

12:58 p.m.

In a discount store that has been shutting down since you came to Australia, where a prerecorded baritone booms over sunglasses,

T-shirts for tourists, men's and boys' underwear in plastic boxes, and Cadbury Fruit & Nut bars, a never-ending closing-down sale goes on and on, right in the heart of Sydney.

"Because this is the final, I repeat, final sale. Everything must go, shoppers, everything must go. Come in and take a look. This time it's for real."

What are you looking for? the Lebanese woman asked Danny. No, she replied, they had no menthol lozenges of any kind. Didn't even know what they were. But yes, they did have kitchen knives.

KENNEMANN KITCHEN KING
NEVER NEEDS TO BE POLISHED
LIFETIME GUARANTEE

Picking up one knife from the bin, Danny imagined touching its tip through the plastic cover.

He could see the King of the Nile again: that face dark and glowing like anthracite, those black reading glasses that he always kept raised over his wavy semi-silver hair.

Danny's fever vanished, and his sinuses glowed the way Uncle Shankar's must have when he inhaled that menthol spray—so light, and in good health. He dropped the knife back into the bin, where it fell on other six-dollar knives.

"Because this is the final, I repeat, final sale. Everything must go, shoppers, everything must go."

On the pavement outside the store, in a cluster of funky hairstyles, sat young Indians fresh from the homeland watching a cell phone, while separated from them by a waste bin, and processed by the West, raw into refined sugar, bulkier Indians in business suits and suburban pompadours had gathered around their own mobile screen. The ones in the suits were locals, icebox Indians, and they were ignoring the immigrants; but *both* of them, Danny noticed, were watching the same Bollywood song.

Sliding down Park Road, down the inner-city grid, Danny came to the Hyde Park intersection.

From where he stood, he could see the three chambers of the heart of Sydney: ocean, park, and hill. If he walked to his right, he would reach the Opera House and the ferries leaving for Manly Beach; in front of him, he could see the banks and insurance buildings arranged around the green lozenge of Hyde Park; but he was looking beyond ocean and park, and at the hill. Rising abruptly from the city, a road named William Street ramps up to an old-fashioned Coca-Cola neon sign, which pulsates from dusk to dawn, and which marks the start of a densely populated part of a mostly empty continent—the red-light district of Kings Cross.

Danny knew that sign well. How many times had he stood right there by the big Coca-Cola sign, up there, while the doctor and Radha were making love, and he had nothing to do but wander, ending up there, at the forehead of the city, looking down a row of glossy palm trees that divided traffic entering the tunnel, and thought: I know something that none of you know. A secret. Because House Number Five and House Number Six were having an affair: and in this never-ending city of Sydney, only he, an illegal immigrant, possessed this fact.

Danny-down-here cursed Danny-up-there: *Crack. You are the world's biggest crack.*

Didn't he once calculate that Radha and Prakash must have spent over five hundred dollars on him in free food and soft drinks in bars while he worked for them? And now, he thought, they are making me pay back every single dollar.

White hieroglyphs—numbers, zizags, dots, and dashes—lay in a mass on the road, painted information for cars driving up to

Kings Cross. And beyond that giant Coca-Cola, tucked away in Kings Cross, was the Clinic. Radha called it that because Prakash spent so much time inside it, playing his games and drinking.

Danny could see, on the flesh of his palm, what he had himself written there: *1-800-330-000*

Eel, silverfish, avocado, and tuna distracted him. To his right, he saw, beyond flowers, newspapers, and water bottles for sale, and through the darkness of an open door, an intermittent glint on a revolving sushi train—everything just three dollars, just three dollars.

But no samosa here, not one samosa.

He looked up again at the gigantic Coca-Cola sign.

In front of him, a pole studded with a silver button was emitting the rapid beat that said, *Cross the road* now.

1:12 p.m.

Beaten, the bull-faced monster had become numb: its eyes were closed, its skin contracted in thick pain as the Greek hero, placid, naked, small-penised, twisted its horn. A mynah, having dipped itself in the fountain, perched on the fallen bull and, in a bid to stir him awake, shook its wet wings, forcing Danny to step back and leave the circle of tourists admiring the bronze giants in the water.

He had failed to do it: failed to break this new taboo. Instead, folding in on his own path and returning to Hyde Park, he had come walking down a promenade of fig trees, until he heard the fountain. Beyond its wet giants, beyond the trees and tourists, Danny saw the russet towers of St. Mary's Cathedral, which sat like a bookmark on a frivolous, pleasure-pursuing city; and again he turned away and walked back into the park, thinking, Gandhi.

Someone twanged at a stringed instrument, and there was woodsmoke in the air.

Gandhi, yes: that was a person the doctor loved to talk about: in South Africa, see, they had a statue of the young Gandhi, with all his lawyer's robes on, in the heart of their big city, which is called Johannesburg. Dr. Prakash had stood before it and clicked a photograph. *Gandhi! Clothes!* That's *civilization.*

And don't you remember how he had placed red tulips in his own window in Potts Point to show that he was in love with Radha. Turn around, Danny. Kiran Rao is telling you, mate, to turn around.

Describing an invisible circle around the fountain, a jabiru stalked with a bent head and exaggerated movements of its scaly reptilian feet, as if mocking the solemnity with which humans were taking photos of themselves.

On either side of its body, the jabiru had a yellow tag printed with a surveillance number, and the wind blew burning forests deep into Danny's nostrils.

As the smoke in the air loosened his bowels, Danny felt that he really really had to shit soon.

Someone was watching him: high up on a stone pedestal, a greenish old Britisher with a telescope, possibly Captain Cook, looked down on him and his cactus; but as the wind blew stronger, the jabiru thrashed its wings, preparing to fly, and the statued Englishman changed right before Danny's eyes into a young, fully clothed Gandhi.

Merrily merrily merrily, the young mother sang as she went up William Street with her child strapped to her chest, *life is but a dream. Merrily merrily . . .*

Following behind her, pressing a cellophane-wrapped cactus to his T-shirt, Danny walked. He was now halfway up the hill. Halfway to the Clinic.

Slowing down in the shade of the banks and the buildings along William Street, he quickened when he had to cross the sunlit intersections. The arch of the Harbor Bridge was visible to the left, and made waiting at the red lights bearable. The whole time, from in front of him, the singing continued.

Life is but a

Patting the baby, the young mother sang: *Merrily merrily merrily, life is but a. Life is but a.* Warm in her shadow and song, the baby glanced at Danny: and the eye that regarded him was as hard, cloudy, and blue as a Sri Lankan street marble.

Danny wished the baby would look elsewhere. They had crossed at three red lights like this, but at the fourth, the mother and child went ahead.

Danny had stopped by a pub that had tables on the road.

On one table, weighed down by a coaster, a newspaper fluttered, alive in the breeze. Everything now had fever. Somewhere inside those fluttering pages was Radha's murdered face.

The table outside the pub was moist, but Danny found no clean water anywhere—the only moisture was a ring of lager. He wet his finger and touched the newspaper and wrote.

Someone else

Meaning, *Someone else will tell the police*

He scratched, with his long fingernail, Tamil words over these—

வேறே யார்

But who else . . .

And scratched those words again

வேறே யார்

126

Who else knew about the two of them?

They changed bars a lot, and no one really knew who they were. That was the point of switching from bar to bar. Their affair would never be caught out, right?

As if wishing to say something, the phone buzzed: and Dr. Prakash had something to say.

H6

I have a flight to catch today. Would be good if you cleaned the flat soon

Dr. Prakash, why don't you stop bothering me?

Toilets esp need work. If I remember you were very good at toilets

Danny sat down on one of the cane chairs outside the bar.

From where he sat, he could look into the bar, where the TV was showing images of the murdered woman: and even from outside, and interrupted by traffic, Danny could listen to the voice on the TV.

The body, said the police, was found last night at a creek in Toongabbie, wrapped in a leather jacket whose pockets were filled with stones. The police describe the jacket as being of Italian make and . . . in color. They are asking for any information about the jacket or for the owner of the jacket to come forward.

Did they say black? Danny went closer to the glass door. But the roar of a powerful truck, going up the hill, blocked out the TV's sound.

They *did* say black, didn't they?

As if in response, the glass face of the building opposite presented a twisted and palsied image of an endless beige tower, like the one Jack climbed up, and Danny knew it was his own heart he was seeing.

From where he sat on the slope of William Street, the Opera House was just about visible, as was a glimpse of the ocean. *Are you going back to your country so easily?* the blue water asked the man. *Whether it's you or the white people here, it's all the same to me,* the water told the man. *I'll go on shining just like this.*

Already forming the words *Tables are only for customers* on her lips, the young Australian woman swung open the glass door but found no one at the table outside, just a newspaper stained by damp finger-marks and held down by a Victoria Bitter coaster: no Aussie bartender was going to catch Danny.

He stood at the next traffic intersection. Didn't William Street have more red lights than any other street of this length in Sydney? He made a note of this to himself—and then laughed.

What is the use of information like this if you're going to be deported tomorrow, Danny?

He felt he would gladly shave off all his golden hair and make an offering of his vanity to God: if that were the price of just one more day in this city.

As the gigantic red Coca-Cola sign drew him to it, the messages seemed to arrive faster

I do have to go to the airport by six. Off to South Africa today. Can you hurry?

To which, to be safe, he texted back

I am on my way. Just in Kings X now.

Imagine, thought Danny, that he actually did it. Killed her. And now what? He's sitting in a pub, texting you? That makes no sense.

Merrily merrily merrily, the Aussie woman singing to her child, *merrily merrily merrily,* walking at her own motherly pace, now passed Danny again.

The child was now smiling vertically up at the Australian sky.

Danny saw the smiling child and thought: I *could* go see Sonja.

His cleaner's singlet stuck to his chest.

At the top of the hill, the Coca-Cola sign stood like a referee between Kings Cross, the red-light district, and the road that led to St. Vincent's Hospital, where she was working today. Instead of going to the Clinic, if he took a right from here and walked past the yellow pub and the Thai restaurants, he would get to St. Vincent's Hospital, Darlinghurst.

He looked at her number, number 16, on his phone's list:

Sonja

And felt better already.

You *could* text her.

Can you see me just five minutes. There was a fountain in front of the hospital, right by that memorial to the murdered Chinese doctor. Fresh cool water. Five minutes. Drink the water. Explain every lie to her.

1:40 p.m.

Decision!

Throwing its mouth wide open, the road demanded: *And make that decision* now.

Because he was at the place where William Street, splitting into curving branches that rejoin at the crest of the hill, allows a concrete tunnel to yawn open, revealing an orange spine of lights leading into darkness, and thus presenting the spectacle of day and night at once, while the Coca-Cola sign, overhead, rules over both realms.

Danny held his throat to soothe it.

On the very next date they had gone on, Sonja knew everything about the Sri Lankan situation, and the Tamil refugee problem, and had even sent a letter to her MP asking for a new policy toward asylum-seekers from that beautiful and troubled island. Danny kept quiet as she explained the peculiar and complex situation in Sri Lanka, beginning each sentence with "*As you well know,* the treatment of the minorities . . ."

Eventually, she let him speak.

"Look," he said, "I reckon we don't need more people to come into Australia."

Grinning, and aware he was becoming ugly, he recited the facts of life to her confused face.

"*As you well know,* there is no fresh water in Australia. *As you well know,* the builders, they're the ones who want more immigration. They're bringing in brown and black people and putting them in slums near the airport and the train stations. To be slaves for white people."

"My God!" She gaped. "Danny is a conservative."

Although she concluded that Danny "could do with a bit of *empathy* on the immigration issue," Sonja had said nothing else. This was just, she must have assumed, in his nature: his deviated septum, his refractory sinuses, his cussedness. Perhaps she liked him all the more for that.

He had told her nothing about the bump on his left forearm. One thing would lead to another, and she would find out in the end that her man was just an illegal. The shame.

Breaking free of the overwhelming Coca-Cola sign, Danny's eyes moved to the right.

He could feel Sonja at once—her fingers in his hair, playing with his highlights, pulling it all toward the back of his neck. Those strong fingers now tugged on his hair from the direction of St. Vincent's Hospital, which was just a short walk to the right of the big sign, saying, *Come. Come. Let's have a coffee together.*

Didn't she love coffee? Three fifty a cup, and she drank three a day. (The way Australians spend money!)

On the other hand, Sonja didn't like to be troubled at work. That was a fact. Their fights usually began with a reference to her work, it was a fact. "A patient pissed on me in the shower today," she had said last week. Danny had asked: "Isn't that a nurse's job?" "What the hell does that mean?" she had demanded. "And if you think you're so smart, why don't you become a male nurse? Or do something other than clean houses?"

But if Danny took a left from the Coca-Cola sign, and walked past the drunks, tourists, and pimps, he would find the Clinic, and in it . . .

Life is but a dream.

Nothing is simple for a man like this one. Not even being helpless. Life is a battle, and though unevenly so, everyone is armed.

He had a story; he had a power. Hefting his cactus in one hand, Danny cracked the knuckles on the other with his thumb.

Life is but a dream.

A fit young female body jogged past. The muscles in her back spoke to Danny of sex, and said, *No, no, it is not a dream. Live today to spend tomorrow with your girlfriend.*

Turn around, Danny. Intelligent Cleaner means a Cleaner who is Intelligent, no?

But then, coming in from the city, circling over the Coca-Cola sign, half a dozen sulfur-breasted cockatoos made a sudden noise before turning leftward.

Following the white birds, Danny walked into Kings Cross—the Central Pleasure District of Sydney.

Third Year as an Illegal

It is an Indonesia inside Australia: an archipelago of illegals, each isolated from the other and kept weak, and fearful, by this isolation.

But after a while you observe that some little islands have joined into bigger ones, and the fear is less here. There is even hope.

On his way back from a one-off cleaning job in Parramatta that Tommo had arranged for him, his astronaut's silver canister on his back, Danny had seen her. That woman who stood at the railway station. Screaming, "Do not turn a blind eye to Syria! Thousands being massacred, raped, and murdered. Sign a petition now! Massacred, raped, and . . ." She looked tough, that woman, she really looked like she could take on immigration and the police.

"So why didn't you talk to her? Why didn't you ask her for help?"

That evening, they had met, the local illegals, in the benches outside the locked Glebe library, and Danny had described the woman to the others. In reply to their questions, he said:

"I didn't like her boots."

"Her boots?" Ibrahim, the Pakistani, asked.

Danny had felt, somehow, that this woman with the long black boots was not really for Syria or Syrians: Pay attention to me, she was shouting to her fellow Aussies, pity the illegal immigrant, but pay attention to me.

Sometimes, it was said, raids in the suburbs were led by social workers, "to protect illegals from exploitation." When they caught you, they asked, "Are you okay, brother?" and gave you a chocolate bar as you were handcuffed. In the end, you were deported anyway. So what did it matter if it was a good-hearted woman or a massive blue policeman with a gun chasing after you? Idealism and corruption flowed side by side in Sydney like parallel streams of sewage. White people would be lecturing you on your rights all the way to the deportation vehicle.

"Didn't like the boots," Danny said decisively.

Smoking his hand-rolled cigarettes, Lin, the illegal Chinese-Malaysian, who made tacos at a Mexican restaurant, said what he always said: "You can get a cigarette packet this thick"—he showed how thick—"for eight ringgit in Malaysia. Just eight ringgit." Yet Lin also said he was never, ever going back to Malaysia.

Lin, who did two shifts a day at the Mexican restaurant, blinked a lot when he wasn't working, as if there were gaps in him where there should be anger.

But once he started smoking, he did get angry. "Kuala Lumpur"— he exhaled smoke away from Danny—"is full of illegals. Ten times more than Sydney. All Muslims. Bangladeshis and Pakistanis and Arabs. The government brings them in. They get their fake Malaysian identity cards. Chinese out, Muslims in."

This was the first time Danny had heard that there were places in the world where the Chinese, despite their numbers, were the weak. But that made sense. He was beginning to feel that there was a reason some immigrants from Malaysia or Sri Lanka or Pakistan ended up driving big cars in the western suburbs of Sydney and others ended up in places like this, outside the Glebe library, whispering to each other. Two illegal Nepali cleaners he had met one day in Surry Hills hadn't looked like he expected Nepalis to. Darker and shorter. Maybe they were the poorest people in Nepal.

Does it work like this? You're not wanted to begin with in your own home. Then illegal immigrants come to your country, take what little you have, and force you to go to Australia and become an illegal there.

He asked Lin: "Those people from Bangladesh and Pakistan who are now in Malaysia—they're the ones to blame, then?"

Lin shook his head. Danny understood. There must be illegals in Bangladesh and Pakistan who forced them out.

My God. Where does it end, then, and who is responsible for what has been done to us?

Lin smoked the way men did back home: the lit cigarette, in equal parts filter, stem, and ash, hanging from his moist lower lip as he stuffed his hands in his pockets. I too, thought Danny, have fallen to his level.

When you watch the Asian Games or Olympics at home, you are proud of your countrymen who bring a good name to all of you, right? Opposite of Olympics, which is bringing a bad name to their country by breaking the law of Australia, is what they were doing. All of them here outside the library.

"What do you tell them back home?"

The lies were modest, and similar. The Pakistanis claimed to be running the store they worked in. Same with Lin. Nothing about being a millionaire in Australia. The lie was just about their dignity.

"What about you?" Lin asked Danny. "What do you tell your people back home you're doing here?"

"I don't tell them anything. I don't write to home at all."

And now he could see that they wanted to move away from him.

Because there is a difference between us, thought Danny, looking at the other illegals. For them, shame was an atmospheric force, pressing down from the outside; in him, it bubbled up from within. Even if I were granted citizenship in this country, I would still be ashamed of myself.

Sending a level beam through Sydney's hierarchies, the setting sun sank. Then the cloud of gloom, of desperation, that had grown so great and black in front of Glebe library, lifted.

Because Lin had begun talking of food. Of a feast. While smoking another hand-rolled cigarette, he had begun describing an outdoor food market, illuminated by incandescent white lights, a night market such as existed only in cities in Asia, one that went on forever and forever. Dim sums steamed in wicker baskets, glazed roasted duck, glazed chicken, skewered sausages, beef cutlets, fresh and fried frogs, everything you ever dreamed of. The two Pakistanis, excited by this description, added to it. Roasted lamb. On skewers. And those ice creams that come alive only at night and only in the open. All this, said Lin, was going to be placed on a large clean wooden table.

They gorged on make-believe duck, chicken, pomfret, and steam-ing jasmine rice.

Danny had something to add to the feast: hope. There is a way out of our shame, he informed them; the chicken and duck evap-orated, and the illegals gathered around him. How? Come closer. The law of Australia can be broken. How? Even closer. See. Danny had been reading in the library. Back in the 1970s, a man named Malcolm Fraser was prime minister, and one day he announced in parliament, in Canberra, "Illegals of Australia, tomorrow is your amnesty." You know how on Christmas Day, the bus conductor won't check if you punched in your blue card or not? Same thing. You just go in to immigration and tell them, I'm illegal, and they say, No problem. Welcome.

Amnesty. Gates will swing open, manholes will fly, and an under-ground city will walk into the light.

Bullshit, said Ibrahim the Pakistani. He had stopped smiling. Not that way. This is how it'll happen; the only way it'll happen. See, the other day, from behind a picket fence in Seven Hills, the windscreen of a truck had emerged, emblazoned in Arabic and Roman letters saying—BISMILLAH—like a new sun waiting to mount over a new Sydney. A new law. And as he watched that big, noisy, Muslim-owned machine, Ibrahim knew: he knew what Australia's future was.

Why not, thought Danny as night fell, and he walked through a dark crowd toward the Sunburst grocery store, why not. Convert the whole fucking country to Islam. That might make men of them at last.

WORLD FAMOUS LOVE MACHINE ADULTS ONLY
STRIPPERS MORE STRIPPERS
EROTICA BOOKSHOP COME IN AND LOOK
PORKY'S NITE SPOT

1:52 p.m.

The names pulsated in red, green, or yellow wattage:
GENTLEMEN'S CLUB. BADA BING. RISQUÉ ADULT BOUTIQUE.
WELCOME TO KINGS CROSS.

Already, this early in the day, a few women in fishnet stockings
and coral-red lipstick had started gathering beneath the lights.
Concave in the cheeks, goggle-eyed, the palest women in Sydney,
with legs from which the sunlight had long ago been sucked out.

In Sri Lanka, prostitutes show their breasts. Here they show
their thighs. A bull-necked pimp with a shaved head, wearing
black, the outfit of his profession, tried to hand Danny something.
"Michael Jackson!" he yelled, even as two more pimps, both bald,
both wearing all black, gathered behind him. "Would you like to
see a woman right now? Michael Jackson!"

They were referring, he supposed, to his golden highlights.

No, thank you. Not for me.

"Gaaandhi!" yelled one of the pimps. "We got Indian women
here!" And the other two grinned.

No, thank you. Not for me. Danny moved on.

He knew there was a kebab shop here (Five-Star Syria) run
by a man named Haroun: in the old days, when he came here to
clean House Number Six, Danny would always stop by to hear
Haroun, behind his counter, complain about Australia; Haroun
was growing old, working twelve hours a day; Haroun was becoming poor in Australia, spending twenty-five dollars for a packet
of cigarettes—and how this jabbed at Danny's heart, the legal
immigrant's prerogative to curse the land that had welcomed him.

But Haroun was gone, and a younger Arab man with a chop-
per made bright wounds in the mound of shawarma. As Danny
watched, the exposed meat darkened in color again.

Guru Purnima day.

Where are you cleaner? his phone beeped. Danny could see the place from where the text messages were coming.

. . . *on my way, Doctor, I am on my way* . . .

Past the solitary prostitute looking for an early customer, past the dog shit by the trees, and past the branching veins of urine and spit superimposed on the grid of the streets, until he made it to a patio where pale men sat smoking and desperately watching the world around them, while dark glass doors indicated a place of deep privacy behind them.

Danny stood staring at an ellipse of white lights glittering around the word VEGAS.

This was the Vegas Hotel of Kings Cross, also known as the Clinic.

Warning noises came from above.

Up in the air, a seagull, catching a cross-building current, glided over the carnal entertainments of the Cross without moving a feather, only opening and closing its beak and emitting a series of loud squawks. Didn't it just remind you of a cartoon of a village gossip—sitting in a tea stall all day, too lazy to move a muscle anywhere except in his powerful mouth.

Danny, assuming he was the subject of the seagull's gossip, winced. He's free, but that's all he's free for: gossiping up in the air.

Down here on earth, he, Dhananjaya, had already placed his hand on the glass door of the Vegas Hotel: he felt it glued down to the door as if no force could unbind it. There were people behind the glass. He saw an audience of a hundred people, dark, multiplied, expectant. Like Kiran Rao in his fine suit at the Sydney Festival, Danny addressed his imaginary audience: A man without rights in this world is not freed from his responsibilities. They applauded. Suddenly, everything made sense, from his hair down to his shoes, and his dark reflection was illuminated at once: half Gandhi, half pig. Let's see what it feels like.

He pushed the door open and went into the Clinic.

The relief of shade and air-conditioning was mitigated by the tinge of sewage on each dark gust of chill air. The carpet may be moist. Or beer was going bad. Danny sniffed.

To his left he saw the red neon sign VIP ROOM.

And then below it, contradictorily, ENTRY FOR ALL.

He wandered about the machines, observing Aztecs, Zodiac Symbols, Taj Mahals, Bengal Tigers, Lightning Bolts, and Mexican Sombreros. A dozen men and women played at these machines. Some had placed beer glasses on their machines. An Asian woman at one station turned her head robotically from side to side, possibly to stretch her neck. A constant buzzing of mechanical happiness—*bing-bing-bing*—filled the room, now and then erupting into euphoria before subsiding again into repetitive *bing-bing-bing* joyousness.

It was like a snake shrine inside the Shiva temple. The gambling room inside the Sydney pub. Every bar had a quiet room where men watched glowing numbers on a TV screen or scanned newspaper pages with a pen. It was an odd vocation, this gambling, very technical, full of numbers, pencils, and calculations, done by the kind of brawny men who did not seem to be otherwise into thoughtfulness or calculation. Men went into debt because of those numbers. Men lost their homes, their cars, their friends, to those flashing numbers in the quiet room. Whites were the first to go crazy, but the immigrants were even worse. Chinese made up three-quarters of the customers in the casino in Star City. Now brown people were catching the disease too.

And Danny had known the King and Queen, the advance guard of the new Indian gambling elite of Australia, hadn't he?

Dragons Myth; Indian Dreaming; Royal Diamonds; Dragon Master; Mega Moolah; 100 Pandas

Yellow diamonds showed in the dull red carpeting; the cashier, on an elevated desk behind secure black bars, looked like he had a shotgun under his chair. A printed notice read: FAKE FIFTY-DOLLAR NOTES BE ALERT. *The best fakes come from* CHINA *of course. Study the three photographs below.*

Danny walked around Central American faces, cactuses, eagles, snakes, and pink Martian landscapes, until he heard, beneath the mechanical noise of the machines, a human voice.

". . . I was there in 1991, you know. When I was in the army. Four years. They train you in the forest in Queensland. You walk single file in a patrol, and suddenly, mate, watch out! A tree falls down, and everyone in the patrol, we'd look up to see a big hole in the canopy of the rain forest, right . . . and then we'd go on our patrol and return, an hour later, to the spot where the tree had fallen, and you don't believe your eyes. Just one hour gone, and you can see the hole up there in the dark green canopy getting smaller, you can see the leaves of the other trees reaching toward each other to knit the hole in the jungle. Nature heals itself. I love Queensland, I tell you. Even thought of moving there once. Sydney, except for all those rich Chinese people that can't buy enough of it, is a shithole, frankly. Don't you agree?"

It appeared to be coming from behind a Super 100 Aztec gambling machine, and Danny walked around to see.

An Indian man in a white T-shirt, whose long black-and-silver hair was clamped down by dark reading glasses, was sitting at a table talking to a white couple and their little golden-haired daughter.

They were listening as if they could listen to him forever; but the Indian man's smile and grace and kingly manner all crumbled at once.

He had caught Danny watching him.

Below his semi-silvery hair, the Indian man had thick, feathery black brows: Danny had forgotten those brows. And Dr. Prakash's eyes, even in the dim light of the bar, were hazelnut in color.

Eyeshock.

There is a buzz, a reflexive retinal buzz, whenever a man or woman born in India, Pakistan, Sri Lanka, or Bangladesh sees another from his or her part of the world in Sydney—a tribal pinprick, an instinct always reciprocal, like the instantaneous recognition of homosexuals in a repressive society. Because even if both of you believe that one brown man holds no special significance for another in Sydney—a city and a civilization built on the principle of the exclusion of men and women who were not white, and which fully outgrew that principle only a generation ago—which is to say, even if you want to stay icebox or indifferent in the presence of the other brown man, you are helpless. You have to look at him just as he has to look at you. Eyeshock. Danny knew it well, but he had never before felt it in the presence of Dr. Prakash, who, though he was brown, though he was clearly born in India, had been living here long enough to become Aussie.

But today, those hazelnut eyes were again an immigrant's eyes. Both men felt it.

Then Dr. Prakash's eyes, relaxing, expanded in the friendly Aussie manner, and a dimple formed on either side of his nose.

"Well, it's been good talking to you, my lady," he said, and, raising the little girl's hand gravely to his lips, kissed it, and then kissed it a second time. The little girl's jaw dropped.

The parents were amused. Behind the counter, the cashier was amused. Everyone was amused except for the girl, who stood openmouthed in the presence of a god.

Prakash stood up. Danny walked up to him. Prakash examined him and then smiled. "You're half a foot taller today, Cleaner. It's the golden hair."

Shrugging to indicate *But life is full of surprises, no?*, Danny smiled back.

House Number Six had gained a lot of weight since Danny last cleaned his place. His hair had much more silver in it, and he looked like the kind of man you would call, back home, an uncle. It's not him, Danny.

"You came to clean the place, right?"

"Yes, sir," replied Danny. "Yes, sir."

"Nelson Mandela, our cleaner," said Prakash, and suddenly, his voice changed. Now that Danny was closer, he could see the face better.

Prakash had that terrible look of a hungover fortysomething-year-old, now at the stage of his life when the drinking depletes some permanent reserve of strength inside. Is this the celebrated, amusing, intelligent, medically inclined occupant of House Number Six? Danny watched him.

No. This is just an animal inside him. An instinct is sitting here, not a man, and Danny had this same instinct inside him. When the Sri Lankan interrogating officer's burning cigarette penetrated Danny's forearm, and he himself felt paralyzed, like the one alert guest in a hotel on fire, this animal thing inside, this instinct, had responded: told Danny to stop screaming and to bend down and lick the burn on his arm, lick it again and again, to stop the fire spreading, until the interrogating officer with the cigarette, showing Danny some mercy, had himself splashed a glass of water on it. This is all that Prakash is today, an instinct to survive, a black rock in the center of a dried-out pond with letters inscribed on it: I AM YOUR SELF-LOATHING.

His old employer's arms, though, were the same: and Danny's eyes followed them down to where the half-sleeve shirt ended: the brown skin lightening a shade there in the exposed biceps, which were taut and irrigated with veins.

"Let's play first?" Leaving the table and motioning Danny to follow, Prakash walked past a row of glowing machines.

Indian Dreaming. 5 Dragons. Sands of Time. Scattered Pyramids.

"I was packing my suitcases at home. Left everything to come here and see you. At the Clinic," he said.

"At the Clinic," agreed Danny.

"You want to go back right now to the place in Potts Point? Clean the toilets? My flight's at six forty-five tonight."

Does he not know yet? Danny wondered. Maybe he hasn't read the newspaper yet.

But just below the doctor's Adam's apple, there was a fresh red wound.

"No," muttered Prakash. "No, I see you aren't ready just yet. You want to discuss. You want to discuss terms. I get it. All right, Nelson Mandela. Let's play for a while. Pick a machine. Any machine. I'm paying."

You always felt the temperature drop around this man. Danny remembered now, even as the Indian looked at him with his calm face and endothermic eyes, which could cool any Australian beach. What is civilization?

"It's Guru Purnima today. You know what that means?"

"Full-moon day."

Prakash smiled approvingly. "Very good luck, all the Indians in Sydney are gambling today, buddy. We'll gamble a bit too." He gestured about the gambling room. "I've always liked this room, Nelson: reminds me of the mines. I worked at the mines, you know. There's just one difference."

"Ambient light."

Prakash drew his lower lip in, closed his eyes, and nodded. "Yes. You remember everything, don't you. Sit down and play on that machine. It's a good one. As far as machines in this city go."

"I don't do gambling. No."

"Sit."

Danny saw the face of an Oriental goddess set in a row with pyramids, hawks, golden ankhs, and other Egyptian emblems. This was the Queen of the Nile, and Danny had been ordered by the King to play it.

Holding up a dollar so Danny could see, Prakash dropped it into the machine. "Go for it," he said. "I'm going to watch. Wait, wait, wait, I'm coming . . ."

Okay, thought Danny, maybe he hasn't read about Radha's death. Maybe he's broken up with her. That happens.

Danny kept jabbing a green button that flashed, even as the machine simulated the sound of real cards being flipped (*dob, dob, dob*), while under the watchful eyes of a sultry Queen Nefertiti, the electronic screen glowed with the symbols of Egypt, and swallowed, in increments of two cents, the dollar coin that had been fed into it.

IS GAMBLING A PROBLEM? CALL THE HELPLINE. 1-800-858-858.

Sitting perfectly still, his head bent low so Danny saw his mop of partly silver hair, Prakash watched the screen—like an exam invigilator, thought Danny. Nothing rash or crazy about him. The King of the Nile.

The door of the pub opened, and an Indian man in an olive uniform with a bubble-wrapped parcel walked in, glanced around, checked out Danny and the doctor, and then squinted at the parcel's address.

Every day one set of brown men wearing shorts crisscrosses the roads of Sydney to deliver letters, wrapped parcels, fresh flowers, and furniture, but before they can do this, they are intercepted by another set of brown men in starched shirts and black trousers, walkie-talkies in hands, wires spiraling into their ears, guarding every door and gate in the city.

Moving or watching brown, Danny—friendly or surveillance brown—which one?

Some white guy probably stabbed Radha out there in the creek in Toongabbie, and here you are, putting your bum down on the seat in front of the one Indian you know, to accuse him.

"Busy day," said Danny. "Very busy day for me. I should go back to work now."

"Legend," said Dr. Prakash with a smile. "You just came. We'll have lunch, and then you can clean my place. That is what you came for, isn't it?" He held up another golden dollar coin. "Play once more."

So Danny had to do it all over again, at the Queen of the Nile, in front of the coruscating rows of pyramids and sacred hawks, and lose that dollar too, until Prakash, satisfied, said: "Your luck really isn't very good today, is it. C'mon. Let's try something else."

Leaving the machines, they sat at a wooden table picked by the doctor. Ketchup bottles, salt shakers, pepper shakers, Johnnie Walker coasters; and in between these things, racing forms printed in red, with a black sign above them that said:

$2 could now win $5 million.
A game every 3 minutes

A blue pencil rested in between the urgent red forms.

Two TV screens near this table showed a rugby match, and there were more screens behind them in a darker alcove that was reserved for hard-core punters: where men, pen and paper in hand, were performing the calculations, the scratchings on white paper, the professional-seeming rituals of the self-ruining gambler. Beyond, there was a black door leading to the street.

If I run now.

This is not the man, Danny told himself for the third or fourth time. He's just an uncle in a pub.

Danny looked at the door of the pub.

Prakash scratched at his left jaw with his thumb.

"Want a glass? Red wine."

"Don't drink."

"Right. You never drank. Just watched other people drink. Right? Yes, I . . ." Prakash smiled. ". . . remember you, Nelson. And you were funny. That's why we kept you around. You said that funny thing about the peacock, didn't you. What was it you said about the peacock?"

He remembers. What a great memory he has, for an Australian. Maybe he just hasn't seen the TV. And he will see it later on. Let's go, Danny. Up, up.

But when he turned to the door of the pub, a bus sped right past, and the sun's glare ricocheted off its white sides into Danny's eyes; he blinked, and then another car drove by, again irradiating his eyes.

"You okay, Intelligent Cleaner?"

Angling his body away from the door, Danny used his left palm as a shade.

"Too much light," he said.

Right outside the door, the bright burning cars kept going by and going by; protecting his eyes with the purdah of his palms, Danny searched Prakash's face for the truth.

"Cleaner." Prakash lowered his voice, as if in sympathy for his painful eyes.

Excellent. Some evidence of human feeling. This was a normal man. This is what you came to establish, isn't it? Now run.

"We wanted to say goodbye to you." An Australian man brought along his daughter, the one whose hand Prakash had kissed. "This young lady is very impressed."

"Would you like me to kiss your hand again?" asked Prakash, and the little girl held it out. He took it to his lips, and her jaw dropped again.

"I bet no one's ever done that to her before," the girl's father said meanly.

Lowering his spectacles over his eyes, Prakash smiled. "I'll be over to visit you one of these days in Queensland. I sure will. May even move there for good."

Danny watched the father and his daughter leave the pub.

"I said, Cleaner." Prakash summoned him nearer with his fingers, looking around, and whispered: "After you, we never had another cleaner." He grinned with a nod. "I did it all myself, you know. I cleaned that damn flat. Even the toilets." He laughed. "Certain people made me clean and watched me do it. You shouldn't have left, you really . . . I don't blame you, though, Nelson. I know what you are. I know your secret." He winked.

Prakash handed Danny the racing page from the newspaper and indicated, *Read,* but Danny shook his head.

". . . don't know anything about betting."

"Well, I do." The doctor smiled. "Take a look at the dogs."

Although he usually had a silver pen in his pocket to do this, the doctor today used his finger to draw a circle around the list of racing dogs.

"Punt on one." He turned the newspaper toward Danny.

Danny pointed at the first name on the list.

Prakash clacked his tongue. "Nineteen to one, that's no good, no good at all. You know how I play? By assuming a mispricing in the system, but only"—demonstrating a space between his thumb and index finger—"a reasonable mispricing. At nineteen to one, the odds don't work for me. Pick another one. Then we can go back to the place and clean it. The toilets really need some work."

This was rational, sensible, and reassuring. Leave at once, please. Just an uncle in a pub.

(Danny remembered an underground Internet café, right underneath the cinema at George Street, filled with Asian kids wearing white headphones and playing computer games for seven-hour blocks. If only he were in that computer cave, where, for ten or eleven dollars, he could sit all through the burning day. Koreans were strong and tight-knit. They'd protect him today.)

"No?" Dr. Prakash grinned. "No bets today? As you please. I'll put the paper away."

(But he also remembered Sydney Harbor as he had just seen it, on his climb up William Street, sparkling and silver: how it reminded him of the lagoon of Batticaloa, which he had seen from the rooftop of his Catholic school. It was the same great ocean, come all the way from Batticaloa to Australia, with no living space on either end of it for Danny.)

Prakash rubbed at something between his teeth with a finger, then ran it down his Adam's apple. His thick eyebrows contracted. "Where's your vacuum? You always brought your own along, didn't you? Professional Cleaner."

"I like Australia," said Danny abruptly. "I like Australia very much." Now the conversation could meander and digress, and then Danny could just slide out of the bar. What do you say?

Right above the bar was a TV screen that pronounced:

NEXT GAME IN 0:43

But only one man here had the power to change this conversation. All at once, Prakash, with a smile, asked, "Buddy, what do you do for Medicare? I mean, instead of Medicare." Now the doctor looked up. "What do illegals do when they fall ill?"

Danny stood.

"Sit.

"I said fucking sit."

Some great strain had ended: Dr. Prakash was no longer acting. Danny looked at the door of the pub and then sat down.

NEXT GAME IN 0:58

"Don't look at the door," said Prakash. "Look at that man, Cleaner." He pointed.

Leaning his head back, a bald stocky man in a black T-shirt was glancing up at the TV screen with the horses and the flashing numbers.

"Look at his neck, Cleaner. See how the base of his brain is glowing: the creamy fat packed into the occipital lobe, the root cunning? That's called the Reptile brain. The Swamp brain. Now, that's a gambling brain there."

The bald gambler moved closer to the TV screen . . . The layer of fat at the base of his neck was throbbing again.

"That's what you never understood, Nelson fucking Mandela. How to place a bet."

Prakash gritted his teeth. He kept looking at the bald gambler as if he meant to assault him; but Danny felt the weight of a finger on his wrist, and that finger's weight told him: *Your intuition was exactly right. It is me.* That finger's weight on his wrist lowered Danny back into his seat. Prakash withdrew his hand and stopped gritting his teeth.

Everything seemed normal; and only the tension in the doctor's jaw, the slight trembling of his white-and-black hair, and the growing pressure of his hand on Danny's wrist indicated that this man was no longer living at that safe distance from reality that we call reality.

Turning to Danny, Prakash smiled.

"Tell me how you did it, Danny. Your secret."

"Did *what*."

"You walk in the open," the doctor asked, "and no one ever catches you? I know what you are, Nelson illegal Mandela. Tell me why the police don't catch you."

And he tightened his grip on Danny's wrist.

Now you get it, don't you, Danny? It happens to you too. Some mornings you wake up, and you've forgotten everything you've done. Same with him. See, this morning he wakes up, and it is like waking up on Bondi Beach: five seconds of paradise, then he remembers. *Then* he thinks, No one will connect me to the killing. Maybe he believes her body has sunk to the bottom. Because he filled the pockets of that Italian jacket with stones. And even if it is found, so what, who can link me and that body? All the time he is thinking, Maybe, just maybe, I've gotten away with murder. Then you call, Intelligent Cleaner. Today of all days. Think about how he feels. You call, and the nightmare starts again. His heart thumps like the horses at Randwick. He hasn't escaped. Now he *has* to deal with you. And he will. The man who killed last night will kill again today.

Why didn't you stay up in the storeroom with the panda bears tucked in to your sides?

Still holding Danny by the wrist, Prakash reached over and extracted the wrapped-up object from his other hand.

"Cactus?" He slowly unwrapped the object from its cellophane cover and sniffed around its base. "Cactus?"

Lowering his glasses from his head and placing them on his nose, Prakash peered through them at Danny.

Before Danny could say it, Prakash had responded to it.

"No." He slapped both his hands on the table. "*You* called me."

The table moved about, and the glasses on it and cutlery shook.

The bartender, who had been wiping beer mugs, turned to them.

At once Prakash leaned back, as if he had lost a point in an encounter. *You're right, Nelson. I can't draw too much attention to myself.*

Removing his glasses, he threw them, almost casually, on the table, and then he reached into his wallet; Danny felt his heels raise themselves off the floor.

His hand in his wallet, Prakash paused to ask:

"You haven't been to South Africa, have you, Cleaner?"

"No, Doctor."

"Then you haven't seen civilization. They've got honest casinos there. Honest machines. I'll win the Flexi Trifecta again."

"Yes, Doctor. I'm sorry. Very sorry."

"Don't fucking call me that," Prakash said. "Don't fucking call me that. I am not a doctor. Don't insult me."

"I'm sorry," said Danny, "I'm sorry."

Prakash breathed out and smiled again. "You can beg, can't you, Nelson." With his finger, he pushed a piece of paper on the table toward Danny. "South Africa today. This evening. See. This is the plane ticket. Look at the time on the ticket, Cleaner. Look at the time."

Departing SYD Arriving JNB

18:45

Gates close half an hour before flight

Premium Economy

34F

Nonsmoking

Danny saw Prakash again wearing his dark-rimmed reading glasses as he awaited a reaction to the ticket.

"Look at the time on the ticket."

"Six forty-five p.m. Today," said Danny, reading off the paper in front of him. "Is this a confirmed ticket?" he asked the doctor.

"Confirmed ticket?" Prakash smiled. "You haven't flown in a long time, have you?"

"Four years," replied Danny.

Outside on Darlinghurst Road, a white bus moved through white sunlight; the beer glasses on the table refracted its beams and cast a watery shimmer on everyone's hands. Danny closed his eyes.

Doctor, she used to call him. He must have hated it as much as I hated being called Nelson.

He heard someone say: "It's too bright here, isn't it? Let's move."

Danny knew a strong hand was holding him by the wrist and guiding him. He felt himself moved down to the darker alcove at the end of the bar, meant for the serious punters. Killer, Cleaner, and Cactus sat down at a new table.

Maybe Prakash just *knows* who did it, thought Danny, settling into his chair. He didn't do it himself. Maybe his right leg is also shaking right now.

"Don't worry about a thing, Cleaner," said Prakash, sounding normal again. "We'll have lunch, then go back to the old place. In Potts Point. And you're cleaning it. The toilets. Okay?"

But he tightened his grip on Danny's right hand, and that grip said: *You and me are connected, Cleaner. You know my secret, and I know yours.*

"Okay, sir. Okay."

Now you have to do what you always do, Danny told himself.

NEXT GAME IN 0:18

Now you have to tell a story.

In the alcove, four conjoined television screens seethed and spilled over: chestnut horses on one screen, greyhounds on another, white women in wide green hats on a third, then a fourth pulsating with numbers, and all four arranged around another, giant TV screen, which was further subdivided into four smaller screens, each febrile with colored data, like the distinct compartments of a heraldic device. Danny remembered the Jesuit coat of arms over the doorway of his school. *Lucet et Ardet*.

"Do you know the fishes sing in my hometown? In a lagoon?" he said.

"What the fuck are you talking about?" asked Prakash. "Let's order lunch. They have steak here. You want that?"

Three white Australians sat in the alcove with paper and pen; Danny wondered how they'd respond if Prakash began yelling about an illegal immigrant.

The TV screens began showing live images from a greyhound race. The dogs were ready for the hunt and awaiting a signal.

The doctor now had the cactus in one hand; with the other, he was still holding Danny's wrist.

Prakash smiled. He was like one indicating that something very long and painful had only just begun for both of them, and they might as well be comfortable. And have lunch.

Like an electronic compound eye, the TV screens now examined Danny synoptically. The numbers flickered and changed and the big TV at the center of the cluster showed a close-up of a man examining the hooves of a chestnut horse.

What if he still has the knife with him? Has he got it under the table or in his pants?

"No steak," said Danny. "I want vegetarian food."

That caught Prakash's attention, and he looked straight at Danny, who said at once:

"Doctor. What is an illegal?"

"What?"

"Illegal means legal who is ill, no? That's a joke, sir. I thought you'd like it."

Before Prakash could respond to these unexpected sounds— vegetarian, or illegal, or the joke—Danny pointed to the bump on his left forearm.

"Do you see this? This . . . ?"

Prakash nodded. First he placed the cactus down on the table, and then removed his thick-rimmed black glasses and placed them beside the potted plant. "What is it?" he asked.

"Did Radha tell you what it was?" Danny asked.

That caught the killer's attention. Danny felt the grip on his wrist tighten.

Prakash squeezed his brow to focus his eyes; he looked at the spot on Danny's forearm.

"What is that thing?"

"I'll tell you, sir. We have an airport, Doctor, in Sri Lanka. Bandaranaike Airport, international airport. I was in Dubai for a year, in a hotel, working in a Deira business motel. Did you know?"

"You've seen the world, Danny. Haven't you?" asked Prakash.

Danny laughed sardonically. Sure.

Dubai! Yes, he'll tell you about Dubai, Doctor. Danny, from his little city along the lagoon, went out to meet the world and discovered the great Muslim city in the desert. He worked in a hotel. He wore a green suit and green tie and stood behind the desk of a business motel in Deira, Dubai, that was his job. Millions of men would kill to have a job like that. Brown men.

When he wasn't updating the computer records, or delivering the morning's newspapers to each door in the hotel, Danny spoke to his guests, one hand on the green tie, answering their questions about entertainment in Dubai, sometimes extending his answers into discussions of Shakespeare's identity and the truth about America's ambitions for the Middle East, if they were in a mood to listen. There was a little white bar in the hotel, and on any given evening, an Arab in a caftan from one of the more repressed emirates, still reeking of desert wind, would be sitting there to utter one word over and over again: "Whiskey." When the day ended, Danny changed his clothes and punched his time card. Filipina prostitutes clapped their hands right outside the hotel. Standing in front of one of Dubai's crazy glass towers, Danny thought, When I go back home, they'll have a small function for me. Dubai Danny. A felicitation. *Cross the road now.* Gray lizards from the desert, twice as thick as Sri Lankan geckos, sat on the posts at every traffic signal, and when the electronic beeping began, it was as if reptilian diaphragms were pulsing, *Cross the road, cross it at once.* Danny returned to the hotel to clean up the little white bar and then slept in a room behind the reception with four other workers. His father sent him a letter each month amending a list of warrantied goods, mostly electronic, he was expected to bring home at the year's end.

Around Christmas, the workers became tense; they had been promised, in their contract, a year-end 20 percent bonus. At the start of December, the bonus was canceled. The workers were powerless. They had been made to surrender their passports to the employer—that was the law in Dubai—and now the passports were held as ransom.

All that was normal in Dubai, it turned out. The employer even had the nerve, when returning Danny's passport, with his salary but without the bonus, to say, "Would you like to work another year in this job, son? Customers enjoy the way you talk to them. The women, especially."

"I said, 'No, I don't want another year of working here in your Dubai.' Maybe I'll try to go to America again, I thought, you know. After working every day for a year, except Sunday mornings, I had two full free days in Dubai. To do shopping for my father."

Danny felt Prakash's grip on his arm loosen.

"Not for yourself?"

"No. Not for myself."

"What a bastard. Not you."

"I bought what I had to for my father, and then I flew home. But when I came home to Sri Lanka, someone stopped me at our airport, which is Katunayake. A customs officer. I told him I had bought nothing in duty-free, thinking that was the problem. But it wasn't. You follow?"

Watching the killer's face, Danny raised and lowered his voice and posed rhetorical questions, knowing from experience that his manner of telling them turned true stories into false ones. He knew that he was always too eager to please.

"So why was he stopping me if it was not about duty-free goods?"

On the TV screen, the horses were getting ready to run. Two other men came into the alcove and looked at the screen.

"The customs officer called me to a room. He asked some questions. Then another officer, not a customs man, came in and asked the same questions while flipping through my passport. More men came like this. Right? After two or three hours, they drove me out of the airport, saying they had to get something sorted out. This whole time I still have no idea what is going on, right?"

Danny explained: the next few hours happened in a daze. He was in a room where he could still hear planes in the distance. Men came and left, asking him stranger and stranger questions.

"I start to understand that they were looking for an LTTE man who was supposed to come from Dubai on my flight. Was I the man? You know . . . LTTE? Tamil Tigers? Rebels. They asked, 'Are you a terrorist? Were you raising money in Dubai for bombs?' No, I kept saying, no, just a Dubai business hotel assistant manager. Then I fell asleep. In the middle of the night, the lights came on in the room, and three new men wearing a different kind of uniform came in and started asking me the same questions. Terrorist? Money? I was very hungry, but I answered them."

"Excuse me, mate—" An Australian man asked them for the racing newspaper.

"Want a cactus instead?" Prakash smiled as he gave him the paper.

"Listen, Genius Cleaner." Prakash leaned forward the moment the white man left. "Is this a story or is this real?"

"It is real. It happened to me. Now listen. And be careful about the cactus," Danny said. "Don't joke about giving it away."

Radha Thomas's murderer placed both hands on the covered cactus, moved it back and forth, and smiled.

Looking at the cactus, Danny explained. Though the interrogating officers changed every hour, the confidence with which each one kept telling Danny that he was a Tamil Tiger—and not just any, but a very specific and real Tiger, one given to use the nom de guerre Danny, also known to pose as a hotel manager in Dubai and fly back to Colombo on Fridays, also known to have a father in Batticaloa for whom he would be bringing back electronic gifts that could be recycled into bomb timers—and their utter imperviousness to his denials—meant that in the breaks from the interrogation, Danny did little other than speculate about this terrorist (also Danny) whom he had somehow been mistaken for upon his return to his own country: what did this other Danny dress like, which street in Batticaloa did he live on or claim to live on, who and what did he fuck; and as a new officer came in and the questioning resumed, becoming more and more specific ("In Kuala Lumpur, how long did you spend at the Tune Hotel on the twenty-third of last month?"), Danny felt like he was in one of those Tamil suspense movies where the hero falls asleep one night in his flat and wakes the next morning in a king-size bed in Bangkok in a blue jacket—finding himself the head of the criminal Mafia in Thailand. He touches his new face, fiddles with his jacket, counts his guns and minions, and has no idea how his life has changed in an instant, how he got to Thailand, or why people assume he is a Mafia boss. After a while though, the hero, confronted by photographs, begins to realize that he *is*, and has *always* been, a Bangkok don: and that his earlier life in Tuticorin or Salem as a simple fun-loving youth was the real illusion.

Then his next interrogator came into the room.

"This fellow was always going to be easy to remember," said Danny. Because this officer had a tic—the right side of his lips twitched upward as he spoke, even as his right eye contracted—like a man who had to squeeze words out of his mouth.

Danny demonstrated; Prakash nodded. He knew the type.

So this officer with the twitch in his lip sat there with a cigarette in the fork of his fingers, looking at Danny.

"What is your name?" he asked. And the same questions again and again. "Do you know the terrorist named Danny? Do you know *any* terrorists? What is your father's name?" And then, without any change of expression, he said: "Write your name on this paper."

"I wrote it. He said, 'Not in Tamil.' I wrote it in English. 'Not in English,' he said. 'Write it in the national language.' Sinhala. I picked up the pen, and my hand was trembling as I wrote. He said, 'That's not the way you write it in the national language, I'll show you how to write Danny in the national language,' and he stubbed his cigarette into my forearm. As I was screaming, as he kept his cigarette held down, I could hear him ask the same questions again. What is your name? What is your father's name? What is—"

"—Crazy shit," Prakash whispered.

On the TV screen, the horses had begun running down the track. Danny could feel through the man's tight grip on his arm their hooves thumping down his own pulse. Then he felt Prakash's grip loosen.

In the dark, Danny thought: The story is good.

Moving his head back, Prakash retorted: "I don't believe. I don't believe the cigarette. I've seen you smoke. You're not scared of cigarettes."

"Yes, I used to, Doctor. You're right, I used to smoke." Danny showed him his teeth. "You see, I began smoking after what they did to me with a cigarette."

And *that* hit the animal's heart. Isn't that just how humans are? Prakash let go of him entirely.

"You see, when I went to see the doctor in Batti about my wound on my arm, he said, 'You also have a blood pressure problem. One forty-nine over one oh three.'"

"Is that . . . is that . . . ?"

Prakash began moving a finger slowly toward the bump on Danny's forearm.

It never reached. With his free arm, Danny rammed a small potted cactus into the murderer's face, knocking him off his chair and onto the floor of the pub.

By the time the man got up, it was too late—the door of the pub was open, vibrating, and Danny was gone.

Remember that boy in the blue sarong.

That Muslim boy, the one who wore a skullcap and a blue sarong, kneeling before an army officer on a halo of burning sand. A month earlier, the tsunami had struck Sri Lanka. It was 2004. Thousands died in a day. A new curse on this island, which had already had a civil war, and how the people responded: like heroes. Men and women who had been sending their sons to kill Tamils now sent money to save Tamil lives.

Danny too had caught the do-good fever, and he went around the coast volunteering in the relief efforts, helping get food and medicine and water to the people who had lost their homes. One particular village of fishermen, all of them Tamils, had lost everything and were living in a church with some blankets, boiled water, and packages of food in plastic. A bucktoothed Muslim in a blue sarong was the one who was bringing them the food and water.

Danny joined up with the Muslim. Remember how things were between Tamils and Muslims in the East back then. Reprisals and counter-reprisals. The cycle never ended. But this goofy Muslim boy on a bicycle that was wobbly with food had become, no one knew why, the savior of these Tamils. Bananas, boiled rice, lemon pickles for the refugees, and fresh milk for the children. Everyone loved this Muslim. A cunning devil, they discovered he was, collecting supplies from the army *and* the rebels, each of whom distributed food and water on the strict condition that it should not be handed to refugees who were taking aid from the other side. After one day off for the tsunami, the civil war had resumed. The local army commander found out that the refugees taking his food were somehow also receiving food from the rebels; and one evening the church was burned down while the refugees watched. The army commander called the Muslim boy to him: "Don't help the Tamils for twenty-four hours. They've been eating our rice and the rebels' rice at the same time. This is punishment. Understand?"

"Understand, understand," replied the Muslim boy in his awkward way.

"You know what will happen," said the commander, "if you break my law?"

Next day the army men in their jeep drove down to the burned church, found that the Muslim boy was still distributing food packets to the refugees, and stopped in front of him. One of them ordered: "Get in."

Danny was there too, helping, but hid and watched as they took the Muslim boy around the block to where the army camp was, by the water. Here they made the boy kneel in front of an officer who sat on a plastic chair. From a safe distance, Danny spied. The abject sight of that Muslim boy in his sarong, prostrate before the Sri Lankan army officer on that halo of burning sand, the blue Indian Ocean behind and infinite humiliation ahead of him, remains in Danny's mind—and let it stay there: as an emblem of the fate of a do-gooder in our world.

This business of helping others will make bigger monsters of us than greed ever did.

Rights? You have the right to run, Danny.

You have the fucking *responsibility* to run.

And that's all.

1:50 p.m.

STEP BACK DANGER

He had come charging down William Street, taking one street to the right and one to the left to throw off his pursuer, until a man in an orange fluorescent vest stood in the middle of the road with a red round sign.

Danger.

Danny gaped at the man with the STOP sign, who looked ready to scream if he came nearer.

Behind the man who held the sign, another was being lowered into a manhole by a metal pulley to which he was strapped by a green harness; three colleagues in orange watched from behind a sign that said, STEP BACK DANGER BY LAW YOU CANNOT COME CLOSER THAN 3 METRES OF THIS SIGN.

"Sorry," said Danny, and walked away from the sign, even as the worker was lowered into it, and onto another narrow street.

He raised his eyes toward the sky. High up on the shining metal roofs, two bald creatures with drooping beaks looked down on him—the jabiru that had stalked him in Hyde Park had followed with a friend. They were the city's scavengers: they had the first right over every dead or discarded thing in Sydney.

You won't catch *me* today—and Danny ran again.

*   *   *

Hop, skip, and leap. Deep inside a side street, Danny stopped running at last.

No one was coming after him, no one else was in that alley. He was safe. That hungover forty-year-old man, Prakash. Imagine his tremulous chest. Dry throat. The lizard throbbing in the pit of his neck. The confusion in the sunlight.

He was in no position to chase a fit triple jumper. You're safe, Danny told himself, safe.

Although his phone was buzzing and glowing.

Don't touch it, Danny. You know who that is.

But Prakash will phone the dob-in number: Prakash will tell them the truth about me.

H6

"Cleaner," Prakash said breathlessly when Danny answered the next call.

"Cleaner. You hit me. In the face."

"Sorry," said Danny, and almost laughed at his own response.

"Where are you?"

Danny stayed silent.

"Illegal Cleaner," said the doctor. "Illegal means legal who is ill, no?" He laughed.

The voice was concentrated and high-pitched, as if it had been forced into a third of its normal range. He must be seething out there. I got him smack in the nose, I think.

The killer chuckled. "You call me today—you call me, you say you want to meet me, and then you come see me and hit me."

"Sorry, sir," Danny said. "Very sorry. Mistake."

"Well, come back, then. Come and apologize. Then we'll go and clean the flat. I'll give you sixty dollars. You want more? You want more?"

"No," said Danny.

"Danny: I am walking out into the Cross now. I am outside the pub now. If you're around, put your hand up so I can see. No. You're not around. You bolted. Really bolted."

The doctor was panting. He's walking. Quickly. Searching for me.

"Sorry, Doctor. I'm sorry I ran."

And sorry if you were too stupid to see that blow coming. Ha.

"You think I'm a killer?"

"Yes," Danny said. The directness of the question caught him. "No, no," he protested at once. "No, no, no, no. You're not—I don't think you are the—"

The phone went dead.

When it rang again, Danny heard no voice on the line.

"I'm sorry," he said. "I'm sorry. I'm very sorry."

Heart pounding, he thought: The average weekly take-home pay, according to the Australian Bureau of Statistics, is one thousand one hundred dollars, and I'm not even 60 percent there. If he had to say sorry to the doctor a thousand more times, he would. That must be how Kiran Rao did it—though he never mentioned that in his book.

"You know where I am, Nelson?"

"The Clinic?"

Prakash's voice became soft. "Should I call the police, then?"

"No."

"Mr. Police, Mr. Australian Police, the man who hit me in a pub, his name is Danny. This is what he looks like. This is his phone number. And just because I was going to dob him in, he starts saying horrible things about me. That I hurt someone. Yes, he's a bad man, this Danny. Shall I tell them that?"

Danny kept quiet.

The man with the advantage spoke.

"There is an immigration dob-in number, buddy. You know

about it, don't you? Wait. I have a question. I have a question, Cleaner. That lovely story . . . about the cigarette, buddy, did it really happen, or was it just made up? No, I think it did happen. It sounded right to me. Come back here, Cleaner, and I'll hit you in the face with the cactus. Deal?"

Even if you called them and informed them the killer was in Kings Cross, in the Vegas pub, right now, the Aussie police would not believe you. Never. A man killed a woman last night, and dumped her body in a creek, and this morning, he is sitting in the pub, smiling and playing the pokie machines? I find it hard to believe, son. Danny touched the bump on his forearm. Of course, no policeman in Australia, for all their firearms and powerful physiques, for all the heavy gear they wore on their blue shirts, had that bump on their forearm. Their understanding of the world had not been expanded by a few hours of torture.

"Here's *my* story, Cleaner. In return for your lovely cactus story. It's called Cleaner Does Deportation. The story is this: You'll be a hero for a minute on Twitter, and then everyone's watching football while you are deported for the rest of your life. You think it's a tall story I'm telling, Cleaner? Sure, no one will want to be the one to say, 'Send the brave little cleaner back to Sri Lanka,' and some may even ask, in customs and in immigration, 'Shouldn't he get a fair go?,' and hundreds in the street will hold up signs for you, and some may even starve to death for a day or carry a little bomb on a Qantas flight or hold a painting show for you in Melbourne, but in the end, they'll go home, and you *will* be deported. Am I lying? Am I fucking with you, Sir Cleaner?"

"No," Danny replied.

He was right. Prakash was right. No felicitations, no garlands, no shawls, and no gold medals: doing the right thing was like turning the light off.

Do you feel whole again, Cleaner?

His left leg trembled. He smelled broccoli being boiled from an Australian kitchen somewhere nearby.

"Villawood. Yeah. That'll be fun, won't it? And you know where you go from there? Christmas Island. You heard of it?"

Danny nodded. Christmas Island. He had heard.

"People will eat nails, and drink things, and cut their wrists to get out of that fucking place. You'll live *pretty* well in there, yes?"

The doctor had asserted the full force, the brute power, of his Australianness in that *yes*. Danny replied with:

"Please." He lowered his voice. "My father spent all his savings to send me to Australia, and I must pay him back. I have to go to Rodney Accountant's house and clean it, please. Please. He has a 'No Uranium Mining' sign on his fridge and he's a good man. Please."

"Danny, you know your voice trembles whenever you lie? Where are you? Come back at once. To the Clinic."

"No," said Danny, and switched the phone off.

Now an echoing *no* came at him, as if from the Coca-Cola sign but in truth from behind it, from the hidden back ways of Kings Cross, a place where men cried like nowhere else on earth—outbursts from bodies that had been untied by alcohol and heroin, and which spread like invertebrates on the pavement—until they suddenly found the strength to sit up straight and howl: *It will never end, Danny. Your civil war will never fucking end!*

Danny ran again.

He ran until he was between a tunnel penetrated by train tracks, and a raw sandstone cliff on top of which stood tiers and tiers of glass balconies. He was hidden from the Coca-Cola sign and from Kings Cross.

The phone had been ringing all the time. Pressing his head against the sandstone cliff, he answered it now.

The line went dead.

Why *did* you tell this man everything, Radha? I bet you told him about the dob-in number too. I bet you did. Why?

To calm himself down, he began moving from side to side along the cliff, plucking the ferns.

How did Prakash put the knife in? Danny struck the sandstone again and again, in imitation of a murderer's blows. I don't know how a knife goes in, but I do know how a cigarette goes into flesh.

Merrily merrily merrily, came the voice from behind him, and he spun around.

It was just the wind sweeping dry leaves along.

Life is but a dream.

When the phone rang again, Danny let go of the ferns and looked up at the blue sky and yelled loudly enough to be heard all the way up to the Coca-Cola sign: "I don't think you killed her, Doctor. I said it wrong."

"Okay."

Closing his eyes, he tried to read the silence on the phone.

"Intelligent Cleaner." After a pause, the killer laughed. "You always were an intelligent cleaner."

The line went dead.

Danny laughed too. Crazy man still wants a way out. The King of the Nile still wants to escape.

Fern and grass grew in patches on the cliff; Danny plucked at the leaves and breathed it in, the fragrance of the continent underneath. It felt, for a second, as good as menthol. His nostrils cleared up.

Top-top-bada-daba-daba-bum-bum . . . Danny's lips trilled; he played with small ferns growing on the sandstone cliff.

But it had started again: the phone was buzzing again.

H6

Danny looked at the phone and clapped. Go away. Leave me alone.

In response, the cliff began vibrating.

The train to Kings Cross station was passing on the tracks down below, and Danny stepped back from the sandstone cliff. At the same time, his phone kept buzzing, as if it were being battered, again and again, by someone's powerful muscles. As if it too were demanding, like the cliff, like the train thundering below, *Why* did *you tell Radha you were illegal? Why did you trust an Australian?*

Because she promised to help.

"Cleaner," Radha had shouted over the roaring of Danny's vacuum, "we won't be going out tonight. I'm sorry about that. Prakash and I are going to a concert in Centenary Park. It's for asylum-seekers. I'd invite you, but we've already bought tickets."

"Okay," shouted Danny. "No problem."

Asylum.

Maybe it was that word: because Danny felt his forehead shift and his jaw tighten. He polished and cleaned everything twice as well that day.

When he was done, he found Radha on the phone, a beer in her hand. "Yeah, I want to know if I can place a bet on the phone? I'll be going to a concert today. Can I call in there, or do I have to come in person? Great."

When she put down the phone, Danny, gathering his courage, told her, "I need asylum."

She laughed. "What?"

"I need asylum," Danny clarified. "Because I don't have Medicare."

The skin between the Aussie woman's eyes wrinkled. "Why not? Everyone gets Medicare in Australia. It's the law."

Danny shook his head. "I don't have superannuation. I don't have a tax file number. I don't have a passport, and I don't have a driver's license."

Radha's forehead furrowed again. You could see her mind examining Danny from another angle, like a parrot going upside down with an odd fruit.

She asked: "Why not?"

She said: "Oh, shit. You came here on a boat?"

He had *not* come here on a boat: he had flown into Australia on Malaysia Airlines, economy-class ticket, and that was the problem.

For three days after Danny returned from Dubai, his father looked at him with a new sympathy, an unknown kindness, as if his son's horror story had moved him; but before the week was over, he was gossiping with the brazen neighbor up on her first-floor terrace: *Men from Sri Lanka, Tamil men, in Canada, Norway, and Germany, have built fortunes, own fleets of motorbikes and cars. But this boy—he goes to Dubai—and returns with what? A black mark on his arm. He doesn't have anything from the list I asked him to bring. Not even the two-in-one DVD player. He's claiming it was police torture, but I ask you, why will the police do this to a man unless he is hiding something? Why?* The way Danny looked at him made his father shut up. "Come inside for a moment," said Danny, and led his father back into the house. Closed the door. Raising a wooden chair from the dinner table over his head, Danny smashed it into a cupboard, making a large black hole in its cheap plywood. Then he dropped the chair and broke it too.

He lay in his bed all day, and when it was cool in the evening, he walked about Batticaloa, stood on the Kallady Bridge, and looked down on the lagoon. Sometimes Kannan, his first cousin, joined him on the bridge and, while the cars and bicycles went past noisily, talked to him in a low voice.

"Everyone's trying to get out of here. I was waiting for you to return so we could go together."

There were two options for leaving, Kannan informed him—Canada or Australia. They were the only countries still taking in Tamils from Sri Lanka. Europe and America were turning back people.

There was a boat that went to Canada every week from Rameswaram in India—they would have to pay the smugglers, and it was risky.

Australia? A boat went there too, but there was another way to get there, Kannan said.

Legally.

So, early that Sunday, the two of them took a bus to Colombo to attend the Study in Australia Education Fair, held each year in a hotel by the oceanfront.

About Australia, other than the advertising images found inside the head of every human being on earth (red sand, white beach, infinite sex appeal), Danny knew only this: that a Tamil doctor had emigrated there decades ago, now owned a mansion in Melbourne, and invited visitors from Sri Lanka to play tennis with him and his Aussie wife on his private clay court and later to swim in his private pool. Wasn't Australia thick with racists, though? the guests asked when his wife left. Don't they have a law called the White Australia law? By way of answer, the doctor opened a safe-deposit box and invited them to see his collection of twenty-four-karat gold coins, which included half-sovereigns embossed with the faces of British kings and genuine South African Krugerrand.

On a merciless summer day, the conference hall inside the hotel—dominated by a giant STUDY IN AUSTRALIA, YOUNG SRI LANKAN poster—glowed with white lights and perfect air-conditioning. Danny and Cousin Kannan scratched up and down the goose bumps on their naked arms. White men wearing wool suits had brought photographs of their colleges, and in a corner of the hall, one of them stood with his right hand over a TV screen showing *Mission: Impossible* 2, featuring the one, the only, the legendary Tom Cruise. Set in the city of Sydney. "Now, we can't *guarantee*," said the square-jawed, carrot-haired representative of the Mackenzie Technical College, but added sotto voce, "but let's just say I'd be *a little* surprised if you didn't get a job and a visa at the end." He looked at Danny and Kannan and added, "That's irony, by the way."

Is he telling the truth? Danny thought about it for a second or two. Didn't matter, did it. The next time he left Sri Lanka would be the last time he left.

The cost of the course, the carrot-haired man added, was $17,400, which was cheaper than anything you'd find in Sydney (but Wollongong, with its vibrant nightlife, is just a couple of hours away). You'll need a one-semester deposit and a $320 OSHC charge for six months. Overseas Student Health Cover. "I'm in good health," Danny protested, and that was the first time he was told of this thing. Australian law. OSHC had to be purchased or he would not be given a visa: it was the Law.

"I don't have that kind of money," said Cousin Kannan on the bus back. "The smugglers, they don't ask for this much."

They had four days to decide, Kannan said. The boat left on Thursday evening. Danny thought about it, thought about it, and thought about it.

Kannan did not think. He went on his own to Rameswaram and bought a seat on the boat to Canada.

Sharks—smugglers—it was all too brazenly illegal. Honest Danny couldn't do that. Besides, he had the money to go to Sydney—just about.

To his Dubai savings, his father added nearly eight thousand in Australian dollars. Now that the civil war was over, land prices were rising, and his father had recently sold a flat that he had kept all these years for this very moment. When he and Danny would go abroad for good. It was a lot of money to spend on a dodgy college, true, but Danny didn't think he would need all of it, because he was going to Australia with a plan—a clever plan, which he explained to his father. The moment he arrived, he would apply for refugee status. His father, who had been avoiding him ever since he smashed the hole in the cupboard with the chair, expressed a mild form of skepticism. Look at him avoiding my eyes, thought Danny. This little man has been scared of the police and the state all his life, and now he is scared of me. I know, insisted Danny, what I am doing. "I meant that it is a good plan," said his father. "First you go, Danny. Then I will come over. Then the cousins will come. You will bring us all over one by one."

In Dubai, a fifty-six-year-old Pakistani waiter at the hotel, asked to tell stories of his roaring youth in Karachi, shouted back: "*When was I ever young? Tell me when I was ever—?*"

I will, Danny promised himself, become young in Australia.

So, Sydney. After a fitful sleep came a red dawn, and deep blue water penetrated by green bays of land that had the pattern of a frog's splayed toes, before the plane turned sharply to reveal buildings that grew taller and whiter by the minute, creating in Danny's mind the impression that he was, like Jack in reverse, descending into a city of new giants.

The airplane landed hard.

After arriving in Sydney at 4:30 p.m. I took the train and reached the Mackenzie College on a Thursday evening. The city called Wollongong is about 95 to 100 minutes from Sydney Central Station.

Three days later, Danny composed to his father, via email, a progress report on what he had to show, so far, in return for spending $11,300 of the family's money on himself.

I checked in to my room by eight p.m. [the Mackenzie College was a further forty minutes from Wollongong, on the first floor of a brick building—a warehouse; part of the ground floor was derelict, and the other part was full of fridges and washing machines; you went up the stairs by the side to classes] *and by 10 that very evening, just before the college library closed, I sent a letter applying for refugee status via the Australian Immigration Office's website.*

Within twenty-four hours, the Commonwealth of Australia had responded to Danny:

Re: Change of Status from Subclass 500 to Subclass 866

Dear Mr. Rajaratnam,

We have received your request for a change of visa status from Student (Subclass 500) to Protection (Subclass 866). Please be aware that we have zero tolerance for vexatious and/or fraudulent protection claims. Upon reviewing your petition, we find that although you claim to be the victim of torture, and have included a photograph of your left forearm as evidence, your story appears to have a few holes in it. Sri Lanka is a diverse, multicultural nation, and we do not believe that any Tamil should fear to live there. If you were a victim of torture, it was more logical that you should have caught the boat, as quite a few of your fellow countrymen have done. You have clearly had the financial resources to fly to Australia as a full fee-paying student, and you have apparently purchased private health care as required by law, and it was only within the country that you have decided, it seems, that you are a victim of state persecution in your homeland. If you do apply for a Protection visa (Subclass 866) now, inside Australia, be aware that in the light of the zero-tolerance policy you will likely

have to spend some time in detention, and your case may well be
rejected after.

On the first day of classes, there was banging and yelling just
outside the classroom because the Middle Eastern students
found out that they had been charged twice what the Asian
students had been.

The college gave each foreign student a job, to train for a new
life in Australia. Danny was assigned to a curry restaurant on the
first floor of a pub. A Tamil man named Venkat ran it—the other
kind of Tamil, from India.

Now, Indian Tamils are *loud*; they don't stop talking; and *that*
is the difference.

Danny, my Sri Lankan brother, how nice to speak again in
Tamil to someone, said Venky. He added: I have lots of DVDs
from Malaysia, latest movies, tip-top condition, as he walked
over pieces of blackening cardboard, avoiding plastic buckets
brimming with soiled dishes, and entered the kitchen. Danny
followed and listened. Four-week training period comes first,
thambi from Sri Lanka, said Venky. Unpaid, of course. Oozing
bilgewater, the cardboard pieces trembled as Danny stepped on
them. I thought I was done with *this* in Dubai, he thought as he
smiled back at Venky. *Being cheated.*

One more thing, said Venky. The legal quota is just twenty
hours of employment a week for a foreign student (or forty hours
in two weeks), but we can work around that, at ten dollars an
hour, "a bit" less than the legal minimum wage, okay?

Little ways existed to get even with Venky as he washed dishes
in the kitchen, and Danny knew them all from Dubai. He stole
plastic cutlery, tissue paper, and condiments. Why not? Every
foreign student in the college was doing the same thing. Getting

even. Some downloaded essays from Google and handed them in. Some were not even bothering with classes, just looking for work as fruit pickers in orchards.

This was the racket: Mackenzie College wooed foreigners to Wollongong and sucked fees from them for two years, at the end of which, arming them with framed certificates of post-graduate competence, MBAs and MTechs, it turned them loose to tar roads, install windows, and wok-fry noodles around Australia. White people were cheating foreigners, and foreigners were cheating white people, and no one in the college seemed happy, except for a Chinese girl who hugged a backpack to her chest and always had a big smile on her face, like Jesus Christ with a lamb in his arms.

At the start of his third month at Mackenzie, Danny saw an Asian student striding out of the college building with a dictionary in his hands: a hardbound edition of *Merriam-Webster's Collegiate Dictionary*. He began following the dictionary boy. "Hey!" shouted Danny, and the Asian boy stopped, and changed into a Japanese-Brazilian man with long black hair and a goatee: name was Abelardo Nishida, but you could call him Abe. Rhymes with sake, mate! He was from Rio, Abe explained, so he did not speak much Japanese. Just a bit. As he walked, he kept offering Danny cigarettes. Free cigarettes. Thank you very much, said Danny, lighting one up.

"How do you have money for cigarettes in Australia?" asked Danny. Abe, the abseiler, just tapped on his forehead with an index finger.

Danny walked behind as Abe led, drumming on the big dictionary. This Japanese guy looks like a fellow, thought Danny, who has no blood pressure at all.

Three days after this meeting, the Japanese-Brazilian stopped attending classes in the college.

*   *   *

On Saturday Danny took the bus into Sydney and followed his map down to Castlereagh Street, the heart of Sydney's CBD, where he saw, up there, on the glass skyscraper, the smiling Abe (rhymes with sake!) now transformed into the Legendary Abseiler. Someone had to keep the city clean, so Abe, in broad daylight, glided down glass windows on Castlereagh and Pitt streets, wearing his blue helmet and all his hooks, loops, and chains around his waist, showing his 100 percent illegal arse to all the Aussies down below. Just like *Mission: Impossible 2,* Danny thought.

They paid him in cash.

Into a green slot machine Abe dropped a blue bus card; then he turned and signaled to Danny, *I'm paying for you,* and they were both taken by fast bus from Taylor Square to a one-room studio in Bondi full of ashtrays and sea breezes and an unimpeded view of ocean, where Abe swam every morning far, far away from, he explained, all the bloody Asian tourists.

Abe lit a cigarette. Abe had made a long list of observations about Australia, which were accompanied by tapping on his forehead. For instance, "Have you seen how the two-dollar coin is smaller than the one-dollar coin, and the fifty-cent coin is bigger than both of them combined?"

No, Danny had never thought about the meaning in that.

"Do you know how big this country is?" asked Abe. "See this." He opened the dictionary and showed Danny a map of the continent they were on.

From the window, Danny could see waves creaming at Bondi Beach. Creases tightened around his eyes, making him feel simultaneously wiser and more juvenile. Then Abe offered Danny a cigarette and asked about *his* life.

"I am never going home," Danny said, summing up his life.

Abe looked at him from the corner of his eye and nodded. *Okay.*

"Let's go," he declared, and brought Danny, after a bus, a train, and another bus, to the Sunburst grocery store in Glebe.

In front of the spray-painted mural of a strange-looking Lord Krishna, an old white man, alerted by phone or simply by scent of the illegal, stood waiting for them: glossy-faced and shock-haired, Tommo Tsavdaridis looked as if life had been good to him, and he had been good to life. With a grin, Tommo led them into his Sunburst grocery store. Inside, though, his froggy-white hands struggled to open the big glass jars in which he kept plastic-wrapped sweets, each as hard as glass, which he tossed one each to Abe and Danny, an apparent token of his goodwill.

"Glebe is a very good area"—he said to the chewing men, as if advertising real estate to rental tenants—"buses take you everywhere from here Central, anywhere if you can pay for it. So where are you from? Ah . . . following the cricket, surely? No? No?"

A touch of arthritis, just a touch, you see, meant that Tommo Tsavdaridis could no longer quite do all the work in his store, he explained as he showed Danny the storeroom, up the metal stairs, thrown in as living space for whoever worked in the Sunburst store, at just $120 a week.

"Only one thing," the old store owner added. "Last man from India I had, he was working here—months." He held up three fingers. "One day the store is smelling, and I come in, asking him, 'Vikram, Vikram.' He says, 'I make coffee.' Okay. You make coffee, but why the bad smell.' Then I see: he is boiling milk in the kettle, and who has ever done that in human history? You must never ever do that, Danny," the old man said, smiling, "never boil milk and make my store smell bad. Or I murder you."

Honest men are all honest in the same way: each rotten thing on earth emits its own special stench. This white-haired Greek grocer was not like Venky. His desire for exploitation was, Danny sensed, much more ambitious.

Your call, Abe the Abseiler replied when Danny expressed his reservations. They were back in Bondi, walking along the beach. Danny was thinking of the map of Australia in the Merriam-Webster's dictionary. As big as the Roman Empire. As big as America minus Alaska. And most of it red and *empty*, which somehow tripled its size.

In Dubai, Danny had seen what happened to illegals. He had seen it at the airport. Two Filipino men, handcuffed to each other, due for deportation, had been made to sit in front of a boarding gate. A uniformed South Asian guard sat with them, and the men had to ask permission from him when they wanted to drink water from a faucet. As one deported Filipino tried to bend down to drink, the other, handcuffed to him, had to twist his body contrapuntally. Like two chained monkeys.

Go back to the college, Danny. Go back and give the college a chance.

Standing above the sands of Bondi, Abe watched the women who were sunbathing, providing a running commentary—bikini on this one, towel on that one, and guess what's on that one—nothing!—while Danny listened to another commentary. At the edge of the beach, a sulfur-crested cockatoo sat on top of a Christmas pine like a rooster on a weather vane, saying, *Fuck you, fuck you, fuck you* incessantly to the seabathing bodies, now extending his neck and now contracting it, as he kept cawing, *Fuck you, fuck you:* to the beach, to the ocean, and to the slender airplane moving through the immense sky, while Danny sensed for the first time the power of a new continent, raw, red, and pagan, which was yelling at him in that cockatoo's voice, *And fuck you too, for being a coward.*

"If you are scared, go back to the college," advised a Japanese-Brazilian he barely knew. Abe explained how that racket worked too. "You switch from one course to the other every semester, right? Two years at the college becomes four years. Even five. You can earn money on the side as a fruit picker. After five years, who knows?"

Danny kept looking at the cockatoo on top of the Christmas pine.

He didn't go back to the college that night. Nor did he drop out. For three days and nights, he stayed with Tommo Tsavdaridis on an experimental basis, working in the Sunburst grocery store, putting toilet paper and condensed milk on their proper shelves, and sleeping in the storage room, thinking, I'm sick of being cheated. I can't keep paying the rip-off college all that money. On the second evening, he picked up the two panda bears, discarded on the pavement outside, carried them in, tucked them under his arms, and slept tight with them. But in the morning, he saw Australian policemen right outside the store, and his left leg trembled, and *no*, his throat whispered down into his stomach, *no*.

No, you can never fuck the law and get away, he thought, going down Glebe and Broadway all the way to George Street, phantasmagoric George Street, a current of healthy young people of various races, Malays, Indonesians, Arabs, and Pakistanis, until pushing through them he discovered the open plaza of Martin Place, the financial center of Australia, a sandstone brag about the wealth of a young continent, full of oversize carved lions and unicorns and emus sitting on top of bank doors, but what made Danny gape here was a man, a white man who did not seem connected to the banks in any way but was nibbling on something from an open paper bag, and looping aimlessly up and down the open plaza, raw freedom radiating from him like the odor of sweat from an athlete's legs: and the next thing Danny knew, he was again at the *mugathwaram*, the magic breach in the lagoon that had encircled his whole life, and the wide silver ocean was just a leap away from him. In the distance a clocktower watched. His two hands were trembling. *But what more can anyone do to you here, Danny, after what they have already done to you back home?* Knowing that there is no way in life to be slightly less fearful, is there, no three little jumps this time, is there?—Danny clutched his hands and leaped. Into ocean. He wrote to the Mackenzie College saying he would not be paying his fees, and hence was dropping out, but he knew he was not going to leave the country. Twenty-eight days after he sent that letter, he became free forever in Sydney. Twenty-eight days after he sent that letter, he became trapped forever in Sydney.

"And now you give this man half of everything? Half of what I give you? O-kay," Radha declared, shaking her head. "O-kay. How much does that leave you a week?"

He told her. Yes, he knew. It was not much. "But I'm free," he said. "I'm free in Sydney."

"But you live in a grocery store."

Danny shrugged. "I live on top of it."

"O-kay . . . Where is this place?"

Danny smiled. It was too late now: why stop. Why stop. "Glebe. I'm next to the Sunburst grocery store."

"I *know* the store. I've been there. It has the famous weird Krishna mural by the side, right?"

Yes. That mural. Point one, Danny didn't approve of the way Hindu gods appeared on these murals in Sydney. What can you do, though? Everyone everywhere makes fun of Hindus. But point two, there *was* art, real merit, in this mural, in the way Krishna had been reimagined as a dreadlocked surfer with a Rastafarian dharma, no denying that.

"Yes, it's that store. Sunburst. It's been in Glebe for thirty years."

"I've been in there. I've never seen you."

He smiled. Because I'm just the brown man working at the back of the store.

But Radha was making important discoveries about the city she'd been born in and lived all her life in. "I guess you're not alone here. Other day I was in Carlingford, and six Chinese guys in singlets look out from above the restaurant, just for half a second. Then they go back in. They looked like monkeys."

When you're an illegal, you are exactly that.

"Clean that up," said old Tommo Tsavdaridis, pointing at the moist dog shit on the pavement outside the store, about two hours after Danny told him he was going to stay. "Yes: clean it up. Customers shouldn't step on that when walking into my store." Danny went down on his knees with white tissue paper and wiped the resinous gunk, holding his breath as he carried the paper and its contents to a public waste bin. He returned to placing cans of tomato soup on the shelves. Half an hour later, Tommo called him again. Dogs had begun shitting four times a day outside the Sunburst store. They must have heard there was an illegal there.

In the evening, the old store owner laid down an iron rule: Danny was not allowed to talk to customers. The Persian woman with the hair salon across the road? Has the same rule for her Chinese girls. The illegal ones.

At nine in the evening, with a click—a patriarchal click—Mr. Tsavdaridis turned the lights in the storeroom off. "No noise, Danny," he whispered, "or I call the immigration." A roar of laughter.

Twenty minutes later, when Danny, his toothbrush and Colgate in his hand, began walking down the metal steps, the old man came and shouted: "I said no!"

"Toilet," protested Danny.

"Immigration!"

Back in the storage room, Danny held on to his two pandas and shut his eyes. If he were writing his own story, he thought, he would call this moment "First Hour of Understanding What It Is to Be Illegal." He closed his eyes and pressed the pandas into his sides.

He felt his blood pressure going up.

The metal staircase outside tittered. Perhaps the grocer had come around to check that he was in his cage. Yes, Danny thought he could smell the man.

He thought his BP must be at 150/110 already. Even higher. But Danny knew a few old tricks to deal with a bursting bladder. Because when he was a boy, his father never let him go to the toilet once the lights were off.

Things to do when you're lying in the dark and your bladder is full and about to burst open. First. Breathe. Close your eyes. You are sticking a long straw down your throat. When the straw pierces the wall of your bladder, suck hard. Your mouth is full of fetid piss. But your bladder is light, oh, so light. Second. Crawl to the mattress's edge. Lick the ground until you find a large crystal of sand. Twirling the sand crystal on the tip of your tongue, intone: "This is a grain of rock sugar slowly dissolving in my mouth. This is a grain . . ." The thought of sugar will soothe the limbs, relax the mind. Third. Flipping over on your belly, contract your thighs, and . . .

. . . the whole time he could feel his fingers walking down his forearm of their own volition, until they touched the bump there, and then his fingers, thinking for themselves, asked, What *more* can they do, Danny, after what they have already done to you.

This was the second hour as an illegal.

Getting up, opening the door of his room again, Danny left his storeroom, walked down the steps, entered the store, went all the way to the back, and used the toilet that was behind the shampoo and conditioner and coconut-cream soaps. Tommo gaped at him with his legal Australian eyes and said nothing. He didn't call immigration. In the morning, he didn't even talk about it.

Weeks went like this. Danny followed some of the rules of the Sunburst and broke some. After three weeks, Abelardo Nishida phoned. There was an opportunity for freelance work.

That evening, after stacking the tomato cans, Danny confronted Mr. Tsavdaridis: "I have to go out on Tuesday. A lawyer in Erskineville has a vacuum cleaner in his house, but I have to bring everything else. If he likes the cleaning, he'll pay me fifty dollars."

Old Tommo just gave him a look. *Have you gone mad, monkey?*

No, he had gone to the library.

"I was reading the law in Glebe library, Tommo. And you know what it says? Any man who employs an illegal and knows he is doing so is going to jail. They'll put *you* in jail if you put *me* in jail."

Me no dob, you no dob.

He agreed to pay Tommo 50 percent of everything he made. And to work late into the night when he got back on Tuesday.

His career as a legendary cleaner in inner-city Sydney had begun. "Because of me, every illegal in Glebe now asks for more from the boss. Every single one."

That ended the story, the Australian woman clapped, and Danny found himself, for the first time in Australia, felicitated.

"You're a bloody revolutionary. Like Gandhi."

"No."

"Yes. Yes. Like Nelson Mandela. This country needs people like you."

Her limbs pulsated with a sense of his freedom. She saw an athlete of the underground.

Danny sensed this, her exultation at his story, and he shared in it. He was the tiger of her eyes. But no, he wanted to tell her, no, this is all wrong. Because even when he was playing the game Abe had introduced him to, even when he was beating the blue-uniformed policemen, even when he was winning, Danny had been losing. He had not even played the game right. Because he *was* in a game—a big, international World Cup or Olympics. In this game, people were running from countries that were burning to not-yet-burning ones; catching boats, cutting barbed wire, snuggling into containers at the bottoms of ships, while another set of people were trying to stop, stall, catch, or turn them back; and though it was all chaos on the surface, it turned out there were definite rules in this game: either you braved it, got on the boat, got caught by Coast Guard, went to special jail—in which case there were lawyers, social workers, and people like the librarians at Glebe and left-wing women at train stations who would help you (would *rush* to help, then to post photos of their generosity on Facebook)—or you arrived by plane, legally, with a visa printed on your passport, went to their dodgy colleges, said *Sorry sorry sorry* when they yelled, and cleaned their toilet bowls for five or six years, before becoming a citizen in the seventh, when you could finally tell the white people to fuck off. What you did not do was fall in between these two by coming to Australia legally and then sliding under, appearing to be one thing and then becoming another, because *that* made you an illegal's illegal, with no one to scream for you and no one to represent you in court. And this custom-made cell within the global prison was Danny's own: a personal hot coal he had forged for himself to stand on.

But *that* was not the story she wanted to hear, was it?

"Tell me, Nelson Mandela," his Australian employer raised her voice, "tell me who's after you. What do they do. Tell me everything."

"Who's after me? They all are."

"Who's *they all*?"

"Customs, cops, the Department of Immigration and Multicultural Affairs, which they renamed Immigration and Citizenship, and then renamed Customs and Border Protection, then renamed Immigration and Border Protection, plus the ABF."

"Who?"

"Australian Border Force, plus they now have Immigration Taskforce Pegasus, and Taskforce Cloudburst, specially for illegals."

"What are you talking about?" Radha asked. "I never heard of these people."

"Rule number one," said Danny, "is they have your tax file number, so you have to close your bank account. Rule number two is you absolutely can't work at a twenty-four-hour shop like City Convenience or 7-Eleven. Always being raided by immigration."

"No shit?"

"No. Another place of danger is any Hindu temple in the city. Immigration raided one last year and arrested everyone, including the priest and the holy peacock."

"Hilarious. You are a fucking *legend*. Next time we go out, you have to tell Prakash everything you just told me. This is incredible."

But now Danny shrank in size and begged: "Please don't tell Dr. Sir my secret? That I am *illegal* . . . ?"—and the effect of that question was to demolish some image of him that she had constructed for herself, for she said in a weary tone: "Sure. I'll keep it a secret. And we will help you, Nelson. Sit down." She pointed to the spot.

"Everyone wants Radha to help them, don't they? And no one does a thing for me, Nelson. Fine. I *won't* mention any names, but I'll ask a friend of mine at Legal Aid. Hypothetically. No names. No address. Promise. But you know"—folding her arms, she arched her back before smiling at him—"that the moment you came here to work for me, you implicated me in an illegal act, do you understand?"

Danny nodded.

Arms still folded, she leaned from the hips toward him. "And what *do* you say when you put other people in trouble, Nelson?"

"I am very very sorry," Danny replied, and then, "Thank you very much," and waited, but she didn't mention it the following week. And he realized that she had never meant to tell anyone about his situation—except Prakash, that is. She must have told the mad doctor about Danny again and again, discussing his case and all its gory details. We should help him, shouldn't we? We should save him, shouldn't we? Let's do it tomorrow. Tonight we'll have fun.

Which was why Prakash remembered everything.

2:31 p.m.

Write me your name in the national language, son.

Danny's heart stopped.

A brown man, normally given to interrogating suspects in Sri Lanka, was today in a lime-colored vest, searching among the parked cars, holding a cigarette in his forked fingers.

But the man turned, and he was again a stranger, with CITY RANGER written on his fluorescent green vest, taking photos with his cell phone of the license plates of cars parked on the left side of the road.

"Hey," Danny shouted at him, just to talk to another brown man. "What time is it?"

Cigarette between black lips, the city ranger consulted his cell phone and held up a certain number of fingers.

"Thanks!"

At once things, small green things, began hitting Danny. Moving along the ferny cliff, his body had disturbed the burned grass: each drying clump exploded into green atoms, four or five at a time, grasshoppers disturbed from their summer sleep, which zapped Danny before each of them disintegrated into four or five more green atoms. He swatted at himself to be free.

The first number on his phone rang.

Sunburst

"Danny," said Tommo's tired old voice, "I told you never bring friends here."

"I have no friends," replied Danny. "What are you talking about?"

"Danny. Your friend is here. He says his name is Prakash. I give him the phone."

There was a shuffle, and a cough, and an apology, while a different voice took over the phone.

"Nelson. You ran away. So I came to see you."

His left leg, Danny noticed, was shaking.

How did Prakash get to Glebe this quickly? But he's a normal Australian, Danny. He has a car. He just drove down into the city and into Glebe.

"But how did you . . ." asked Danny, though he knew.

"Next to the painting in Glebe. Everyone knows the famous

painting in Glebe. It's not Ganesha. *Krishna*. Right. Jamaican Krishna. I've seen it whenever I've come for the Saturday market. Nelson. I have your cactus here. You know which one. The one you hit me with. That's how your employer here . . . *Tsavdaridis*, is that right? Is that how you say it? Tommo. Okay, that's how Tommo here knows I wasn't joking. I am really your friend."

He's parked outside the Sunburst store. While you were hiding here in East Sydney, that man with the ravaged, hungowver face went to *your* clinic.

Blood makes them smart, doesn't it. After you hit him, Prakash didn't panic. No.

After the moment of surprise, after getting up from the floor, righting himself in the pub, telling people around him, "It's okay, I'm fine, don't worry about me," the half-mad doctor didn't run after you. No. He used his finger and drew circles on the racing page. Assessed Dhananjaya Rajaratnam like a professional punter, found the dog reasonably priced, and placed his money. The full moon glowed on Prakash's face. As he bet he could control you.

Danny ran his fingers through his hair.

No. It wasn't just when I hit him. That isn't when he started planning. Prakash's cool brown eyes had found me long before that. Nelson Mandela. Our old cleaner. He'll see the news on TV. What do I do about him?

House Number Six would have called me today if I hadn't called him first.

From high above Kings Cross, spreading and widening, Danny saw a dark net, like the ones tossed into the air by the fishermen at the Batticaloa lagoon, spreading wide and falling faster, threatening to snare and drag him into the tunnel underneath the Coca-Cola sign, down through the spine of orange lights into blackness.

"Nelson," said the voice on his phone. "Are you okay?"

Danny transferred the instrument to his left ear. "Sorry, Dr. Sir," said Danny, surprised to hear his voice trembling.

"What should I do about the cactus?"

"I don't want it, Dr. Sir. I don't want anything. Me no dob, me no dob."

"Right." Prakash laughed. "Right. You keep saying that. I'll wait here. I'd like to see you again, Nelson. Before I fly to South Africa. Right? Listen." He dropped his voice. "I'm not going to live here like the stingray, under the glass boat. I told you that once, didn't I. You take a glass-bottomed boat over the reef and you see the filthy hiding stingray. That's not me. Never me. I've lived well." His voice almost broke. "I've lived *really* well. You understand, Nelson?"

"Yes."

"I don't blame you for anything that happened over there at the Clinic, Nelson. For hitting me. I don't blame you at all. You know who I blame?"

"Who?" Danny asked.

"Your boss."

"My boss?" repeated Danny. "Tommo?"

"No. Not him. Your real boss. You're just a cleaner."

"Sir, you are right. I'm just the cleaner, and it is an honor to be trusted by you." Speak as if this were the hotel in Dubai, Danny told himself, and you were behind the desk again. "Sir, I will never forget what we have agreed upon."

Prakash hung up.

At once Danny thought, I have to tell Sonja. That's the only thing left to do now. I have to tell her at once.

He ran his fingers through his golden hair.

But what was he going to tell her, exactly? First, in two minutes, let me tell you that I am an illegal and how I became one; and then, in another two or three minutes, let me tell you about the murder that I am mixed up in today.

My history of lying in five minutes. She'll never forgive me.

Where is that cactus when you need it? Would've felt good against his chest now. Right.

But he *had* been so close to telling her, so many times.

Once was at the movies, naturally: that was on a Tuesday, cheap-ticket day, when they went to the cinema in Parramatta Westfield, where he blankly refused her suggestion that they watch the Tamil movie. They saw something with Tom Cruise in it, and he kept looking at Sonja and wondering if he could just whisper: "I am in Australia because of him."

Or he could have told Sonja just a fortnight ago when they went together to Bondi Beach. While she swam on the north side, away from Asian tourists, Danny sat on the towel and watched. "I don't like swimming," he explained. What? Didn't you grow up in some sort of lagoon? "I don't like swimming," he said, and she knew by now not to argue. He watched her as she swam by herself. Because the shoreline was the line of taboo now: he could never swim in this part of the ocean. Abe had come swimming here in Bondi. He did not want to remember Abe.

Sydney had become a city full of bad magic and interdictions, places he must never visit again: there was an intersection in Rose Bay, for instance, where a policeman's horse snorted, dilating a vein over its nose, as it found Danny through blinkers. That shopping mall in Burwood where the woman with the green umbrella had spotted him was still off-limits after three years. Just a month ago, waiting for Sonja, Danny had begun walking about on his own along a new part of Parramatta River, till the sight of a distant metal structure made him remember the Kallady Bridge in Batticaloa. A whistling rose, as if the fish in Parramatta River had learned to sing as well as those back home: *You abandoned your father. In his old age.* Parts of Parramatta were henceforth also forbidden. Labyrinth of remembered errors: or the world's most beautiful city, Sydney.

"What a weird man you are, my Danny," Sonja said when she'd returned from her swim and, having washed herself under an open-air shower, sat down for him to dry her hair. Danny covered Sonja's head with a white towel and said: "Ready?" As he rubbed it vigorously, Danny looked up at all the houses, at all the windows that glittered in the evening light like fool's gold over Bondi Beach.

Dried and changed, Sonja drove the two of them up the hill to a vantage point where she insisted that he step out of the car. If he didn't want to swim, fine. But he had to see.

Beyond Bondi Beach, a rocky promontory extended into the water, a lion's paw of the continent resting on the ocean. Beyond it stood another rocky promontory, another beach. Danny saw, in all her authority, Australia.

Dark green waves crashed into the rocks below.

Sonja, a driving woman, had rented a Ford for the day, and she drove them next to see her mother. It was the first time Danny had taken a long car trip in Australia. Various shadows fell on them as she drove, a school of birds, the massive dark rafters of the Harbor Bridge, before they were in new country: North Sydney. In a living room on the sixteenth floor, Sonja's mother gave them a bit of English conversation and lots of Vietnamese vegan soup; she stared at Danny's hair all through dinner. Afterward, under powerful lights, mother and daughter showed Danny some of what they had knitted: sweaters, wool socks, and mufflers. Next, Sonja's mother brought out her Medicare card, senior card, and library card, placing them all in a line for Sonja and Danny to inspect: it was her idea of propriety and Danny's idea of happiness. So that, thought Danny, is how it looks like from *their* side.

Seizing the bump on his forearm, he probed it with his sharpest fingernail. He remembered those thatch-work shadows of the massive Harbor Bridge that fell on him as Sonja drove the car, and felt how those shadows webbed but did not support him as they supported her.

"Are you a Muslim?" the old woman asked.

"Mum. Not *again*." Sonja turned to Danny. "Look at his smile. Why are you scared of him?"

Danny let go of his forearm. "I am not a terrorist," he replied, "so explain this to your mother, please."

Now the old woman understood that she had given offense, because she told her daughter a long story, which had to be translated for the boyfriend's benefit. "Mum wants you to know this." Sonja looked from the old woman to Danny. "Back in Vietnam, when my father was trying to get her attention and he was too shy to talk to her, he came to the village market, but he couldn't say a thing to her. So you know what he did? My father shaved his head. To prove his love for her. And she understood what he meant."

"She wants me to do that?" asked Danny, and the women laughed, as if he were very stupid.

"Next year," Sonja said, holding a piece of shortbread from the after-dinner platter her mother had made, "we are going on holiday to Cairns. Aren't we, Danny?"

He ate shortbread. His passport had expired three months ago, and he would need some form of identification to go on a plane, surely. He dodged the issue whenever she talked about Cairns and snorkeling around the Great Barrier Reef, a place that he suspected would prove to be an overpriced version of the Batticaloa Lagoon.

"It's Sri Lanka up there in Cairns, so tropical, you'll love it there."

"How do you know what Sri Lanka's like?" he retorted.

"YouTube."

"Right. Right." One day, he told Sonja, he would tell her about Sri Lanka, the world's most beautiful country. Then she would stop talking about this Barrier Reef and whatnot.

She turned to her mother to say: "If he doesn't want to go to Cairns, that's fine. I say, 'Let's go to Sri Lanka and see your home.' But he won't even talk about it. Always changes the subject. He thinks I haven't noticed." And that reminded Sonja that she should really get Danny an herbal spray from that ayurveda place in Harris Park run by that lovely lovely Sri Lankan family. For his famous deviated septum? By the way, what a beautiful accent those Sri Lankans have. Why isn't yours like theirs, Danny?

So Danny did it again, changed the subject, but cunningly: instead of Sri Lanka, Batticaloa, or the mystery of his nearly Aussie accent, he began telling Sonja's mum about Tamils and Aborigines.

Yes, ever since that day, on a deserted street in Campsie on a summer's morning, when Danny had seen a brown man and a girl who were dancing to no music but the sunlight—he shirtless, she in a bikini top and blue shorts—wearing, in fact, nothing except their glistening heat-resistant skin—and had drawn nearer and nearer to the two of them, only to realize at the end that they were not Indian, not Sri Lankan, but Aboriginal. How they danced. Ever since then he'd been researching at the Glebe and Newtown libraries. And he'd found out all this *stuff* online.

Sonja did the translating into Vietnamese as Danny talked.

"Listen to *this*, Mummy. It's a great story. See, he's saying that brown people, or Tamil people in particular, were here in Australia before anyone else, because Aborigines originally spoke a kind of Tamil. Mummy, he says it's true. The scientists, they have the facts to prove all of this. This kind of scientist, he wants you to know, is called a linguist. See why I love this man? Now he's saying that next time he and I come over the bridge to North Sydney, he will bring a linguist with him to prove scientifically that everything in Australia originally was Tamil."

Sonja shook with laughter. Even her old mother no longer thought Danny was a Muslim. He was a legend. *More* than a legend. He was eating their shortbread, and they were eating his stories.

You could have told her even then. This is what I really want you to know: my own story.

But to tell her everything *today*? Today, of all days?

We have been together two years, and you never told me you were illegal? And now you're mixed up with some murder? she might scream at him. Even worse, he could imagine himself crumbling, begging: *Don't tell anyone I'm illegal—please.* And her: *Don't tell anyone? I fucking took you to see my mother, Danny. And she was right about you.*

Murugan.

Turning to his right, Danny saw a great fig tree sparkle in many places inside its dark canopy of leaves, like a thing that knew its own heart.

2:36 p.m.

When the phone rang again, he realized he hadn't moved.

"Nelson. I'm right outside your place. There's a library here. I bet you come here, don't you."

"Sir. I am very very sorry. Please don't tell the police where I live, sir."

A man laughed.

"You really know how to beg, don't you, Cleaner. I never told you what happened after you left. When they made me clean the place myself. I learned things. Yeah. I learned about black drops. One day I pick up the toilet seat to clean it, the way you must have done, and I find black piss drops on the underside. Now I'm clean when I piss. I'm an army man. Never leave drops. But here I'm seeing black dried-out drops. Someone else's urine on my seat. My toilet seat. Someone's had my view of the Opera House as he pissed in my pot. And then he may have used my bed. It wasn't you. No, I never blamed *you*. It was your boss."

Is he talking about Tsavdaridis? Danny wondered. Is he going to kill him now?

The doctor's voice quivered. "It's really hot here outside the library," he said. "I'd better move inside to the air-conditioning."

Danny heard the creaking of a door being opened.

"Public libraries, they're all a fucking waste. Most people's IQ, it's fixed at age ten, right, and it can't increase." Prakash paused. "Did I tell you of the incident at the mines, Nelson?"

"No."

"Well, I'm not going to tell you now, am I?" Another laugh. "Man. This is nice in here. Air-conditioned."

There was a sigh, and then a noise, and Danny thought that Prakash had sat down. Maybe on a chair in the Glebe library in front of a computer.

"You know you're driving on the bloody Mitchell Highway for the long weekend and you see that red Toyota smashed and you wonder what happened to the people inside? That was me. Are you listening?"

"Yes. Is this the incident at the mines?"

"No. This is another one. I was driving on the highway. I told you. It was winter. I had a jacket on. Leather. Canadian goose feathers inside. Expensive. They slit my leather jacket open and laid me on a hospital emergency bed. When I woke up, snowy feathers were floating about, and there was a big disc of light above me, and I thought, I've become an angel. These are feathers from my wings, and that big shining disc up there is my new angel's brain. When I learned I was still alive, I tell you, my eyes filled with tears. Her father—there was a woman in the car too—her father didn't see me as an angel, of course. When he accused me in the hospital, buddy, I tell you . . . First the mine and that accident, and now this—but I never gave in, I tell you. I never apologized. In court, the judge and the lawyers made me tick this box—that box—and then I was free. The gambling started after that, and next time when I got into trouble, they sent me to this rehab thing, right. That is what they wanted from me. Do you feel sorry for me, Nelson?"

"Yes," said Danny.

There was shuffling, and he heard Prakash say, "All right, I'll go out. All right. I'll go. I won't say sorry. I'll go," then continuing, "Fucking librarian. Wants me to leave. All right. I'm out of this shithole. You know they treated me badly at *your* library, don't you, Nelson?"

"Sorry, sir."

"I don't blame you for a thing. Just the fucking Cleaner. There's a flight at six forty-five p.m. I can't stay in Glebe forever. Have to go back and do the packing. And the cleaning. Don't you think you owe me, Nelson? They made me do it. Now you come and clean up one last time."

"No," Danny said, and hung up.

That was a mistake. It upset Prakash, who texted back.

whats the dob in number oh yes 1-800-009-623
I hear its terrible inside Villawood all those gangs
People kill themselves rather than stay there

From the bushes all around, grasshoppers flew into Danny's legs.

The phone began ringing again.

Unknown Number

Sonja, Danny hoped, using a landline at the hospital? His fingers moved to the button . . . No, she wouldn't call from a landline.

It kept ringing.

Unknown Number

What can they do to you, Danny—he pinched his forearm— that they haven't done already?

"Yes?" he almost shouted as he answered the phone.

2:46 p.m.

"Mate," the voice on the phone said after a pause, "this is Detective Sergeant Michaelos from Homicide. Who am I speaking to?"

Falling through leaves, a magpie swooped on a branch near Danny; the point of its beak, glistening in the sun, turned into a knife.

"Yes." Danny began moving at once. "Yes. Yes."

"Who am I speaking to? I'm calling you in connection with the investigation of a murder. Can you tell me your name, please?"

He did.

The voice on the phone informed him that his number had been found on a cell phone belonging to a Radha Thomas, who was murdered last night in Toongabbie, and could the police please ask a few questions of him. For now, just on the phone?

"Yes."

"Name, occupation, address. Yes, suburb will do for now. Phone number?"

Bunching up the ferns and pulling them out in clumps, Danny moved along the cliff face as he answered each question.

Then: "Were you a friend of hers? We're calling everyone on the list."

"I used to clean her place," he said. "That's all. But it stopped a long time ago."

"How long ago?"

"Eight, nine months ago." He consciously added a month to the estimate. "At least."

"I see." The sergeant asked: "Is there anything you can tell us that would help in the investigation? Anything suspicious you saw?"

Danny tried hard to remember. "No," he said.

Think, Danny. Raising his ferny hands to his face, he inhaled the cool scent. If the police were checking her phone for numbers, then they'd find Prakash's number. And they'd catch him on their own, wouldn't they? Someone *would* remember an Indian man who wore a striped tie to a pub. Some white Australian would have wanted to smash his nose in. He'd remember. He'd know it's *his* duty to tell the police.

Me no dob, you no dob.

When Danny glanced up, he saw a pair of Chinese eyes trained on him. A man in a blue-striped sailor's T-shirt leaned out from the glass balcony of a building above him. Yawning up there, the Chinese observer scratched his arms, and he grinned.

Mate, can't you read a calendar?

The Asian man kept smiling from up there.

Danny saw through the open door of the balcony a view of cool upholstery, electronics, an earthern urn, and the sure hint of a wife more beautiful than the man.

Stay in Australia, Danny.

Danny wished he could shout up and explain. See: he felt the pulse pounding against his sore throat. That made him want to go back to Sunburst and lie down on the sofa. But see, it also made him think of Radha's throat and Justice.

From up on his safe perch, the Chinese observer began chewing something and watched Danny with moving jaws.

Did the cop call u too

Prakash had texted again.

Yes, Danny replied.

What did you say

Nothing

At once the phone rang and the killer asked: "What did you say?"

"I told you. Nothing."

"Really?"

"Yes."

"Really?"

It was a plea. Danny could finally hear Prakash for what he was: Gambler, King of the Nile, Boss of the Sydney nightlife—and someone who was now beyond all hope of remission or amnesty.

"Yes, Doctor. Really really."

"Stop calling me that. I'm no doctor. Don't insult me."

Prakash waited. Then he asked: "You really told him nothing? Good. I never blamed you for a thing, Cleaner."

The killer sounded almost grateful. With some luck, thought Danny, he'll stay in a civil mood for the rest of the day.

A second later, though, his voice had changed. "Nelson. You— you hit me in the face."

"Sorry. I'm sorry. Ten times sorry, Doctor. Twenty times sorry."

A pause, and then: "I don't blame you, I know you're just a cleaner. It's all fixed at the top-top level. We know who fixed it, don't we?"

"Who?"

Instead of answering, he said: "I'm flying this evening, Nelson. I have to get in good shape. You know where I'm going? What time?"

When Danny had answered those, the murderer returned to his earlier question.

"We know who did the fixing, don't we?"

"Who?" asked Danny.

"The top-top man."

Danny waited.

"The people selling this country out. That's the top-top man."

"Who?"

Hissing, *"Top-top,"* Prakash hung up.

Who is he talking about? Danny wondered.

High up in his redoubt, the Chinese observer nodded, as if he too were wondering the same thing, then stretched his arms over his head and yawned before walking back into his dark home.

An ambush. Two dozen black hoods gleamed at Danny from an open shed. In the middle of a deserted street, halfway down the hill that led from Kings Cross to Woollomolloo, Danny stood gazing at sleek, evil European things—an Italian car showroom.

Right outside the showroom, he saw a crushed thing—a rat (or some marsupial version thereof)—and now the shock of this country, the horror of white people, their use of toilet paper, the stench of broccoli, the obsession with rugby (*never* call it rugby), presented themselves in that pulverized rat-or-rat-like thing.

Hop, skip, and leap. Jump over the rat and move, Danny.

Ten feet away from the showroom, high over a concrete bridge, he saw the tall, stony pinnacles of the Gothic cathedral superimposed over the weblike steel cables of the Centrepoint Tower. How scary it looks, thought Danny, who saw it almost every day.

Things must seem like that to Prakash now. The world in a murderer's eyes must be as shiny and terrifying as in an immigrant's. No Australian policeman would understand that.

From around him, Danny heard gnawing: the gnawing of the night kangaroo . . . chewing on bones for living salt.

He turned back to the Italian showroom. Three cockatoos with their split sulfur crests held on with their gray claws to the hood of a black car, like the logos of a nervous new luxury brand—and Danny's phone was ringing.

Unknown Number

Again?

"Yes?" said Danny, looking at the cockatoos on top of the car.

It *was* the police, yes—but not the same police as last time.

"Look. I'm Detective Chief Inspector Jeffries, and I'm the squad commander, which is to say team leader, on this case, you should have gotten the call from me, not from Detective Sergeant Michaelos. I'm sorry about that, it wasn't correct procedure. I hate it when that happens, and I'm sure you do as well. I appreciate that you have spoken to Sergeant Michaelos, but I have to ask you a few questions again. Now: can I ask you a few questions, sir?"

"Yes, sir," replied Danny, and answered the questions again while walking under the bridge.

How long did you know this woman?

Did you clean her place often?

Did you ever notice anything unusual?

"No, sir," replied Danny.

Do you know anyone who might have wanted to harm her?

"No," said Danny, and more confidently this time, though his leg was still shaking.

"Nothing at all to tell us?"

"Nothing, sir. Can I go now? Have to work."

"Yes," said the policeman after a pause, "you can."

Danny knew that eyes under the concrete bridge were looking at him, perhaps observing his humid discomfort, his lie-perspiring face, but there was nothing to worry about: they were the eyes of homeless Australians.

*   *   *

"When immigration finally catches you, Nelson, what you need to do is look those fellows in the eye and tell them, free me and I will do your plumbing." Rubbing her face with cold cream, Radha Thomas walked into the bathroom one day while Danny was on his knees, scrubbing the ring of stains inside the tub. "Nelson, did you hear me? See: we only *appear* to like rules and regulations. What we really like is plumbing."

Danny kept scrubbing away. He never knew, with half the things she said, was she joking, was she serious? Or was she in that place in between, which seemed to be what Australians called irony.

After a while, though, the jokes, or irony, or whatever it was, dried up in Radha Thomas.

"The accountant keeps asking," she began to say, "where is that money from that flat going, and he's going to mention it to Mark one of these days." Nothing can escape rent in the city of Sydney—not even a wild love affair. Prakash must know that the moonlit bhangra was coming to an end. A good time, Danny thought, for me to leave as well.

Yet Danny stayed.

And stayed.

She paid like an honest woman, on time and with tips, didn't she? Never made him clean the dog poo on the pavement outside, did she?

Week after week, he had put off the decision to tell Radha, just smiling at her when he was done cleaning her place; until one Tuesday six and a half months ago, *Bada-bump-brrrrrump*, after cleaning the carpet, doing the toilets (with special care), after making sure that everything in the flat was just right, and then accepting his sixty dollars, he took a breath, tightened his back, and told House Number Five he had to quit cleaning here. For good.

The windows were open that day: she stood near her red tulips, punching at her cell phone, without looking at him. She had a copy of the racing newspages with her.

Beyond the open windows, Danny could see the back of Daryl the Lawyer's flat—House Number Four—and it looked like peace of mind and relief.

He stood running his right hand through his hair and grinning. Finally, to get her attention, he spoke.

"I have to quit," he said, "this job."

He knew his grin was *so* ugly that day, because when she finally understood what he meant, the third time he said it—quitting this job—she asked: "You think we're freaks, don't you?"

She went over to the sofa and sat down. "You hypocrite. Do you even know," she said, "there are these people locked in Villawood writing poems about suicide, and here you are, going about Sydney town dressed up, cashed up, and enjoying the whole Aussie lifestyle. You bloody hypocrite."

Danny stopped smiling. And now *he* felt brave enough to say: "Prakash is a little crack, Miss Radha."

"Crack?"

He had already turned around when she snapped: "Hey. You can't say stuff like that and leave. What *do* you fucking mean?"

So he explained: it was just what they said in the Tamil films, what Danny's father told the neighbors about him when he came back from Dubai ("My son is a little crack").

Crazy, it meant. Like the boy in school who tells tall stories.

Radha placed her phone facedown on the table before the sofa. "Crazy?" she said. "Is that what you think of us? You were like family for us, you know: for Prakash and me. I . . . *have* spoken to people about your illegal status. I have . . . asked people to help you."

Danny replied, "Thanks."

"Crack." Radha folded her arms and looked at him. "Don't fucking grin. You look so ugly when you do. Listen. Prakash and Radha, Radha and her Prakash. The Indians over there in the western suburbs, they hate Prakash, he can't go there. They hate us *both*. Because we're Oscar and Lucinda. We're not living the Indian lifestyle in Sydney, which is what, just buying bigger and bigger cars and celebrating Hindu festivals louder and louder each year in Parramatta. Stop fucking grinning, I said."

Her phone buzzed, and she picked it up and played with it, talking to Danny the whole time. "He's from an Indian background, his whole family are surgeons, and that's what he felt he had to become, like his brother. Instead, do you know what he's had to go through, the army in Queensland, then working as a miner in the Kimberleys. He's been around the whole world, you know. The whole fucking world . . . are you"—she smiled and looked up at Danny—"listening to me, Cleaner? Life *owes* him. He could have been Gandhi. Or Fred Hollows."

"Or Nelson Mandela," Danny said—with a smile.

"Are you mocking me?" Radha looked at him. "Are you fucking mocking me? I invented you. You didn't even *exist* before you worked for me. Look what I found online, Cleaner."

Danny stopped smiling. She showed him the cell phone screen—and she had not been betting after all.

"Look. Read. 'Anyone who is aware of an individual, business, or employer who might be facili—facili . . .'"

Danny took a step closer. He looked at the phone.

"Facilitating."

"Don't do that again. 'Facilitating visa fraud or illegal work is urged to contact Border Watch at Australia dot gov dot au slash . . . border slash slash . . .'"

Radha slapped the phone facedown on the table. "Slash slash," she said.

Danny stared.

After the silence, she said, "I didn't mean that. You made me say it. You don't know the first thing about Prakash. All the terrible things he has been through."

". . . I can't clean here anymore."

"Nelson. I mean, we could go to Hong Kong. There's a job there for me, it's the job of a hospital administrator. But I can't leave this light. Sydney, the light is too strong, you can't leave it so easily. Sometimes I think he's going to hurt me, you know. He's going to hurt himself and then hurt me and then hurt Mark too. He's becoming so jealous."

"Go to the police," said Danny. "Tell them."

She turned to him and let out a sardonic laugh. "Police." A shake of her head. "There's *nowhere* to go. Nowhere to hide in this city. No one will give me a job or a fair go. I know they're talking about me everywhere. That crazy woman in the Medicare office. Who stole money from the government and ran, and her own husband dobbed her. The police *got* me into this mess."

She let the phone drop on the table. "All we do is gamble all day, and we can't take one bet on ourselves."

She wiped away her tears with her left hand. Danny tightened his hand around his cleaning bag, in which he had a box full of paper napkins.

"'Prakash,' I keep telling him, 'a man in prison has a choice: either break out or make his cell as big as the world.' I keep telling him."

Danny looked at the door. When you have two lives, you simply double the number of places you want to escape from.

"Nelson. Do you know Randwick? Of course you do. It's from *Mission: Impossible* 2. That bloody movie, it's all you talk about. Listen. There is a flock of black cockatoos, living in secret in the heart of Sydney, and every summer evening, around six or seven, they make semicircles over Randwick, just in front of the big pub there—and you're watching the sunset sky, these crested things, their black wings outstretched, they're like the fucking Spanish armada. If you ever see those black cockatoos, think of me, think of Radha. The woman you didn't want to help. Now get the fuck out of here if you want to."

Should I beg her again, Danny wondered, not to tell Prakash that I'm illegal?

Ten minutes later, when, after warning him to stand right there while she went into the bedroom to bring him the business card of a woman she'd met on the train the other day who just happened to be an amazing immigration attorney, Danny left the apartment.

She did call him many times after that, true. His phone had vibrated, and he had seen that it was:

H5

Maybe she told Prakash everything she knew about the wonderful Cleaner, that he was an illegal, because she was angry. Maybe when they got drunk, she rang up the immigration hotline in front of Prakash, and nearly told them everything—before pulling back, and hanging up, and laughing with him.

Maybe that's why she betrayed Danny's confidence. To get even.

She may have betrayed you, but she's dead now, Danny told himself. Do not judge her. The Queen of the Nile.

By the base of the sandstone cliff, in a clump of succulents, caught by a strand of spider silk, a small leaf was being spun round and round in that windless spot by its own torsion. He got down on his knees to watch it.

Her? No, she was not the one who needed judging—not Radha Thomas.

For months, she had been right there behind Daryl the Lawyer's home—the window with the red tulips was right there, behind or across the road—and, holding tight to his cleaning gear,

Nelson the Cleaner could have gone over, could have said hello, just to see how Radha was. Five minutes it would have taken.

But that was one black line he had never crossed.

2:52 p.m.

Danny was still squatting by the succulents. Like a perpetual-motion machine, the leaf trapped in the spider's thread kept turning round and round.

2:54 p.m.

Not murder: calculation.

Not madness but the calm sweat after a mad rage. That's why he killed her.

Down on his knees, watching the little turning leaf, Danny could see a scar on the doctor's neck; it was more vivid than ever, a fresh red semicircle, something that was no shaving wound. As if a fingernail had cut deep into it. And growing brighter and redder. She had fought him to the end.

What did she say to get him angry?

Did she say, for instance:

Fine. We don't have to go to India. You can get a job and make a new start right here. But we can't continue like this. You're staying for free in Potts fucking Point, and who can live in Sydney without paying rent? You have to start again, Prakash.

Was she trying to help him, as she tried to help Danny? And is that why he killed her?

That man with his private school ties, that obsessive gambler, cut off from community, but one who liked to roar up in his cage in Kings Cross: one day he attacked Radha, the way a lion attacks its tamer.

Grasshoppers again flew into Danny from the disturbed bushes, and he kept swatting at them, knocking some of them down senseless, missing others.

Or maybe . . . *he's* doing the talking. Yes. He's been telling her that he's going to stop drinking and gambling . . . and they have to run away to South Africa, and why don't they go along together . . . and suddenly, she replies, *It's over, Prakash, you have to leave the Potts Point flat, the fucking accountant is really asking questions . . .*

It's Guru Purnima tomorrow, he says. *You're throwing me out on Guru Purnima day?* But she says: *Mark is starting to suspect something, and you have to leave that place. You have to move into a lodging house or something, I can pay a part of the bill, but Mark is getting very—*

Don't fucking mention his name.

His name is Mark, all right?

Don't mention his name.

Does Prakash now look up at the night sky, hoping it will calm him down? Yes. He does that. The clearer the stars, the more disturbed he is. Yes. He puts his hand inside his red jacket and finds—he has a knife there. Excellent. And how smart of him to bring it along. *Come right down to the water, Radha. Yes, come right here. Shall we try the Lindy Hop again?*

Maybe they danced by the water—yes, they certainly did.

And just when something cool and rational inside a madman whispered, Do it, while she kept saying, *Poor Mark, I had better tell him I am out late, I'll just text him a moment, poor Mark,* because she mentioned his name, or because the stars had shifted their positions, he shouts that she is no rock star, just a forty-year-old woman, and it's that whole show-off Indian culture he can't stand out there in the fucking suburbs, and even then he did not want to hurt her, maybe he held her down to the ground with his powerful arms, and only then did he discover that he had brought along a knife with him, what a fine thing to have brought along, and as he stabbed at her again and again, did he chant—*What is civilization? What is fucking civili—?*—before he covered her with an expensive leather jacket, filling its pockets with cold stones so she would sink all the way down. And then all the ambient light went out of Sydney.

Danny's phone beeped.

Message from your phone company

As we continue to build a mobile network for the future, we will have to say goodbye—

In a single motion, Danny took the phone out of his pocket, raised it high up, and smashed it down on the road: where it broke into pieces, flying into the succulents.

I am *never* going back home.

2:55 p.m.

In response, from above came the three-and-a-half-note birdcall (*short-short-looooong-half*) that had always sounded to Danny's ear, amidst the incessant firecrackers of the Sydney aviary, like the firearm of a trained shooter. Even as he turned an eye up into the canopy of the tree and searched for the bird, the three-long-and-then-a-half-note call sounded again. . . .

Danny laughed at himself. In the middle of the summer day, shivering from fear and with heavy hurting sinuses, he clapped his hands, again and again, over the wreckage of his phone.

It won't happen this way, Danny. You can't start the day again.

Down on his knees, he reassembled the phone, strapping the battery into place with the Band-Aids, and turned the machine on. It cheerfully came back to life. It could not be killed or murdered. It was too cheap.

Message from your phone company

As we continue to build a mobile network for the future, we will have to say goodbye—

But the time on the phone now said

0:00

and blinked. How long is it from now to 6:45 p.m.? Danny thought. Wondering if he could ask someone the time, Danny turned toward the bridge and saw one homeless man offer his friend a choice of five exquisite cigarette butts to pick from, a gesture of mateship. Danny watched, ravished. He wished he could go nearer. Even the smell of tobacco made a man more rational.

Fucking madness, this. Changing your mind in the middle of a busy road in Australia.

Having started to cross William Street, toward an epic pile of governmental sandstone, whose face was covered by scrolls illustrated with giant red spiders from the Outback, Danny stopped, remembering that the building must be a museum of some kind, and that if he went too close, he would find tourists from Sri Lanka or South India or Malaysia there, and that was why he had not gone near that place in years, and although he knew that the lights had changed, he stopped, turned, and recrossed William Street, running just ahead of oncoming traffic, with the cars blasting their horns—for a moment the Sydney road became as loud as a South Asian one—and kept running, driven by the momentum of his own misadventure, over the pavement and past people, and then over a green bank and up a pair of steps. These steps jagged sharply to the right and deposited him, of their volition rather than his, before a great church.

Ten feet ahead of Danny, an Asian woman in a white wedding dress posed with a bouquet of red roses outside St. Mary's Cathedral, while a man in a tuxedo crouched and photographed her, and for a moment, Danny thought he was in an East Asian version of Disneyland—before the leash tugged again at him.

The phone buzzed in his trousers.

H6

"Cleaner. Where are you right now?"

Danny said nothing.

"You won't tell me. That's fine, Cleaner. Guess where I am? Your boss wanted to get rid of me. Tommo. Isn't that his name? So he said, 'Go to the library and wait for Danny there.' This must be a favorite spot of yours, right?"

"Yes."

"Are these other men sitting here illegals too?"

"No," said Danny.

The Asian woman was being photographed again, this time while holding a bouquet of yellow roses to her chest.

"You don't want to get them into trouble. That's good of you. Where is this house that you're cleaning right now?"

"Newtown," said Danny. "Vroom vroom."

The murderer considered his answer. "How do you get into these places you clean?"

"Key's usually under the welcome rug. Or in the mailbox. Under the first letter."

"And the money?"

"They leave it right on the desk. Sixty dollars. Cash." Danny paused. "They trust me."

"People didn't trust me," said Prakash. "Some people made me fucking clean the place after you left. But I tell you what. I'm not going to clean the place today. And at six forty-five, I have a flight to catch. And if I'm not going to clean it, guess who's going to clean it? Fucking Nelson . . ."

The bells of St. Mary's struck, and Danny turned the phone off.

With the first four peals of the bells, Danny grew weak, because he remembered Sonja, and with each subsequent peal, he became strong again.

An Asian bride clapped with joy, and the phone rang again.

If you have no idea where you are going, he told himself, you might as well go see her at the hospital.

When Danny looked up, he could see through the buildings on William Street to St. Vincent's Hospital. It would be lunch break now. She'd be walking with two other nurses in indigo uniforms up to the coffee kiosk on the green hill outside St. Vincent's.

"So it's a soy latte, skinny cap, and a big flat white. Correct?"

I was not a vegetarian when I joined VeggieDate to meet women like you. I was a smoker too. After meeting you, I became a vegetarian and, what was much harder and required much more willpower, a nonsmoker.

I cannot, however, through willpower alone, become legal.

Soundless above the sandstone buildings, a flock of cockatoos soared, perhaps the same flock that had led him into the Cross, preserving the shape of a white cloud, like a thought bubble over the city.

Get back to work, Cleaner.

Fifty-three Brown Street, Newtown. Rodney Accountant's building, which he entered by punching in the numeric code: 1987.

Of course, Danny didn't have his vacuum on his back, which meant he would have to use the old one on the accountant's shelves. Suboptimal, he told himself, seriously suboptimal.

If the church weren't enough stimulation for the tourists, a glass roof allowed them to peer into a public swimming pool beneath their feet. The tourists understood that this was the real religion of this country: *swimming*. Down below, in the underground nave that paralleled the one in the church, pilgrims with goggles were thrashing up and down their aqueous prayer lanes.

Standing by the glass roof and looking at the swimmers in their lanes, Danny now saw a dead woman, alive . . .

One morning she and Prakash, to do something different, had driven Danny to a swimming pool near Central . . . and he had held the two-dollar visitor's ticket in his finger and stood watching while the two of them, in their trunks, swam into the kids' section to frolic about underneath a spreading snake, a *Nagadeva* of colored mosaic tiles, while the Aussie children in their goggles watched the two happy Indian swimmers; and then, calling Danny near the water's edge, Radha and Prakash had splashed water on him: *Redneck! Redddddneck, come back!*

House Number Five. You must have fought hard when he stabbed you. You were a strong woman. A strong swimmer. A mistress of two households.

Won't someone else call the police and tell them who killed you?

As Danny stared down through the glass panel into the pool in the depths, the blue water gaped, and swallowed the swimmers in a blink.

A month ago, he had been sitting on the bus to Marrickville, when two men who wore blue shirts, as if they were policemen, got on—"Ticket checking"—and Danny, almost proudly, showed them his ticket—like all illegals, he was scrupulous in these things, and *Fine, sir, you're good,* said the checkers. But in the row right behind Danny, a young Aussie proved not to have a ticket. At once the ticket policeman turned into a cartoon figure, raising his eyebrows and emitting a stream of high-pitched outrage, as if he thought he had to look and sound like a clown before he could dispense the law; but his manner only incensed the ticketless young Australian man, who protested more and more, until the blue-shirted ticket policeman and his colleague—"I said *now*"—just seized the offender and almost carried him off the bus. That poor citizen boy, thought Danny, didn't he look as if all those giant piles of sandstone blocks, all the nineteenth-century government buildings banked up against Circular Quay, had slid down on him, crushing his life breath. If he'd had a newspaper at that moment, Danny would have dipped a finger in water and inscribed over its Australian English in Tamil: *A legal is just someone who is unwanted in the same way everyone else is.*

A long fingernail scraped against the glass. Down in the swimming pool below St. Mary's Cathedral, young Australian bodies rematerialized: summoned by Danny's touch.

The Blue-10 bus card slipped quickly into the green time machine, which, after grumbling and rejecting the card, suddenly reswallowed it and noisily printed something on it before grudgingly releasing the card.

15:31:12

After smiling at the Arab-looking driver, Danny went to the back of the bus. He looked at the fresh black ink on the back of the plastic bus-travel card and reread the time the traditional way. Three-thirty.

Danny was back at Central Station. The four-faced sandstone clock tower was somewhere behind him as he walked down the bus, looking for a seat that felt safe. Forget that Coca-Cola sign and everything behind it. Forget the long walk up the hill to Kings Cross. Danny had wound this day back to where it had been at eleven in the morning: he was back in the flat, honest part of the city. He was going to work.

A bearded Indian man in the middle row raised a two-liter carton of whole milk and took an endless drink from it: Danny's mouth watered. But Prakash is also doing that right now, he thought. Drinking and getting madder and madder by the moment.

He sat down.

Sun hit the windows of the bus. Scratch marks in the glass, cut with a schoolboy's keys or with the bottle cap of a first beer, glistened like loops and loops of silver thread all around Danny.

3:39 p.m.

The bus moved through construction noise—the same keening of giant drills that could be heard anywhere in the itchy, restless city, though when he glanced out the window, Danny could see only two compliant earth-digging machines, their metal heads bowed as if in mock deference to the passing humans, and high over them, beyond the green lawns, a series of unattainable sandstone peaks: the University of Sydney.

The air-conditioning in the bus was not working well.

On the university's lawns, next to a flowering jacaranda, stood a gray North American totem pole. Topmost on the pole was a ferocious eagle with a yellow beak. A mop of silvery hair appeared on the eagle's face, and black-rimmed spectacles now framed its giant hazelnut eyes. Danny sweated from his roots.

3:49 p.m.

The bus stopped to pick up a group of Chinese students wearing fresh new University of Sydney T-shirts. Each stood with his finger inside a red passport with golden stars on the cover as if he expected the bus conductor would ask to see it. That must be what life in China is like, thought Danny.

Their faces were too raw, too terrible, for him, and he closed his eyes and tried to imagine it.

Home.

Sometimes in his dreams he still saw her, their neighbor in Batticaloa: a woman with close-cropped white hair whom he had nicknamed the Brazen Starer, because from the day "Dubai Danny" had returned, this neighbor had stood with her hands on her hips, elbows thrust out, on the first-floor balcony of a new building that had come up opposite his house. She stood like that and she stared at him. From her balcony, she commanded a view of the door of Danny's house, and didn't she know it. Danny did obvious things with his teeth, but the Brazen Starer just didn't care. Below her on the street, people came and left, like changing denominators to her constant hands-on-hips numerator. Anytime Danny entered or left, this creature, a permanent grin on the face, stood up there watching—no, *sucking* up his image, as she must have sucked up his story, so many times over, from the other neighbors: Dubai? Torture? Our Danny? Oh, tell me again. Dubai? Torture? Our Danny? Gossip back home was so dense, so cementlike, it ought to be renamed. *Goddip*. Belly-filling Tamil *goddip*. Imagine, even if you somehow survived Villawood, extradition, the flight home, the Sri Lankan army, and intelligence men—imagine, after all that, having to go back to your home and endure the Brazen Starer's wide grin from her first-floor balcony: Australia? Illegal? Arrested and sent back? *And* he was mixed up in some murder? Our Danny? Tell me the story all over again.

Danny was sure he would rather kill himself.

3:50 p.m.

"It's hot out here in Glebe, Danny. Why don't you come over?"

"I have to work now, sir."

"I said, Come over right now."

Looking around, wondering if anyone would guess he was talking to a killer, Danny dropped his voice. "I'll be there in the evening. I have to sleep there in the grocery store."

"But I'll be in South Africa by then. I'm flying premium economy tonight. Good legroom, Nelson."

"Right."

How can you talk of premium economy today, Danny wanted to shout at Prakash.

But maybe he already knew the answer. Remember, Danny told himself. He remembered a morning back when he was six or seven, standing in a crowd at the market in Batticaloa, watching a moist yellowfin tuna. The fish was three and a half feet head to tail. A man with a boat had caught it in the ocean and brought it here to show them: after displaying the monster to the public, the fisherman, removing the scales, sliced it open with a cut into the gills, then carved deep into it, piling pink fillets on the scales and more wet pink fillets on top of them. The boy stood on tiptoe. At the end of the performance, when the monster was just a string of dark wet organs attached to a tuna head, the fisherman held it up again for his audience—not that they would buy it, no, but so that, as they clapped, they could feel once more the thrill of being counted among the living.

That's why you fly premium economy on a day like this.

"Nelson. You're thinking of something. You didn't answer me."

"Sorry, sir. What did you ask?"

Slowly, as if giving him plenty of time to think, the doctor repeated himself: "How did all this start, Mandela? Why did you call me today?"

"Because I forgot, sir."

"What did you forget."

"That I was an illegal here."

The killer breathed out. "Cleaner. Where were you this morning when you called me?"

"I was cleaning. The lawyer's place. The police came in asking about her. The lawyer's flat is in Erskineville. Close to . . . her place."

"*How* close?"

"It's just behind her place. Thirty-six Flora Street."

"Right. And?"

"I told you, the police came and asked questions. That's how I knew she'd died."

"Why didn't you stay there? Why did you get mixed up in all of this, Nelson?"

"Because of the blue ball."

"What?"

Danny sighed. "Nothing."

And the phone went dead.

Danny calculated. The flight is at 6:45. International flight. He has to be there by 5:45. So, well before 5:45, Prakash will pack a few of his ties in a suitcase and start to move toward the airport. Just two hours left for Prakash to be gone. Danny clapped his hands.

The bus at once filled up with young Asian students, which meant they were close to the university, which was not far from King Street, the central avenue of Newtown.

Hope is a kind of rigor. Despair is sugar. Remember, Danny reminded himself, the mistake you made at Mackenzie College. Seduced by Abe the Abseiler. Do not despair today. It's just two hours. Let Prakash go.

He glanced a last time at the bearded Indian man with the milk carton, whose face, milk-fortified, radiated the calm and peace of a South Asian village.

But if everything does go wrong in the next two hours, they *will* have ice-cold milk in Villawood, won't they? Even if they send me from there to some Pacific island, there will always be cold milk to drink. Life will go on.

Danny pressed the red button to indicate that the bus had to stop.

His card punched out

15:51:56

and then he got down on King Street. He could barely move. The door of the furnace was wide open now. Blowing as if through a desert, the wind hit him in the face. They certainly won't have cold milk for you back in Sri Lanka, son.

4:02 p.m.

If it has names like flat white, latte, or doppio, if it is hand-brewed by men or women who wear aprons, and served in porcelain at a cost of four dollars a cup, then it is what white Australians call coffee. They insist that this coffee is very good—perhaps even the best in the world—or at least good enough to prove (along with universal health care, gun control laws, and a sense of irony) that their country is not America, not *American*, and not just a remote refueling stop for the U.S. Pacific Fleet.

But for the immigrant to Sydney, coffee is what comes out of a self-service machine made in China and imported into 7-Eleven stores throughout the city. The cost is a dollar for a plastic cup, black and strong. The machine even pours you milk if you press a button. Yes, *hot* milk.

A line of taxi drivers, foreign students, and backpackers invariably stand waiting for coffee in any 7-Eleven, but this particular store on King Street was empty, and Danny, walking in, found out why: MACHINE BEING CLEANED, read the sign.

In any case, Danny watched the black drops dripping from the machine and changed his mind. He could feel his blood pressure rising. Maybe 145/110 now. Coffee made that worse.

He should have kept his Black & Gold cheese slices with him.

Next to the cash counter, beside the warm evening-edition newspapers that probably had a murdered woman's photo somewhere inside, he saw a golden corn muffin in a plastic wrapper. It was marked two dollars, and he knew it was stale. Just by looking at it.

It was exactly the kind of muffin sold at the Sunburst store.

"Gluten?" He held the plastic-wrapped muffin in between two fingers and showed it to the young brown man, who looked North Indian, behind the glass counter. "Gluten?"

What? The man behind the counter grimaced. *Who?*

"Gluten is bad for my sinuses." Sonja had told him that. "Does this have gluten?"

The Indian behind the counter shrugged.

Danny sighed. "Give me a discount."

If the Indian man hadn't heard of gluten, he certainly hadn't heard of *discount*.

Tearing apart the plastic cover, Danny ate the two-dollar golden corn muffin on a bench right outside the 7-Eleven. He was aware that his phone was buzzing. Prakash, probably.

He picked up pieces of corn that had fallen on the bench and licked them off his fingers.

He had gluten and common sense in his guts now, and his odds of survival again felt good to Danny. He kept licking. Prakash will leave well before six. I just have to go clean Rodney Accountant's place and keep myself occupied.

After eating, he always had to crack his knuckles. Danny almost began doing it and stopped. He looked around. White people did not like the sound of knuckles being cracked. "Stop that," they said, as if he were spitting in public or farting.

"Fuck off." He said it out loud. And began cracking the knuckles of his right hand.

Glancing sideways at Danny, a white man wearing a black suit but no tie, holding a leather black diary in his hand, walked past. Then another man, dressed identically, holding the same black diary, followed him. Danny got up and followed them. Both walked up the steps and into a grand building with a sign on it that said, as if it belonged in a children's game of Monopoly: COURTHOUSE.

Danny walked up the steps and entered an Australian court of law.

Six lemon-colored globes were suspended from the ceiling, and they cast a twilight glow inside a large hall full of wooden benches. A dozen people of various races were spread about the benches. Above a raised wooden podium, and beneath a wooden pulpit mounted by a golden lion and a silver unicorn, sat a man in a black gown who was, Danny assumed, the judge.

"Sixteen traffic offenses in fifteen years is no small thing," he said into a microphone.

"Yes, Your Honor, but . . ." Down below, placing his hand on the shoulder of a perspiring overweight man who looked like the defendant, a young lawyer tried to respond to the judge. "Not one of those offenses was committed since 2004, you will note."

"True, but for this particular offense he was driving on the highway," responded the judge, who looked, Danny thought, more and more like the old prime minister Malcolm Fraser.

"Without denying or diminishing his guilt, Your Honor, I ask again that you consider the defendant's family circumstances. He is a good father, and I assure you his two sons love him. . . ."

It was like a scene out of Kiran Rao's book come to life: everyone was being logical and civilized. Though he could have played the bully up there, the old judge, abandoning pomp, speaking plain English, making the Australian accent sound more attractive than it had ever before to Danny, seemed to be trying his best to understand why the man on trial had made the mistake he had. When it was the lawyer's turn, the judge held his jaw in his hand and listened.

Asylum! Danny had so often pleaded his case before an imaginary audience, but this was the real thing. The lion and the unicorn up there were the law: and they were not menacing, the way any symbol connected to the government of Sri Lanka was. As he listened to the judge and the attorney spar with each other, Danny felt once again the attraction of the law of Australia, its promise, more elemental than any ocean he had seen: fairness. But where did it come from, this fair law? Danny looked around the courtroom. White, or black, or Arab, the people who lived in Sydney weren't particularly decent or civilized.

So who built this wooden hall, who suspended these six lemon-colored lamps from the ceiling, who created this expectancy, which everyone sitting here seemed to feel, that justice was the likely outcome of this hearing?

And isn't this, Danny thought, the obverse side of the question that he had asked every day in Sri Lanka. Because individually, no one there ever seems bad, whether Tamil, or Sinhala, or Muslim. But it does exist—evil. A man puts on a uniform, and becomes the uniform. Danny touched his left forearm: this bump in his forearm was real.

If you accept the mystery of evil, why can't you accept the mystery of a more-or-less just law?

"You are now free to leave," said the judge, liberating someone else in that hall, but Danny's heart, too, beat faster.

Maybe he could walk right up to that high wooden seat and demand that Malcolm Fraser up there feel the bump in his forearm, and then argue: "That's a pretty good case for asylum, don't you think, mate? Next, I want to tell you all about a man named Dr. Prakash. Will you listen?"

It was as if the court answered him directly. A wooden door swung wide, and a man in blue wearing a vest that stated SHERIFF walked into the hall, hitched up his black belt, and looked around.

This person too, thought Danny, who will in a minute start talking and acting like a figure out of a TV cartoon—bullying and shoving people around—had his place in the order of things. The thorns are there to protect the roses.

But when Danny, opening another wooden door and slipping out of the hall lit up by the six lamps, had left the twilit court-house and reentered the summer afternoon, he began cracking the knuckles on his hands once again.

ARAVIND ADIGA

4:10 p.m.

Sun-baked fissures widened in the tar, and as he crossed the road toward the accountant's place (53 Brown Street), he half expected to see smoke rising up from below him. Why not? He'd seen it happen before. Roads in Sydney in summer often steam up when a little rain falls on the hot asphalt. Do it, Danny dared the small-hearted city of Sydney, do it, he dared the petty road—burst into smoke, become a bed of live coals while I'm walking. I'll survive. I'll beat you again. (But he also thought: Let someone *else* walk on these coals today. I've been on them for four years.)

Fourth Year as an Illegal

"They'll never catch us," Abe had begun to say. "I know this country by now."

For eight months, Abe the Abseiler was nowhere to be seen on the skyscrapers of Pitt and Castlereagh streets. He had left Sydney, gotten on Greyhound Australia, and traveled into the countryside, working illegally. Cattle farms, painting fences, picking fruits, for eight months Abe worked anything that was available. Stuffed with Aussie dollars, he returned to Sydney.

"Did you see kangaroos?" asked Danny.

Kangaroos, bulls, horses, rabbits. Every other living thing has its head down, gobbling grass all day long, except the roos, which stop everything they're doing and just look at the passing bus, and their ears are up (Abe demonstrated) like this. "They know we're bad."

After two days on the bus, Abe shouted: "Stop, driver." They had reached a place where there was pink fire on all sides: cherry trees

222

in full blossom. Mildura, the place was called. Abe picked cherries for cash, and it was like the United Nations on that farm—the cherry pickers were from Vietnam, Indonesia, Tonga, Fiji, and not one white man around except the boss. The farm was not far from a river, and now and then, when the farmer blew a long whistle, the workers left everything and ran down to the water. It was a prearranged code. Immigration officers were raiding the fields and they had to hide. The river was called the Murray, and dead white tree trunks stuck out of it. Abe and the others huddled along the river, waving at Chinese tourists who went by on boats, sipping from glasses of champagne. Then came another long whistle—meaning, immigration was gone, and they had to return to work.

"I lost," said Abe, jabbing at his tummy, "five point eight kilograms when picking fruit. It is the kind of weight a man loses and never regains."

"Don't the farmers out there ever get arrested for hiring illegals?" Danny asked.

"No." Abe laughed. "No one's going to fucking arrest an Australian farmer. He's a bloody legend. You know what he does? He gets poor Malaysians to water his plants, pick his cherries, pack them into boxes, and then ships those boxes to Kuala Lumpur, where rich Malaysians buy them, paying any price that's demanded, because they think white people grew these cherries. That is legendary."

See: Abe had solved the riddle. Rich Asians and poor Asians don't seem to talk a lot to each other, and that's how Australians make most of their money.

"All the immigration officers out there are rotten, right. They just watch the whole season while you work, and the day you are supposed to get paid, the farmer phones immigration—and immediately they come, with their dogs and vans, picking you up."

Immigration wasn't the real danger in the countryside, anyway. You could always run from the fat men in blue and hide by the river and watch the black birds sitting on the dead white tree trunks in the water. But one day Abe was walking up to an orchard where he was working, right, and a black pitbull terrier started following him. The fellow looked sunburned, or confused, or hungry. When Abe stopped, the dog reared up on his chest. When he moved, it nipped and took small bites of his jeans. It growled. Abe thought, If it bites me and I have to go to the hospital, they'll find out I have no Medicare. He stood by the highway and tried to stop a car. "Help," Abe shouted, "help me." The moment you shout help, Australia becomes empty. It's a fact. After Abe ran from the pitbull for half an hour, a policeman came along on a bicycle. "We wouldn't want that dog to be hit by traffic," he said as he led it away. (It was only when the white policeman stopped his bicycle in the distance and glanced over his shoulder that Abe recognized the look in his eyes: the look of a people losing their grip on a continent.)

After leaving Mildura, Abe kept going along the Murray River until he got to South Australia. Here, you saw plenty of white boys picking grapes. They were all young European backpackers. In the evening, after slogging on the vineyards, the white boys went back to their hostel, dialed a number, and then a middle-aged brown man came sweating on a bicycle, carrying sixteen boxes of pizza for them. Sixteen boxes! The white boys, stripped to their undies, stood on the balconies of the hostel, yelling, "Faster, faster!" They ate all those pizzas in twenty minutes and then dialed that man for more pizzas and waited on the balcony so they could yell "Faster, faster!" once again. All day long, these white boys were the farmer's slaves, but at night this brown man was their slave. Wasn't that funny? Abe had thought so. But that's the problem with Australia: there's never anyone to share a joke with, because no one sees a bloody thing.

In a town called Berri, in South Australia, Abe had met this fifty-two-year-old fruit picker from Malaysia, Chang, and he had been illegal for nine years. The Malaysian Chinese, they were the best *at staying illegally. Abe, out of respect, began calling him Chang Uncle.*

Nine years, thought Danny. If a man called Chang Uncle had made it for nine, Danny could make it for ten.

Twenty!

And then, just like that, a week after returning to Sydney, Abe the Abseiler was arrested. Immigration raided the construction company even as he was strapping on his abseiling gear. Tom Cruise was kept in detention for two weeks and then deported. He phoned one day from Villawood. "You know, Danny, the funny thing is, everyone who stayed at Mackenzie College did get a job in the end. I keep seeing them wherever I go. They've even bought cars. You'll be cleaning their houses one day. Isn't that funny?"

Which was how Danny knew that it had always been a game for Abe. That guy probably left Australia shaking hands with immigration officers.

Two days later, reading a local newspaper, he learned that an illegal immigrant from Senegal had died on the last seat of a bus; the police said he was diabetic but probably too scared to get medical attention in time.

It rained that night, and wandering down Glebe until he could see the twin white buildings, the Portals of Sydney, Danny watched the green globes on top of each building—blurred in drizzle and mist, like two glowing miniature earths held up by invisible giants, and each saying the same thing: But you abandoned the worlds you had to carry, Danny. And what did you get in return? A pair of Chinese pandas to hug at night.

Danny awoke in darkness and splashed water on his face in the bathroom at the Sunburst store.

Honest Danny. Brave Danny. Intelligent Danny.

Danny shook the water off his face and wiped it dry with Tommo's towel.

He had his regular cleaning job in Rose Bay that day; from there, he took the bus into the city. The bus moved through the heart of Sydney, going past East Asian–run canteens that fed white people junk food toward white-run boutiques that fed East Asians luxury goods. Freedom, fine leather, suits, Danny observed them all go past. At Central Station, he stood on the platform watching a train with a glowing Villawood sign pull in; how it pounded, his heart.

"Murugan," he prayed, "bring me back to this very spot on the platform."

He helped a mother lift a pram with a child over the edge of the train, while a man in a blue uniform walked by, wearing a dark pistol holster on his belt. The three bodies—child, mother, policeman—overlapped like an essential truth.

Then he was on his way to Villawood.

"Murugan," he said each time the train came to a station. At the last stop on the train, he got off, saying, "Murugan," and walked to the Villawood Immigration Detention Center and stood outside and folded his arms. Inside its thick brick walls were Greeks, Muslims, Chinese, Indians, Pakistanis; their strong eyes burned through the brick wall and said, It's only a matter of time, Danny. No one ever beats the law here.

In the open, in Australia, Danny turned his head to the side and spat. No. I'll find a way. I'll stay out. Somehow. But I won't say sorry for what I did four years ago, and I won't live in fear ever again.

4:12 p.m.

The white cat was waiting, and as soon as he entered the accountant's flat, on the fifth floor of the building on Brown Street, it made straight for the door, forcing Danny to kick the door shut behind him. Thwarted, the cat rubbed its furry sides against the closed exit, purring seductively as Danny removed his shoes and placed them on a bookshelf to protect them from the animal's vengeance.

Had to remove your shoes before entering Unit 6, 53 Brown Street, because street dust triggers allergies. As do pollen, wind, flaxseed, most flowers, all bees, rust, bark, asbestos, and many other things.

Rodney Accountant, House Number Eight, had been extensively tested for nervous weaknesses, and employed Danny once a week on the strict understanding that there were various conditions to be adhered to, including that Danny not use synthetic deodorants or nonorganic soap on the morning of his visits, and Danny, who had followed a long string of careless cleaners, had managed to stick to all of these requirements for six months and two weeks.

He knew there was an asthmatic vacuum in the allergen-free closet, behind the fridge with the progressive slogans. He found the machine, plugged it in, and went about the room, thinking, Maybe I shouldn't take sixty dollars today from the accountant. I'm not doing a good job. Maybe fifty dollars is enough.

Forty-five. That'll do. I'll explain next time. My sinuses were bad. As an allergy man, he'll understand.

From here, Danny could see the pay phones across from the Newtown library. Across the road stood three side-by-side Telstra pay phones, two of them colored red, the one in the middle pink.

The gray needle of a church rose over the houses.

He closed that blind.

Ba-da-da-dum-dum-ba-da . . . The white cat came into the room with its tail up and watched him.

Of course, the good accountant won't consider the possibility that you, cat, are the source of his allergies. Danny vacuumed his way into the study.

Because of its height over Newtown, each window in the accountant's flat had a view of a large graffiti artwork painted in a different style, from the Renaissance to the contemporary.

LOVE IS THE ANSWER, declared the giant blue-and-red slogan on the back of a white building that could be seen from the window of the study. Maybe not today, mate. Ha.

Into the bedroom next.

Finding the window closed, he tucked the nozzle of the vacuum under his arm and raised it.

He saw it again—on the side of a house, a mural of a deer with curved horns, a heron, and a rabbit, tied up above a butcher's table.

So *this* was where he had seen that image. From this window.

Three animals, three corpses, trussed up by wires from the ceiling of a kitchen, and below them, on the butcher's table, a ram lay, its mouth bound with ropes, its tongue sticking out. The suspended heron in profile had one eye open wide. Looking at the viewer. *This is how the world is stolen. Right before your eyes.* What a terrible image, and painted with such sensuous cruelty, such precision, to say: *You did not even scream as everything was taken from you.*

Cousin Kannan, Danny thought. Cousin Kannan did scream. That is why he is now a citizen in Canada, which he deserves to be.

From down below, a dog barked.

As the vacuum fell down and sucked air from around his ankles, he raised his fingers to his nose. He thought he could smell something on them. Broccoli?

No, not that. Not that, and not shark liver oil.

Blood.

You *will* see her, Danny. You will see her when the clustered white masts in Rose or Rushcutters Bay sear your eye; you will see her when the light falls through the fig trees like soft wood chips on the Domain; and when the banks and life insurance buildings that make a glittering glass mangrove at Circular Quay are holding on to the last of the sunset; or even when a bicycle wheel deflects the light of passing traffic, you *will* see her, as she was in the pool that day, under the *Nagadeva* and splashing water on the children.

Laughter from a murdered woman filled the air.

Letting the vacuum rumble on the carpet, and leaving the white cat to watch over it, Danny walked back to the living room, lifted up the blind, and looked down at the three Telstra pay phones outside on King Street.

Jumping on top of the pay phones, three rats then ran straight up a painted wall before becoming the dark wings of pigeons scattering over the white-hot street.

He picked the pink phone booth, the one in the middle.

4:50 p.m.

Painted white and red, and standing as tall as a skyscraper, a giant crane made a clear geometrical statement high over King Street: a vertical shaft, a horizontal bar, and two isosceles triangles formed by cables that were suspending rectangular containers half a mile above the city, the whole thing topped by a gold-white flag fluttering in the blue sky, like a euclidean republic that had declared independence from the messy human city below.

Danny noticed the structure as he walked up to the Telstra phone booth.

4:51 p.m.

The police hotline was ringing.

He was inside the phone booth now, the pink one, the one in the middle. He had not changed his mind. After finishing his work, he had returned the vacuum to the accountant's closet, lowered his shoes from the bookshelf and laced them on, and then come here and looked at the faded numbers on his palm while dialing

1-800-333-000

As he listened to it ring, he used his fingernail to begin writing in Tamil on the cold plastic handle of the phone.

My beliefs:

Age one to thirteen: No original thoughts. Mother not well. That was the problem. So: Father's creation. Religious, superstitious. No politics.

Age thirteen to fourteen: Does God exist? I begin to doubt. I secretly support LTTE and openly support Che Guevara. One day I find pornography in Father's cabinet. Small black-and-white photos. Woman in a bra.

Age fourteen to sixteen: Total change: 50 percent atheist, 50 percent communist. I eat raw eggs every morning after reading that Muhammad Ali did the same when training.

Age sixteen: 100 percent atheist, 100 percent communist. I stop eating raw eggs.

And now, sliding down the handle of the phone, his finger kept writing over his forearm, edging closer and closer to the bump.

Politics: I start hating the LTTE but not Che.

Age seventeen: Back to 50 percent communist. My voice breaks very late. Father is calling me a "crack."

The line rang and rang, and no one picked up. He transferred the phone from one hot ear to another.

"Got a cigarette on you, buddy?"

The voice startled Danny. He was immediately aware of someone hovering about him, murmuring and moving around him.

Wearing a gray jumpsuit, like an oversize baby, the white man had a medication-stunned face and keen blue eyes, and he touched Danny on the shoulder. "Give me a cigarette, mate? Give an Aussie a cigarette?"

"Don't smoke anymore," said Danny.

The blue eyes of the man-child contracted. "He won't be a smoker, I knew it. If he was a smoker, though, he wouldn't give an Aussie a cigarette anyway, would he."

Danny looked up for relief.

4:52 p.m.

Through the interstices of a fig tree, a bird dropped like a hot white stone.

4:52:20 p.m.

God, make me whole again. Danny overcame the urge to put the phone down. He heard the police hotline number ring again and again.

1-800-333-000

And then it was picked up.

A man answered this time. "New South Wales Police Hotline . . ."

He could see the owner of that voice: seated in his immense chair in his suffocatingly blue uniform.

"Can I help you, sir?"

"Every morning," Danny told the policeman, "my mum put me on a train from Penrith to the city to attend Knox Grammar."

"Excuse me?" the policeman said.

"Thanks to Mum's never-say-die attitude, I now advise Channel Nine on multicultural affairs."

"Sir. Do you know it is against the law to call this number for frivolous purposes?"

Tell them, Danny. He pinched the bump on his forearm. Tell them who murdered Radha Thomas and dumped her body in the creek. Wrapped in an Italian leather jacket full of stones.

There was a sign pasted on the inside of the phone booth.

Attention Foreign Graduates: done with your uni degree?
STUDENT
SPOUSE
MIGRANT
GSM VISAS
INTERNATIONAL MIGRATION CONSULTANTS AUSTRALIA (IMCA)
99% PLACEMENT SUCCESS

4:53 p.m.

"Sir," the person answering the police hotline said. "Sir?"

Sending sullen looks Danny's way, the Australian man-child in the gray jumpsuit still stalked around the pink Telstra phone booth, murmuring, "Won't give an Aussie a cigarette, will he?"

Danny's left leg was trembling again.

Policemen stood across the road.

There they were, on the other side of the buses and the traffic, massive, square-jawed blonds, bearing on their blue belts a locksmith's pride of silver pouches, sashes, and chains, plus a leather holster bulging and buttoned.

Danny felt certain he was urinating down his left leg.

Across the road, he saw one of the policemen looking straight at him.

What is your name, son? What is your father's name?

Write your name for me, son.

Now write it in the national language

Danny raised his eyes from the policeman to the green-painted balcony of an old building.

Be very careful, Danny: that wrought-iron balcony, that turmeric-colored paint, don't they remind you of another city?

He could hear them now, the packed buses spurting out diesel, he could smell deep-fried fish in the air, he could see alcoves on a summer's day that were pitch dark but for the dim ivory of a human figure sitting inside with unsold bread.

Didn't you say you were never going home again?

Danny felt a fingernail scraping over the side of his moist neck.

People do it all the time in Villawood. You swallow something; or cut your wrist; or eat nails; or find fuel and set yourself on fire.

"Sir?" said the man on the phone. "Do you have any information?"

He smashed the receiver down.

He began laughing at once. So you did it again, Danny the Brave. Went to the phone and backed off. So many hours later, Danny was still on that three-dollar sushi belt, alongside chopped silverfish and raw eel, going round and round: and now Prakash was on the belt with him too. The whole city was on that belt.

"Won't give an Aussie a cigarette, will he?" said the Australian man-child in his jumpsuit, circumambulating the phone booth.

Danny, about to say *Fuck off*, noticed that the man-child's eyes were a familiar color.

Hazelnut.

He saw another face superimposed on this Australian one: a pair of fierce eyebrows and thick black reading glasses on top of a mass of rebellious salt-and-pepper hair.

All of Newtown's walls were at once stenciled with hazelnut eyes.

You nearly fucked up, Cleaner. You nearly made that call. And once you make the call, you lose everything.

He ran to the train station.

4:58 p.m.

As the train approached Platform 2 at Kings Cross Station, cool wind blew over him, and he felt Sonja's fingers through his hair, and he knew he had done the right thing.

Absolutely done the right thing.

Sitting on a wooden bench, a boy who was not catching this particular train opened an illustrated book and recited from it to the woman beside him, "We eat chicken and another kind of chicken eats us."

5:12 p.m.

A man without rights in this world is still entitled to love.

Danny stood before a stately building with a double row of pillars that reminded him of government offices back home. St. Vincent's Hospital.

Facing the hospital, up on a green hillock, was a coffee kiosk where nurses in medicinal indigo gowns came to talk to their boyfriends on their phones. Danny glanced up, making sure she wasn't there.

An ambulance drove past as Danny walked into the lobby.

Jai Baby Jai.

Jai Jai Baby Jai Jai.

Behind the glass panel saying RECEPTION, the Indian secretary, her elbows propped up on the white hospital desk, watched a catchy Bollywood song on her iPad.

"Nurse Tran," said Danny. "I'm her boyfriend."

"I'll see if I can locate her, okay?"

The Indian lady turned slowly from her iPad to dial a number on a green phone, and handed that receiver to Danny, who found himself on hold, and thus in a position to watch more of the Bollywood song, until the voice finally said: "Danny, I am *working* today."

"I lost the cactus that you wanted," he said, and she did not respond.

"Sonja," he said, lowering his voice, knowing that this always affected her. "Can we have dinner tonight?"

"No. I have a second shift tonight. You know this."

He said nothing.

She paused. "My first shift ends at six-thirty. Come at six-thirty exactly, okay?"

"Okay."

The Indian lady at reception had begun bobbing her head to the beat of the song as he put the green receiver down.

Steel jaws clicked as Danny came out of the hospital; sticking his arms out of a loose gray smock, a man on a bench tried to cut his fingernails with a pair of trembling scissors.

5:30 p.m.

From the heart of the city, a gun stared at Danny. Leaving St. Vincent's Hospital, he had gone down to Oxford Street and walked to where the street joined Hyde Park, until he gazed, across the road, at an ancient naval cannon.

"This old gun," Danny sometimes said, when he imagined himself standing before an audience of logical, sensible Australians and pleading his case, "has been, for four years, my only family in this whole country."

Four years ago, when he had just come to Sydney and was reading the inscription next to it, he was astonished to learn that this ancient weapon was a trophy of the *Emden*, the German ship that had shelled Chennai in World War I, becoming a byword for terror even down in Tamil-speaking Sri Lanka. *Emden*. A dragon over there, it had become a dodo over here, and was destroyed; and now the last piece of the *Emden*, this gun, perhaps the same one that had set the waters of the marina ablaze and lit nightmares in Chennai for generations, was mounted in a park in Sydney.

Anything can happen in Australia, because the world's upside down here. Danny clapped his hands in front of the monster.

It was still bright here in Hyde Park, but darker up there, behind the Coca-Cola sign. Danny knew that it would be already evening in Kings Cross, and wouldn't the shaven-headed pimps in their black T-shirts just know it. Their hands were growing warmer with every cooling minute; there would be no such thing now as a casual passerby, no innocent man in the Cross. The pimps would be swarming over Prakash as he walked back to Potts Point, to his flat with the view of the Opera House. Yes, Danny could see the situation up there, in that boiling fleshpot on top of the city.

Even as he stood around the gun of the *Emden*, his phone began to buzz.

H6

The voice on the phone said: "Vrooom vrooom."

Danny laughed. He got the joke. The murderer is up in Potts Point, cleaning up the flat.

"Place is a mess, Nelson."

Danny believed that. The private school ties must be lying on the floor.

"Nelson. Did I tell you about the drops. The black drops."

"Yes."

"The black drops on the underside of the toilet seat. I have to clean them before I go. You should have done it for me."

"Sorry, sir."

Prakash laughed. "Premium economy. That's all I'm thinking of, Cleaner. It's almost over, isn't it. Me no dob, buddy. Have the police come for you? Call your boss and ask him if the police are there. He'll say no. I didn't betray you. Although you know what, *he* betrayed you."

"He did?" Danny asked. "Tommo?"

"Tsavdaridis. Yeah. He betrayed you. I didn't tell you this. But you know, before I left the store, he gave me a small sweet. A chocolate. I sucked on it. Nasty. Then he says: 'Glebe is a very good area. Easy to see the cricket from here.' You know what? He's *pitching* his store, Nelson. He wants to get rid of you. Maybe you've been demanding too much? He asked me if I knew anyone who would work in his store. Can you believe that? He asked me. Thinks all of us Indians know illegals. I'm telling you, Cleaner, white people."

"No class," said Danny.

Absolutely no class. He could see old Tommo in his store, already planning to get rid of Danny. All this talk about murder was making him nervous. Yes. He's begun asking people again. Someone else? You know someone else to work in the store?

"Prakash, sir," asked Danny, "do you still have that cactus?"

"Yes. Why?"

"Will you do something for me, sir?"

"What?"

Because somewhere in Sydney, the young Indian or Sri Lankan or Fijian student is still being told, *You will work for half minimum wage and sleep downstairs, okay?* Because next to the mural of Lord Krishna in the middle of Glebe, Tommo Tsavdaridis is dangling his left arm out the window of the Sunburst store with a live cigarette, tapping ash onto the Sydney street. And waiting. For the next young illegal to walk into his store looking for work. And the old man is thinking: Better make the new fellow Chinese. Someone who can't speak English well. That way he'll stay here longer. Because the day in Sydney is just *starting*. As it is out there—in the lush grape lands of South Australia and Victoria, all along the Murray River where nothing will grow without the sweat of foreigners who will then, the day after harvest, as they line up thinking they are about to be paid for their labor, be chased by police dogs and police vans, as if they were vermin.

"Will you take that cactus, Prakash, sir," asked Danny, "go back to Glebe, and kill that old Greek man with it? Before you go to South Africa, will you do that for me?"

I *mean* it. You go there and I'll live here like Chang Uncle. For the next twenty years.

The murderer heard that; he laughed.

"Now I know you didn't betray me, Danny. Now I know you didn't call the police. Did you?"

"No."

Prakash replied: "I'm leaving for the airport now. I already checked in. Don't fuck up now, Cleaner. Day's almost over."

"Bye, sir," said Danny.

Just half an hour left. All he had to do was make sure he didn't give in to a rush of blood pressure and call the police again.

Go to South Africa, mad Prakash—Danny brought his palms together to his forehead in a namaste—and live free there.

Leaving the *Emden* behind him, Danny walked back toward the hospital and then, to kill time, wandered behind it, into streets full of quiet houses. He looped about till he saw an old house with a stucco lion resting its paw on the globe up on the ceiling. The house was so ancient that the electrical mains were in a box beside the door, like in homes in Batticaloa. Ancient, yes, but lovingly preserved, and each of its diverse surfaces glistened; and everything strong in the suburb, in the city, in the continent of Australia, seemed to be at work in this well-maintained structure. Tin, wood, brick, tile, rusticated stone, wrought iron, paint, and lacquer had joined into a commonwealth here; on top of everything stood an inscription, *Maybelline 1924*, and resting above it, the old lion of the British empire.

There was a sturdy bench right outside the fence, naturally.

A cigarette stub, placed upright on the pavement, cast a long shadow like a sundial; Danny scratched at his singlet and sat down on the bench, facing the house. Up there. That cozy room in the attic. That would be their bedroom, up there.

Etta, Etty, he remembered. What was the name of that woman to whom the airplane above George Street was proposing marriage?

Then he took his face in his palms. Etta, Etty.

He placed his elbows on his knees. Soon he had become a parallelogram of pressure points: the slab of a butt on the cold bench, two bones thrusting into his knees, and a scratch of one long fingernail against his right cheek. The rest of him was . . .

Smoke.

*   *   *

Startled, Danny looked up—and found the source of the music. Having lowered the window of his silver-top taxi, a saffron-turbaned Sikh was corkscrewing the rectilinear streets of Sydney with jubilant spirals of Punjabi pop. Danny stared at the passing taxi, and at the house, and knew he was free.

The cliffs around Pyrmont were gone; law is gone, the white circle is gone.

It was past six o'clock now.

Prakash has gone to the airport.

I reckon he has, thought Danny. I reckon he is on his way to South Africa. And now it was time for Sonja's second shift to end.

"G'day, mate," said Danny, coming back to life as an invisible Australian.

6:12 p.m.

As if in celebration, the first bats of the day became visible.

Lord Murugan's peacock, incarnated here in the Southern Hemisphere as a flying vermin, emitting a sharp squeal as it approached. Lifting his right hand, Danny flexed his third finger, with its magnificent nail, in a salute.

This day of the illegal can go on a long, long time yet, Lord Murugan: years.

A brown-red smear of blood was illuminated in the bat's wing for just an instant, before it disappeared behind him. Danny's sinuses cleared up at once.

Some things take time to emerge, like a glossy plantain shining deep inside a dark coconut grove. Some things emerge at once.

Danny could see now that Prakash was certainly *not* on his way to the airport.

He was, in fact, nowhere *near* the airport.

6:13 p.m.

Remember what Abe said.

A black dog attacks you in a field, and suddenly, there's no one around. The country is empty. The continent is empty.

Sonja had said not to come back till 6:30 p.m., so he couldn't go there, but he had to ask someone to look something up on the Internet for him.

Flight times to South Africa.

And of course, they're never around when you need them, Australians.

Then, in the middle of an empty street, Danny saw a discarded white sofa and ran toward it, thinking, Where things exist, there must be people, and as he did so, three men, who looked as if they were waiting there for him, got up from the sofa.

Three white men.

One of them wore a hat, an Akubra hat. "Mate," he said. "Are you part of the resistance?"

Danny looked at the white man in the hat and shook his head.

"Sorry. You look like one of us," the man said. "Your hair." He smiled. "I'm being ironic."

Only then did Danny observe that there was a handwritten cardboard sign on the white sofa

Protest WestConnex

We are being forcibly removed from our homes

Your city won't look like your city in five years

The moment he saw the soft white leather of the sofa, Danny couldn't resist. In a day full of excruciating adult decisions, he took a childish joy in sitting down on the lovely white derelict sofa. He grinned. He felt ready to fart.

Glancing at Danny, a bright red-faced dwarf with probing eyes began rummaging through the waste bin next to the white sofa. Capillaries, like fine red surgical thread, like his knowledge of the law, looped, arced, and semicircled all over his fat right cheek. He moved his hand through the rubbish so volubly that it seemed to speak to Danny.

You are sitting on a white sofa, buddy. An Aussie sofa. Not meant for your arse, legally.

The sofa felt so comfortable. Danny kicked his legs about. Not going.

The older man, the one in the Akubra, read the situation, the unspoken words. And smiled.

"You shouldn't mind him. Sleeping out in the open does nothing for the manners. That little fellow, he knows all about the laws to do with eviction and force majeure, every detail and subdetail. He's going to help us in the press conference, I tell you. He'll be in the nightly news tomorrow. If you're not part of the resistance"—the man in the hat looked slyly at Danny—"what do you want here, buddy?"

Force majeure, Danny said to himself. I should know what that means, but I don't. He looked at the homeless Australians.

"Can someone do me a favor?" he asked. "Flight times. Do you have Internet? On your phone?"

The man with the Akubra hat did, sure. Danny explained again what he wanted. To know the flight times from Sydney to South Africa. The city of Johannesburg.

"Tonight?" asked the man in the hat. Letting go of the trash can, the dwarf came and stood by his side.

"Tonight," said Danny.

"Let's check Expedia. No, you have this other place that tells you all the flights. Just check the airport website. That'll tell you."

The dwarf knew that something was not right with Danny.

"Don't you have a phone of your own, mate? Check the flights yourself. Why, you going there?"

So Danny showed them his phone. The resistance men, passing the phone from one to the other, thought it was "a bit crook . . . a bit crook."

Appalled, the white men agreed to check on their phones for him. "Where are you from, mate? Which country? Don't they have good phones there?"

The hatted man, after going over the options, said: "Can't see a thing. Sorry. Can't see a thing. No flight to South Africa tonight. Next one leaves at . . . tomorrow."

"Are you sure?"

"That's what the Internet says. Does the Internet ever lie?" The man with the hat regarded him. "Why you asking? Going to South Africa?"

On the Portals of Sydney opposite the Lansdowne Hotel, the minute hands on the twin clocks moved together.

He's never been after you, Danny. You were just the cleaner.

Now Danny saw the man whose white face he had observed this morning coming out of the windowsill with red tulips: the one in tears, the one talking to the police. The top-top man.

That's the one Prakash wants.

The one whose name he couldn't ever say. The real estate man. The one who left the black urine drops on the underside of the toilet seat.

Mark, her clueless husband.

Sure, the police were thick around him in the morning. Except the police must have left by now. And it is Guru Purnima. Full-moon night. You know how Indians like to gamble on a night like this.

The moment you called Prakash, you convinced him someone is going to be held accountable. And he knows he isn't going to escape for long, so he thought, Why not. Let me at least get Mark. Two murders are the same as one.

The four dark obelisks, the chimney stacks of St. Peters, rose up once again before Danny's eyes.

From Glebe he must have driven over to Erskineville. Prakash was watching House Number Five right now. He was watching it from someplace across the road.

Or you would say *behind* the road.

36 Flora Street.

You told him the address.

Prakash was probably there now. He certainly knew how to get into the flat. Where's the key left in all these places, Cleaner? Under the welcome rug—or in the mailbox.

Found the key, went up the two flights of stairs, opened the door, and is now at the window, watching the home with the red tulips opposite. He could be doing that.

He's got the blue ball in his hands, maybe.

Or: he's at the desktop computer, having removed the shiny cover patterned with koalas. It's just a question of hitting the return key. He's figured it out. Maybe he's reading the latest racing results on the computer while watching the window. He's placed his thick black glasses down on the table. He's drawing circles with his finger on the computer screen.

Prrrrrmp.

And the moment he sees Mark alone over there, in the window with the red tulips across the road, he's going to run over. *Ba-da-bum-ba-da-bum.* He's going to stick a knife into the chest of that man. The same knife, probably.

"Hey, mate," someone said in a kindly voice. "Mate. Are you all right."

Danny put his head down and covered his ears. He felt the blood pound against his folded earlobes. Top-top.

A man who is illegal dobs in another man who is a killer but is so stupid he doesn't remember he's not legal and is deported. Read and laugh, Australians. Read and . . .

He could see it before him now, the newspaper article. He wouldn't even make the *Telegraph* or the *Herald*. Just one of those two-page community papers they gave you for free at Pizza Hut.

"I think he's not well. What do you reckon?"

From a rooftop behind him, a blackbird cawed. It kept cawing even as he tried to block his ears. He heard the bird cry subside into a low parched note that was almost a gloating croak: he could see behind him the black throat swollen up like a bullfrog's.

Hearing footsteps around him, he assumed it was the dwarf, come to taunt him once again. "I'm not getting up from this white sofa. I'm not . . ."

6:22 p.m.

But when Danny looked up, a girl was staring back at him.

Kadal kanni, he thought at first. Mermaid. A little mermaid.

He got up from the sofa and took a step toward her, and the little girl took a step away from him.

"Sam," a man called, and her parents followed, and the girl, losing her magic, turned into a restless child again before she ran down the road, while her parents followed.

A Tamil man sat there on a white sofa watching the girl.

He was thinking: There is no way, Danny, for you to keep silent today and live tomorrow.

"No, he's all right. Bloke's stood up. He's not crook."

"Could thank us, though, for helping him."

"Maybe he's going to South Africa."

From far down the road, the little girl's giggling could still be heard, though Danny walked faster and faster.

He was headed in the direction of Oxford Street, where he assumed the nearest pay phones would be, when it began glowing again.

H6

No one spoke; but when Danny answered the mobile phone, on the other end, he heard something that sounded like sobbing. Is he crying? Has he guessed, wondered Danny, that I have guessed?

Wherever you're going from here, Dr. Prakash, I hope it's not as bad as where I'm going.

Danny sighed into the phone before it went dead. Looking at it, he realized there was no need to go searching for a pay phone. He could call the police hotline right here, from this ancient thing in his right hand.

Transferring the phone to his left hand, he pressed the numbers one by one with his long fingernail.

1-800-333-000

It rang, and rang, until a woman's voice answered:

"Yes?"

As he heard his voice say, "I have information about a murder that took place last night," Danny was no longer in Sydney: because the Brazen Starer, up there on her first-floor balcony, hands on her hips, was grinning down at him, and next to her was a small and terrible old man he had not seen in four years—his father—and now Danny was pressing the phone so hard to his earlobe that it had grown warm against the side of his skull, even as he said to the Australian woman who was answering the police hotline, for the third time, "Yes, her name was Radha Thomas. R-A-D-H . . ."

7:02 p.m.

Remember the tsunami of 2004? It happened far away from Australia. Many of those dead were in Sri Lanka. There is a city on the coast, a small but famous old city. It was partly destroyed in the tsunami. Danny was going about the country in those days, trying to help people. This old city was a mess when he got there. The water came right into the market and killed all the sellers and buyers of vegetables. A thousand people or more in that city died in two hours that morning. But one group of people in the most affected area survived unscathed—one group of men. You know who they were? There was a cinema in that city up on a hill, and all the people who were watching the movie there were kept safe during the whole tsunami. What kind of movie was showing in that place? It was a blue-movie theater. So down in the market, the honest people died; and up on the hill, the men watching the dirty picture—at ten in the morning—God let them live.

Recalling this story on his way to St. Vincent's Hospital, his old cell phone still warm in his hand, Danny smiled. This, it occurred to him, was irony. The way that word is used here.

Right outside St. Vincent's Hospital, he stopped and looked up at a tree: he saw something with stripes of outrageous color around its neck, like a multivitamin parrot, flying into a gum tree and clinging onto a white branch, upside down.

Lorikeet.

Named correctly, the Australian bird flew away.

7:03 p.m.

Inside the hospital, as Danny was running up the stairs to meet Sonja, someone came running down.

A man with flaps of shampooed black hair covering his ears in the manner of something preserved from the 1990s, and on his back, he had a vacuum pack.

An astronaut—Nepali, for sure, probably from the least prosperous part of that country; and that shiny blue canister on his back was from Kmart, the new eighty-four-dollar version of the seventy-nine-dollar silver model Danny had carried with him for nearly four years. In the man's right hand, a plastic bag with extra sponges and sprays. You knew there was lots of Clorox in there. Maybe this astronaut had just cleaned the toilets in the hospital.

The young man saw Danny—and the eyeshock, which occurs when one brown man sees another in the city of Sydney, occurred.

Then one of them descended and disappeared, while Danny rose up the stairs and into artificial light.

"Weren't you here before?" the Indian woman behind the glass panel marked RECEPTION wondered. She put her iPad down.

"Yes. I'm here to see Nurse Sonja."

"You mean Tran. Sonja Tran. I think her second shift has started. I'll have to locate her."

Danny sat and waited.

His cell phone began ringing, and the cracked display said:
H13

Danny answered it to hear the thin voice of Rodney Accountant on the phone.

"Yes, it's me."

"Danny. I just got back into my place, and . . . I'm not accusing you of anything, mate, but you know there was a whiff in the air when I got back. I was sneezing. My allergies were all triggered. Now, you know the reason we've had this long working relationship is that I've been impressed by your integrity. So I've got to ask, friend, is there anything you introduced into my flat today? New material unchecked for allergens?"

You could tell him, *I used your own vacuum. I did your toilet with your own brushes. Your own cat watched me the whole time.*

"Sorry," said Danny.

"Sorry? You *know* I'm very sensitive to these things."

Danny noticed that the patient in the gray smock who had been outside was now sitting here, in the waiting room, still trying to cut his fingernails.

"I will give you ten percent discount next time."

The accountant said nothing.

"Twenty percent." Danny sighed. "Okay, I give you a hundred percent discount next time."

"That's a bit too much," replied the accountant, "but I appreciate the gesture. Twenty percent will do. And please be careful. That's all I ask."

"No," said Danny, "I'm giving you fucking a hundred percent off next time," and turned his phone off. He laughed.

"What is it?" Sonja came out, removing the baggy indigo tunic that the nurses, even the contract ones like her, wore over their clothes. She put the tunic down on the floor and sat on a chair beside Danny in the waiting area. "You're late. You know that?" She jabbed at Danny.

He jabbed her back. "Yes, I know. I know. I have to tell you something," he began. "I'm not a vegan."

She waited. Then she laughed. "Yes. I know."

Even after a full day's work, she smelled of floral perfume. Smelled great. Just like frangipane.

"What I meant to say is when I met you, I wasn't even a vegetarian."

Sonja smiled. "I know that too. You *told* me. Have you forgotten? It's okay. Vegetarian men are the most self-obsessed men in all of Sydney." She asked, "Did you deal with that huntsman?"

Danny clapped his hands together.

"Oh, you shouldn't have, you really shouldn't. They're harmless," she said.

Yes, she's not scared of spiders, thought Danny, but she was still too scared to come into the Sunburst store that day.

Where do you live? She had been asking him a long time, and she had even dropped by Glebe one Saturday to see him, until he took her near the Sunburst store and pointed up at his little window over the store, and as if she couldn't cope with it, she gaped. *You live in a storeroom? Really?* And because she didn't really want to know any more, she had refused to see his room or his twin panda bears, though he had gone in to get her a Kit Kat bar, which he later repaid Tommo for. Honest Danny, of course.

You could have been Brave Sonja that day—had you come up to the room and seen the truth about your Danny.

Later that same night, they had dinner at Pizza Hut, and then they went down to the river at Parramatta—the two of them rushing together, excited by the prospect of the breeze from the black river at night. "What do you want in life, Danny?" Sonja had asked as they stood on the bridge with a view of the flowing water below them.

"To be felicitated in Sydney," he had replied. "Like Kiran Rao."

"Like who?"

When he explained the idea of the felicitation, she laughed at once; and then, making an oblique but obviously dirty joke, she announced that she would shortly felicitate him, and he would felicitate her in return. Oh, he got it, he got, and reached for her arm—before he stopped. Because a square of the pavement in Parramatta had suddenly moved beneath his shoe. While Sonja watched, Danny troubled the loose square with the tip of his shoe: as it trembled, he felt all of Sydney from Richmond to Manly, with Parramatta in between, tremble with it. "I'm here," Danny told all of those people. "And I'm *never* going back."

"What are you doing, Danny?" Sonja drew closer. With a frown, she watched him shake the square of the pavement, as if she understood; and then, after kicking at his shoe, she shouted: "Felicitate me! Felicitate me!"—and ran down the river. It was just a game for her.

You should have been braver that day, Sonja.

Now Danny chafed the polished floor of the hospital with his shoe. He saw a fingernail down below and was glad that the fellow in the gray had summoned up the strength to do that. Must keep oneself clean, even in the hospital. Even in jail.

"Is there anything else?" she asked. "My second shift is about to start."

"I've got a story for you," he said.

Reaching over, she touched the tip of his nose. "Danny always does. Too many stories. You've got the sinus trouble again, don't you? Your voice is different today."

She traced with her finger the fault line inside his nose. The famous deviated septum.

"I don't think surgery is a good option, you know. We see kids who've got it, and then . . . the problem just gets worse. I don't know what can be done about it, Danny. Maybe you should go paleo for a while, that might help. You know, just fruits and nuts? But I have to get back now. Second shift. I said come at six-thirty. We could have discussed all this. But you are late."

"I know," he said. "I'm sorry."

What a thing to lose she'd be, to any man.

"But I have to tell you right now why I was late."

She leaned back and waited. In the cold hospital air, Danny rubbed his forearms.

"I had a call to make. It took a long time to finish." He lowered his voice. "A very important phone call. There were many things to explain."

She frowned. "Who were you talking to?"

Danny looked at Sonja for a little while before he scratched at his neck with his fingernail and said:

"The police."

The South Sydney Express
Circulation 16,000
First Published 2002

Police have arrested a 44-year-old man in connection
with the murder of local resident Radha Thomas, a
former Medicare executive.

Acting on a tip-off, a team of New South Wales
Police detained the alleged killer at a flat on Flora
Street right across the road from the dead woman's
apartment.

The man, identified as Prakash Wadhwa, a discharged
member of the armed forces with a history of addiction
issues, had brought a knife with him, on which they
found bloodstains that they believe are the murder
victim's.

"We suspect he was waiting for the right moment
to inflict harm on his target, the husband of the
woman he had murdered just the previous night," said
Detective Sergeant J. T. Michaelos.

He added that the person who tipped police off on
the hotline confessed during questioning to being
illegally present in Australia and is now being
processed for deportation to his home country.

(For real estate news, see pages 2—5; property
ads, 8—11.)

Acknowledgments

The exchange between Danny and the Australian immigration officer on pages 39 and 40 is adapted from a real exchange on an online immigration forum that occurred about seven years ago.

The idea for *Amnesty* came to me when I was James Payten's guest at his old place in Erskineville. This novel wouldn't exist without James's hospitality, forbearance, and knowledge of the law, nor would it without Shalini Perera's many acts of kindness.

Jeremy Kirk and Katey Grusovin in Sydney, Stephen Rebikoff in Melbourne, and Keshava Guha in Bangalore read early versions of the manuscript and offered suggestions, as did Andrea Canobbio and Jeff Yurcan.

In Sri Lanka: thanks to Dominic and Nazreen Sansoni; and to the late Father Harry Miller, longtime resident of Batticaloa, who spoke to me about the history of his city.

In Chennai: A. R. Venkatachalapathy patiently answered many questions. My thanks also to Kamal Haasan, the distinguished Tamil actor, for his responses to my queries.

In Kuala Lumpur and Penang: I am grateful to all the people

who told me their stories as illegal overseas farm workers in Australia. I hope each one of them has a chance to return legally.

A series of brilliant suggestions from my editor, Daniel Loedel at Scribner, allowed me, after five years of work, to complete this novel.